Legacy of a Duellist

T. C. Sutton

The Book Guild Ltd

First published in Great Britain in 2017 by
The Book Guild Ltd
9 Priory Business Park
Wistow Road, Kibworth
Leicestershire, LE8 0RX
Freephone: 0800 999 2982
www.bookguild.co.uk
Email: info@bookguild.co.uk
Twitter: @bookguild

Copyright © 2017 T. C. Sutton

The right of T. C. Sutton to be identified as the author of this
work has been asserted by him in accordance with the
Copyright, Design and Patents Act 1988.

All rights reserved. No part of this publication may be
reproduced, transmitted, or stored in a retrieval system, in any form or by any means,
without permission in writing from the publisher, nor be otherwise circulated in
any form of binding or cover other than that in which it is published and without
a similar condition being imposed on the subsequent purchaser.

This work is entirely fictitious and bears no resemblance to any persons living or dead.

Typeset in Minion Pro

Printed and bound in Great Britain by CPI Group (UK) Ltd, Croydon, CR0 4YY

ISBN 978 1911320 586

British Library Cataloguing in Publication Data.
A catalogue record for this book is available from the British Library.

When your legacy is a rapier
Your birthright a flashing blade
& the clashing sound of steel on steel
*　　is the only music made.*
The path of the duellist is a lone one
where your enemies wish you dead
the few friends you have they fear you
fickle fate dictates the path you must tread.

Foreword

A dirty, ragged child wanders through woodlands driven by a desperate need to appease his hunger. Attracted by the sound of laughing and voices, he peers through the undergrowth to be confronted by a scene so far removed from his limited experience it appears magical in his eyes. To this child of the streets, used only to poverty privations and hunger, accustomed to scavenging the mud of a filthy river to eke out a precarious existence, the affluence of an aristocratic gathering was a lifestyle he could not have imagined in his wildest dreams.

Yet even at this moment the hand of fate was resting on those emaciated shoulders. Friendless, illiterate, his short life lived without the benefits of adult guidance, he was barely able to converse, using a series of grunts to make his needs known.

This filthy, ragged scrap of humanity could not know that the finger of fate was already writing his story in the sands of time. Circumstances would gradually draw him into a lifestyle that his humble birthright in the early years of the eighteenth century could never have given him without the intervention of destiny.

He would achieve comfort, knowledge, a family life. As he grew to adulthood he would become affluent, knowledgeable and refined. He would become one of the upper classes that he now gazed on in such awe.

Fate, however, will charge him a high price for the gifts it bestowed on him. He would know the fearful desperation of the hunted felon. He would know unbearable sadness. As a duellist he would have to overcome the doubts and uncertainties that the fear of death brings to all who stand on the field of honour. Worst of all, he will have to endure the lonely isolation of someone feared by his fellow man.

Fate, although bestowing her favours on him provided him with a destiny peopled by powerful enemies dedicated to his destruction. They will ensure he must always be looking over his shoulder, never daring to trust or to give friendship freely for fear of being betrayed and delivered helpless to those who wished to destroy him.

Ultimately the path of destiny would lead him to the final challenge where he will look into the jaws of death itself in order to gain his rightful legacy.

1

An Unlikely Son for an Unlikely Father

The ring of tempered blade against tempered blade was a common enough sound to be heard in a woodland glade during the middle years of the eighteenth century England; however, the source of this sound was not an affair of honour, not a dispute between gentlemen whose only recourse was to meet in the pale light of dawn and settle their differences by the strict codes laid down by custom and convention, guided and controlled by officials. Indeed the combatants who wielded their weapons on that hot summer's afternoon were merely boys, boys as different in appearance as their obvious difference in training and skill with a sword, two boys who could not have been further apart in their social standing. All things being equal under different circumstances they would not have passed on the same street, but here they were, the older of the two as rough in appearance and style as the homespun clothes he wore, he had no shoes or stockings, clad in simple woollen breeches and shirt, his hair untrimmed, his general appearance and physique typical of a deprived and undernourished lifestyle. His attacks on the other boy were enthusiastic and full of vigour but even to an untrained observer it was painfully obvious the weapon he wielded was totally alien to him, his style being more suitable to a cudgel than a court sword.

The other boy was a complete and utter contrast; from his silk shirt and satin breeches right down to his silver buckled shoes spoke of wealth and privilege, his general grooming and overall bearing stamped him very clearly as an aristocrat. Although two or three years younger than his opponent, he had no problem in parrying the clumsy attacks and indeed seemed to be toying with the other boy. It could be clearly seen that his skill with a sword, despite the fact that he was merely ten years of age, could only have been achieved by many hours of skilful tutoring.

The person responsible for this tutoring frowned as he watched the boys, being neither amused, nor entertained by the spectacle before him. He had not come all the way from France to teach the subtle but complicated skills of duelling to his pupil only to see them abused by his charge demonstrating his superiority over village bumpkin boys, who without knowledge or practice as swordsmen had no chance against his trained blade.

All this, he thought to himself, *purely to entertain the boy's father and his empty-headed friends.* He looked across at the noisy boisterous people making a colourful picture as they gathered around the food-laden table placed beneath the shady branches of a huge oak tree, the ladies all flamboyantly dressed in the most expensive silks and satins, whilst the men fluttered among them strutting like peacocks, their embroidered coats and waistcoats as colourful and as carefully chosen as any of the ladies dresses.

Moving respectfully amongst the group were liveried footmen, who administered to their every need, some offering food and drink on silver trays, others standing stiffly and silently to one side, waiting to give their services at the slightest command from their lord and master, Alexandre Victor Theodore Ferailleur, Fourth Duke of Mulgrove.

The only man seated, the central figure in the group, he held court like a medieval king, surrounded by fawning courtiers. Tall and thin with gaunt features, large nose and greyish complexion, there was that about his appearance which suggested a mixture of arrogance and evil, even his friends had good reason to fear him for he was a man of extreme complexity of character. A man of great charm and given to acts of spontaneous generosity, his wit and extrovert personality made him a popular host and dinner companion, but underlying the veneer of affability was a vindictive and evil man whose self interest and possessive ego would send him into unpredictable and violent rages with complete loss of self control.

After these rages there followed days of morose sulks, woe betide anyone, servants or family, who were unwise enough to get in his way. It was not for nothing that he was known privately by the local population as, 'The Duke of Darkness'.

Despite his vast wealth he coveted all of his possessions, his greatest joy being to show his friends the huge mansion with its army of servants and the acres of parklands and woods that surrounded it. It was in these same woods the day's entertainment was now taking place. He sent his steward to the village with instructions to round up villagers with sons of a suitable age who would be used as sport for his son, who would then cut them up for his gratification and amusement of his friends. His son of course was just another possession; it was his avowed intention that he should become the finest swordsman and the most feared duellist in the whole of England. However, he did not intend to take the risk of humiliation before his friends, with the possibility of his son being beaten by a boy of his own class and equivalent skills, hence the use of the village boys, who along with their relatives and supporters came willingly to these events. They knew they would have to take a cut or two and the risks were high, but a good performance, which pleased the duke, would result in a few coins, and the family would live well for a short time.

The gulf between aristocrat and peasant was such that what

the duke spent in an hour at the gaming tables would keep a family 'in what they considered luxury' for a year. It was because of his ambitions for his son that the duke, at considerable expense, had bought the most famous fencing master that France could provide and shipped him to England to be personal tutor to his son.

It was at times like this that Jacques Gerard had his doubts whether he had made the right decision. He had lived all his life by a personal code of honour, but he would not have considered himself to be a good man; in fact, his whole adult life had consisted of battles, fighting and bloodshed. Yet he had never knowingly done anything that he would have considered to be dishonourable or transgressive against the code he had lived his life by.

As a young drummer boy he had fought against the Spanish, fighting for France and Louis the XIV in the wars against the Habsburgs. As he matured on the battlefield, his quick wits and natural ability as a soldier saw him rise quickly through the ranks. He became a respected tactician with an encyclopaedic knowledge of the set piece battle and an acknowledged master of the art of the siege. These abilities were to lead him away from the service of the king and into the more lucrative role of a mercenary, selling his knowledge of all things martial to whoever would pay him the most, thus he became a moderately wealthy man.

However, as the years rolled by, he tired of the carnage of the battlefield and rough spartan life of the solider. Realising that he could not live forever, and that the odds against his survival were getting shorter every day, he returned to his native France and set up home in Paris to enjoy the remainder of his life and the money he had made.

Such a man who has led a life of adventure and excitement does not settle easily to a dull peaceful retirement, as such he found that the brain-numbing boredom of his life led him into the inns and temptations of Paris, where his quick tongue and even quicker blade soon gained him a reputation as the most feared and infamous duellist in the city.

He lived this life for some years, but as age and the odds against his survival crept up on him, he sat back and took a good look at himself and his situation and decided that, without question, he must change his perilous lifestyle.

He took the dwindling remains of his money and bought a building in the centre of Paris, which he converted into a Salle d'Armes and set himself up as a professional fencing master.

Such was his reputation and skill with a sword that the business prospered. Soon his fame spread and he began to enjoy the reputation of the most famous fencing master in the whole of France, but fate is fickle and rarely leaves the successful alone for long. Thus it was, as so often happens to those who teach fencing, during a moment of inattention that a clumsy and inept pupil removed his right eye with an over enthusiastic thrust, which, though meant for the body, ended up going over the top of the parry and straight into the unprotected face.

The loss of an eye, or even complete blindness was not unusual for a fencing master and was considered to be an occupational hazard; but for Jacques Gerard it was the realisation of a lifelong nightmare. All his life he had never feared wounds or even death, but he had always dreaded blindness and now, as he continued with the only business he knew, he was in constant fear he would lose the other eye. Therefore when the Duke of Mulgrove had asked him to come to England as fencing master to his son, it had seemed like manna from heaven. He did not agree instantaneously – his business instincts told him there would be a better price if at first he appeared reluctant. Finally they agreed, to what Jacques privately considered to be a salary beyond his wildest dreams.

So in a state of high euphoria he packed his bags, settled all his business affairs and leaving his fencing Salle in the capable hands of his friend – the lawyer Messier Françoise Faubert – who would run it for him at an agreed commission while he was away. He set sail on the first available ship for England to take up his position as fencing master to the duke's son and heir.

Suddenly there was a mighty cheer and the sound of clapping from the spectators. This jerked him out of his private thoughts and turned his attention back to the combatants; the young aristocrat had just disarmed his opponent and was standing holding him at arms length with the point of his sword pressed into the soft flesh under the boy's chin. The youngster was in a state of terror, as well he might be; he was standing on tiptoe in an attempt to take the weight off his chin, but to no avail, there was already a trickle of blood coming from the indentation where the sharp point pressed into the skin. His arms were pushed out from the sides with the palms facing out and the fingers spread wide in a gesture of helpless surrender, his eyes rolled wildly from side to side as he looked in desperation for someone to help him. The young boy looked to his father for guidance and Jacques blood ran cold, for he knew that a nod from the father would spell doom for his son's victim – the duke's money would buy him out of any repercussions that might follow.

His fears however proved to be unfounded when the duke laughed loudly and shouted, "Well done, my boy. Let him go." He reached into his pocket and threw a handful of coins at the group of villagers who stood apprehensively at the far end of the clearing. This was the signal for guests to do the same and throw coins to the group; the boy scampered gratefully to join his relatives who were searching gleefully in the grass and undergrowth to find the coins that would give a little ease to their poverty-stricken lives.

Jacques felt pity and disgust for these people; he understood their poverty, he had seen deprivation and starvation in all its forms, be it city or village, whatever the nationality the need was the same, what he could not understand was their lack of pride. These aristocrats treated them like dirt. They used them and they abused them and still they came back for more. They came willingly, even appearing to enjoy the humiliation inflicted upon them, even though their children were not allowed within a sword-length of their betters until they had been thoroughly scrubbed.

The boys would be stripped and their dirty ragged garments thrown onto a bonfire, they were then bundled into a large wooden tub and thoroughly scrubbed by two servant girls (who were none too gentle with them), being well aware that the more the boys howled, the more the duke's guests enjoyed the spectacle. At the conclusion of his ordeal a boy would emerge from the tub, his skin glowing red and sore from the attention of the stiff brushes. He would be given a pair of rough breeches and a homespun shirt. These he would be allowed to keep. The duke would often boast of his generosity in giving out clothes to the poor, omitting to mention of course that it was more an exercise in decontamination than in philanthropy. Many of the rustic villagers, without the benefit of a formal education and steeped in folklore and superstition as they were, actually believed it can be harmful to the health to remove coatings of dirt and grime built up over the years; therefore it was not surprising that the boys approaching the tub, with their heads full of dire warnings and superstitious fears, found the experience not just a painful one, but a psychologically traumatic one also.

To say that the latest victim of this most subtle of water tortures was approaching with a certain amount of trepidation was a gross understatement. He was dragged, half walking half carried, struggling like a landed fish to be tipped into the tub like a fish from a bucket. Rising to the surface, gasping for breath, he was gripped by a nameless terror which gave strength to his limbs; his wet body as slippery as an eel, he tore himself loose from his tormentors and in a blind panic ran across the clearing as naked and as pink as the day that he was born.

He dashed across the clearing like a startled fawn, running past the young aristocrat, who stood waiting with sword in hand, seeing a small hay cart barring his way and perceiving it as a possible hiding place he leaped over the back of the cart and with the mentality of an ostrich buried his head beneath the loose straw. He remained motionless in this position no doubt believing that if he could not see then he could not be seen, a viewpoint not shared by the spectators, who were highly amused by the sight of the rearmost part of his anatomy sticking up out of the pile of straw.

The young boy, encouraged by the laughter of his father's friends and finding this a far too tempting a target to miss, struck an exaggerated on guard position, executed a perfect lunge and drove his sword into the exposed rear end. The needle-sharp point entered from the side and, slicing through the soft flesh, penetrated the two halves of his buttocks as easily as a pin going through a peach!

Amazingly the boy did not move. It was as though he had not felt the cold steel slicing through his body. He remained in the kneeling position with his head beneath the straw, the sword impaling him looking as innocuous as a pin in a lady's bonnet. His opponent climbed into the cart and placing his foot on the boy's side he callously withdrew the weapon. Then, waving the bloodstained sword above his head in triumph, he executed a grand salute in the direction of the spectators.

This example of man's inhumanity to man was witnessed with a dumbfounded silence, even these social butterflies, used to treating the peasant classes with a brutal distain, were stunned into silence by this sudden act of cruelty by one so young.

The silence was short lived, for as the sword was withdrawn, it rent an agonised shriek from the boy in the cart as the pain from his wound seared through his body. This was the signal for the whole scene to change: people who had been frozen into immobility were galvanised into activity, each according to their individual loyalties and needs. The boy's relatives and friends rushed across to the cart – a ragged group desperate to help but nervous and uncertain what to do. Jacques Gerard pulled a handful of clean white cloths from his pocket – he always carried them on these occasions. He did not have to come and watch, as a paid servant he was not a part of the social scene and as a honourable man he found these events both distasteful and degrading. Despite his violent life he was a compassionate man with a social conscience and as such felt that he should be present with his extensive knowledge of wounds and the correct way to treat them, a knowledge forced on him through necessity on the battlefields of the world.

Pushing his way through the people surrounding the boy, who had been lifted from the cart and now lay in a crumpled, whimpering heap on the ground, he gave orders to some of the men to obtain branches and showed them how to construct a makeshift stretcher. Having removed the boy's mother, who had been wailing and almost smothering the poor unfortunate lad, he was able to turn his attention to the wound. This was deep and extremely painful but there was no damage to any vital organs. However it was pumping blood at an alarming rate and the task was to stem the flow before it was too late. This he managed to do with the help of his makeshift bandages. Having dressed the wound as best he could, the boy seemed more comfortable and they were able to get him face downwards onto the makeshift stretcher.

The duke in the meantime had viewed these events as part of the entertainment. At first he had been just as stunned as the others, but when his son made the salute, with red face and bulging eyes, he had spluttered at first then the spluttering had turned into gales of laughter. Holding his sides, rocking backwards and forwards, he was in imminent danger of falling off his chair. His guests, equally amused, saw this as a signal to give vent to their own emotions and joined in the hilarity; even they who were not amused joined in, faking laughter so as not to be considered the odd one out and hoping that in appearing to share the duke's amusement they would curry favour and increase their social standing with him.

The fourth duke managed to regain his composure and shouted for the boy's father to make himself known. After some hesitation and much discussion among the villagers a timid-looking figure detached itself from the group and approached the main party in a somewhat fearful manner. The duke wiped tears from his eyes and greeted him jovially.

"Come on now, fellow, what's the matter with you? You and your lad have given us good sport today. Here, take this." And so saying he pulled a leather pouch from his coat and flung it on the ground at the man's feet.

You could virtually see the apprehension draining from the man as he quickly scooped up the pouch. He did not know whether or not he or his son had done wrong but he had feared the worst, and here he was receiving a reward. With trembling fingers he undid the drawstring and emptied the contents into his hand – his heart nearly stopped and his eyes almost popped out of his head. There in his hand were several gold coins, a trifling sum to the giver, but to this man it was a king's ransom. Gathering his wits together he managed to stammer out a 'thank-you' and even contrived to execute what he considered a courtly bow. The sight of the ragged figure attempting to emulate the etiquette of society in such a clumsy manner was too much for the duke, who once again collapsed into gales of uncontrollable laughter.

The man scuttled off, deciding he had better not push his luck too far. Quickly putting the coins back into the pouch, he ran back to his friends to show them his good fortune. There were shouts of laughter and excitement, for good fortune is infectious, and were they not all friends of a rich man now? They would all celebrate tonight.

The wounding of the boy now forgotten, he was the hero of the hour as they carried his stretcher shoulder high. They were a laughing excited group of people who set off down the track to the village. The boy even managed a smile and a wave as they disappeared into the trees. Jacques waved and smiled grimly as they went. He did not give much for the lad's chances. He had seen similar wounds before. They needed clean conditions and regular changes of clean dressings. He had seen the hovels these people lived in, he knew their ignorance and their lack of hygiene. The danger with such wounds was infection. If gangrene were to set in the boy would die horribly. Still, perhaps he was being pessimistic. It was surprising how tough these yokels could be: they had to be to withstand the rigors of their deprived lifestyle, so maybe the boy would survive to enjoy a little of his family's good fortune. Jacques certainly hoped so as he had done his best. The rest was up to them now.

He turned to walk away. The festivities would carry on for some time yet. The duke's party would continue with the eating and drinking. Now that the villagers had gone to their celebrations there was no need for him to remain. What he did not need now was to be reminded. The sights and sounds of the last hour had filled him full of disgust; he wished only to go away and forget them.

Fate, however, had not finished with Jacques Gerard on that day. At the far end of the clearing where the woods were thickest, the heavily foliaged branches hung low over the bushes and the undergrowth merge with the uncut grasses and ferns that edging the clearing. Concealed in this tangle of vegetation, a ragged unkempt urchin had been lying hidden from view, watching and waiting for an opportunity to arise he could turn to his advantage.

His eyes gleamed when he saw the gold coins that the duke had been thrown with what appeared to be such spontaneous generosity, for such a child as this timidity and a natural caution were as deeply engrained in his nature as any of the wild animals who walked or crawled in the woods about him, but the temptation of such a generous gift for so little effort overcame the very real fears the past events of his short life had instilled within him.

Prompted by hunger and need he threw all caution to the winds, burst out of the undergrowth and ran across the clearing, pausing only to pick up the bloodstained sword the duke's son had carelessly discarded after impaling the unfortunate boy in the hay cart.

Continuing his headlong dash he confronted the young aristocrat, waving the sword in front of his face he exclaimed, "Ere y'are, I'll take yer on, guv!"

The young boy stepped back, startled by this sudden and unexpected intrusion, but he was a lad with quick wits blessed with the ability to size up a situation very quickly and to act on it equally quickly. For a few seconds he stared at the gleaming point waving inches from his nose, then with one smooth movement he ducked beneath the others' sword arm, bundling the boy out of the way as he did so. He grabbed for the handle of an ornamental court sword being worn by one of the guests, withdrawing the sword from its scabbard, he turned and threw himself at the ragged challenger, who moved backwards out of the way with amazing speed and agility. Within seconds, the two boys were fighting furiously up and down the clearing.

Jacques turned back and moved to a better vantage point in order that he might see more clearly. He did this not from a sense of Christian charity or duty, as he had with the other boys but more from curiosity. There was something that intrigued him about this one. He moved with a smooth, flowing grace that seemed perfectly natural to him. Jacques had lost count of the number of pupils to whom he had tried to teach this manner of movement only to give up in despair after years of frustrated effort, and here was this urchin who produced it without effort.

He looked more closely at the boy. He appeared no different to the thousands of urchins he had seen, mostly in the cities, who scratched out a precarious existence in any manner they could in a world that turned a blind eye to their suffering. His filthy clothes barely covered his emaciated frame and, through the rents in his tattered shirt, you could clearly count the ribs that stuck out from his undernourished torso. Yet the boy clearly had a brain; it was most unlikely the boy had ever used a sword before and even more unlikely he had any training in it's' use. Yet he was copying the other boy's movements and learning as he went along and even though he lacked the control of a trained swordsman, he was putting up a credible performance.

Jacques suddenly became anxious for the boy, he had apparently mustered reserves of energy and amazingly he was pushing his opponent back, forcing him to defend desperately. At that moment there was a great danger he would inflict some injury on the young duke, and Jacques knew if that were to happen the father would punish and urchin severely and brutally. However he did not have to be concerned on that issue for the young duke was far too well trained a swordsman to be beaten so easily and was now beginning to take control of the fight. He had taken the sting out of the attack and was beginning to show his superiority. Now there was a different element in the fight, something that only an experienced duellist like Jacques Gerard could spot, the young aristocrat was more careful with his attacks, more purposeful with his movements, there was a look in his eye that Jacques knew well. Instinctively he knew the young devil intended to kill his opponent!

This boy did not stand a chance. He was a loser whatever happened: to win he would have to inflict an injury on his opponent, but if he did that he would be punished severely; to lose would mean serious injury or death. Jacques made up his mind quickly: he would stop this fight. With Jacques to think was to act. Unsheathing his own sword he lowered the blade between the two fencers, shouting out, "Halt!" as he did so.

The fencing master was not a young man, being well into his sixties, but he still had an imposing presence. His upright military bearing and the black patch over his mutilated eye gave the overall impression he was not a man to temper with. His voice carried the authority of a man used to giving orders. As a soldier he had given an order and strong men had jumped to obey, therefore the effect on two ten year olds was electric, they stopped and both jumped backwards.

Jacques grabbed the urchin by the shoulder and took both swords from the boys, making sure. The young duke might very well have run the boy through. He was about to lead him away to safety when there was a shout from the duke:

"Bring the young blaggard over her, Gerard."

It passed through his mind he should allow the boy to wriggle free and run away, but he immediately discarded the notion. He knew the duke only too well, and was aware that if he did that it would allow the duke to indulge his one ruling passion, hunting! Hunting in all its forms, a pastime he pursued with a fanatical zeal. He was immensely proud of his pack of foxhounds, one of the first packs to be established in England. He and his friends spent many hours following the hounds laying down the ground rules for a pastime that was gradually becoming popular throughout the country.

A far more sinister side to his passion for hunting were his two teams of tracker dogs. As a magistrate he considered it his duty to keep and train these dogs and the men who worked them. One team consisted of two men, a bloodhound and two English Mastiffs. One man would handle the bloodhound and following the scent, and the other would handle the mastiffs. Once the quarry was within sight the mastiffs would be released; many a poor miscreant attempting to evade the law had been pulled down and savaged by these powerful and fearsome beasts.

The duke of course never missed an opportunity to be present on these occasions and would follow the hunt on horseback, the excitement and enthusiasm he generated on these hunts bore witness to the fact he did it more for personal gratification than for his duty as a magistrate.

It was for this reason that Jacques did not release the boy. He tightened his grip on his arm, far better for the boy to take his punishment now; if he were allowed to run the duke would consider it a perfect end to a perfect day. He would without doubt release the dogs and, with himself and his friends in full pursuit, the boy would be hunted down like a wild animal, standing no chance whatsoever against those fearsome jaws – he would be ripped to pieces and the duke, in his capacity as a magistrate, would concoct some story about his criminal activity followed by a lawful pursuit. Because of the duke's social standing in the community, and of course his wealth and influence, this story would be accepted without question. So reluctantly and with a feeling of guilt Jacques dragged the struggling boy to where he was sitting.

The youngster had not been struggling quietly. He had been cursing with a colourful vocabulary that Jacques was certain he had not learned in the local village, as such oaths could only have been picked up on the streets of a large city. Going by the boy's accent, Jacques judged that he had come from London and had a shrewd suspicion he was a street urchin, but what was a street urchin doing so far from the city and appearing here in the depths of the English countryside? This was difficult to understand.

Now he was facing the duke, who glared at the boy and addressed him in a thunderous voice that shocked the struggling youngster into sullen submission.

"Now then, you young villain, who are you and where do you come from?"

Something in the his tone of voice made the boy realise he

could be in danger. For the first time he showed signs of fear, he looked at him with his mouth hanging open and the words would not come. Jacques spoke for him, he spoke with only the slightest trace of a French accent; although he was a Frenchman who loved his country, he had lived a cosmopolitan life and had the command of several languages, all of which he spoke fluently.

"Your Grace, I do not think this is a local lad. It appears to me he is passing by on his way from the city."

"Ha!" said the duke, "A gypsy or vagrant. Which is it, boy? No matter, either way I'll have you whipped for it!"

By now the boy had found his tongue and stammered out something to the effect that he had not known where he was and did not know where he had come from and he had been trying to find a road.

The duke broke into this hesitant explanation; he had not interest in it anyway.

"Where are your parents, boy?"

"I never had none," said the boy.

"You have no parents. You do not know where you came from. You do not know where you are going and what's more you don't know where you are now." The duke was exasperated.

"Take him away and give him a whipping," he said to a footman.

"One moment, Your Grace…"

Jacques Gerard began to speak in the boy's defence, in the years to come he was to look back many times on this day and wonder why he said what he did, without ever being able to give himself a satisfactory explanation of his actions. He had felt sorry for the lad, but then he had felt sorry for many under-privileged people in his time, but he knew it was impossible to help everyone. Generally he accepted their plight as the way of the world. Maybe he saw a natural ability he could groom into an expert swordsman. Maybe he saw a little of himself in the lad. Whatever the explanation, here he was offering to take the lad on as his assistant to clean his salle and look after his equipment,

"And of course, Your Grace, he will be useful to me in the training of your son, being the same age and size he will be an ideal partner for him to practice his movements on," this said in a final attempt to persuade in his favour.

The duke considered this request for a moment or two then,

"Very well, Gerard. If you think you can use him you can have the young ruffian, but keep him out of my way and for God's sake get him cleaned up."

"Thank you, Your Grace, you are very kind."

So saying Jacques dragged the boy over to the tub and holding him by the scruff of the neck and the seat of his pants he dumped him head first and fully clothed into the water, the laughing servant girls eager for another victim promptly pounced and proceeded to scrub him vigorously. The duke, much amused by this action, returned to his friends in a benevolent frame of mind and forgot the whole incident. Jacques, much relieved that he had got the boy off the hook, retrieved him from the tub and the unwelcome attentions of the girls who had almost scrubbed him raw, fitted the boy out with a pair of breeches and a shirt, took him by the hand and led him back to the manor house.

The east wing of the manor contained the kitchen and the servants' workrooms in the basement. Above this was the dining hall, connected to the kitchen by a narrow set of spiral stone steps. Running directly alongside the dining hall was a gallery. This was the gallery that had been converted into a salle d'armes and was Jacques sole responsibility. At the far end of the east wing stood a stone tower, only accessible through the gallery. It was this tower that had been allocated to Jacques for his personal quarters. At the top of the stone tower under the conical slate roof was a room he had never used; a word from Jacques to the housekeeper and it was quickly converted into a bedroom for the boy.

Having recovered from his fear and realising that no one intended to harm him he tucked into the prodigious amounts of food obtained by Jacques from the kitchen. Jacques got on well with the servants. As tutor to the duke's son he was not expected to socialise with the servants but being a very personable type of fellow not given to ideas of status and class distinction, he would often nip downstairs from his quarters for a yarn and a drink in the kitchen.

As the boy became more at ease with his surroundings, he proved to be quite a chatterbox and Jacques was able to find out something more about his past life. It transpired that he had been telling the truth about where he had come from, he truly did not know. He said that there had been many houses and a lot of people. From his description Jacques surmised that he had been correct in his assumption that London had been his home. He had no recollection of either of his parents and could only remember being with a group of children from an early age. Jacques made a shrewd guess that he had been a foundling adopted by a group of street urchins who had looked after him until he was able to fend for himself.

Living on the streets, begging and stealing to survive, he had fallen foul of a group of travelling showmen who had kidnapped him to use as an unpaid worker as they travelled from fair to fair. He had no means of measuring time and being totally illiterate had no means of assessing it either. How long he had been with these showmen was uncertain but eventually he had managed to escape from their clutches. Wandering through a countryside totally alien to an uneducated boy who had lived his life in the confines of the city, he was lost and friendless, completely bemused by a strange and hostile world. He had finally found himself on the duke's estate without knowing where he was or what he intended to do.

The events of the day had changed his life beyond belief. There he was with a full stomach, a roof over his head, new clothes and, for the first time in his life, a bed to sleep in. He accepted these things without question. Life had always provided for him somehow and if now his fortunes were to change for the better then he was not about to argue with that. So as darkness fell, he snuggled down beneath the bedclothes and slept the sleep of the just.

Below in his quarters, Jacques settled down with a glass of wine and let his mind consider the events of the day. He thought of the boy upstairs and the hardness of the short life he must have led and how fate had caused their paths to cross. At that stage in their relationship he could not have foreseen how close they were to become, that the boy would eventually look upon him as his father, and he, Jacques Gerard, one time soldier of fortune, ex-mercenary and duellist who had never married, the life he had led being too uncertain and too full of danger to allow any long term emotional involvement, would eventually look upon himself as the boy's father.

2

A Debt is Paid in Fire and Steel

Life at the household of the Duke of Mulgrove went in the same regimented routine, as was the custom in the lifestyle of the aristocracy. Downstairs, the servants bustled about in their workrooms and kitchen, working from early morning until late at night, their entire existence centred on what was the all important purposes directing their lives of subservient drudgery, making sure that life was comfortable and pleasant for the ruling classes. The ruling classes for their part gave little thought to why so many should labour so hard for so little, and for the comfort of so few. They merely accepted their position in life as a divine right, in the same way as those who have nothing of their own to give, but their ability to work, accepted their status in the pecking order as an act of God. Rich and poor alike believed that if God had intended them to be rich then they would have been born that way, therefore if they were not rich, then God himself wished it to be so.

A doctrine such as this was most conducive to the running of a great house. Everything ran like clockwork. No one stepped out of line and everyone did their job, contented with the acceptance that this was their role in life. Even if they had not accepted it, there was nowhere else they could have gone without slipping into the life of deprivation they all dreaded. It was, therefore, not surprising that the general atmosphere of the household was directly linked to the moods of its master. With him in a good humour all was well. He would walk about the house amusing himself; every curtsy or bow from a servant would be greeted with a nod and a smile. Servants would bustle about dusting, cleaning and preparing meals, maintaining the house and its grounds, concentrating on these tasks without feeling the need to be constantly looking over their shoulders. These were the good days that did not last. The duke's mood would change and a dark cloud would descend on the house, an aura of fear and apprehension would permeate the community. Everywhere there would be gloom; people would go about their work quietly and without laughter. They who had to work in the main part of the house would do so by maintaining a low profile, slinking fearfully about almost as though they were trying to merge into the woodwork.

The duchess was no exception. She was the recipient of the impotent sympathy of everyone, for though she was universally liked, there was little anyone could do to help. It was she who took the brunt of his rages. Quiet and inoffensive, a woman of great beauty, she rarely interfered with the running of the house, preferring to give her instructions to her housekeeper in the privacy of her boudoir. These qualities inspired great loyalty and affection in her personal servants; indeed she was liked and respected by everyone employed at the manor. But none were able to protect her from the duke, who would beat her without mercy and with little reason whenever he was in one of his violent moods. For weeks after she would be confined to her rooms until the bruising subsided. Her maids would whisper their sympathy to other servants in their quarters, but there was little they could do against the duke, their master who was virtually untouchable and all-powerful.

These fluctuations of mood and atmosphere had little effect on the life of Jacques Gerard. He was king in his own kingdom.

The Salle was his to run as he thought fit and no one, not even the duke, interfered in the running of it. He had been most insistent about this when he duke had agreed his contract of employment. Of course he was aware of the situation in the main house, as during his social visits to the kitchen he would hear of it. He had sat many times with a tankard of ale and listened to the tales of the duke's mood and the dark deeds he had perpetrated, but none of them had touched him personally, closeted as he was in his Salle and his private quarters, insulated from the day to day life of the rest of the household.

Jacques job was not a hard one; in fact, he was under employed. Most of the time he was bored and found that time hung heavily on his hands. His duties were directed to one purpose and one purpose only: the training of his employers son in the art of swordsmanship. Three hours per day were allocated to this task, usually in the mornings. The rest of the time was his-own. In fact this was all the time he required. The boy was a natural swordsman and a quick learner. Jacques had very little doubt he would realise all the ambitions his father had for him.

The duke took a keen interest in his son's training and would often pop into the Salle and join the boy in a bout with the sword. He even did a little training himself and would allow Jacques to improve his techniques with a little coaching. For some strange reason, when he was in his dark moods he would keep away from the Salle and at these times would lose all interest in his son's training completely. This was fortunate indeed, for Jacques was not a man to accept an insult without reply and would take humiliation from no man, be he aristocrat or commoner. Jacques spent much of his spare time walking in the surrounding countryside and in the evening he enjoyed reading; however, since the appearance of the young urchin he had taken under his wing, his lifestyle took on a new purpose and was to change dramatically. The boy quickly settled into his new life and accepted everything gratefully, doing all he was told to do without question, setting to with a will to complete every task that he was given. Communicating with the boy was the most difficult part. At first he could be withdrawn and introvert. There was a barrier of suspicion and distrust that had to be broken down before any headway could be made. After a while the boy began to trust his benefactor, became more open with his attitude and conversation. Jacques was then able to find out a little more about his past life and the privations and hardships he had suffered. It was amazing that a child, quite literally born on the streets, growing up without parents and no means of support, could survive at all in such a harsh environment. He knew nothing whatsoever about his personal details; when he was born, his age, even his name – as far as he knew, he did not have one. In terms of a personal identity he did not exist. Jacques guessed he was about ten years of age and gave him the date of which they first met as a birthday. When talking about the group of children who were among his earliest memories he said they had called him Nipper. The nearest name Jacques could think of to this was Napier, so Napier he became. Jacques added his own surname to it, therefore that the boy became known as Napier Gerard.

Jacques was determined that the boy should receive an education, and so set himself the task of breaking down the barriers of ignorance and illiteracy erected by his past lifestyle. This was not an easy option he had taken up for himself, for the boy had no numeracy and was totally illiterate. Even his grasp of the English language was very basic. His conversation consisted of a series of grunts and swearwords gleaned from the streets.

Jacques however was the ideal man for the task. Time had hung heavy on his hands and his life for a long time had lacked any real purpose. Now with his gift of endless patience he set to work on a job he thought was well worth doing. Despite the fact that he was a soldier by profession, Jacques was a scholar by inclination. All his life he had loved books and had collected and devoured them throughout his travels. He had talked and listened to wise men and scholars in many countries throughout the world; he was a highly intelligent man who could talk with authority on a vast range of subjects. He had a gift for languages, not only could he speak several, but was able to read and write in them as well.

His first task was to increase the boy's vocabulary for he reasoned that until the boy was able to use his own language competently he had little chance of understanding any subject he tried to teach him. This proved to be more difficult than he had at first anticipated. The street language was firmly embedded in the boy's memory and required a great deal of patience and perseverance to eradicate. Once Jacques had the boy conversing satisfactorily, a great change came over him: the street urchin disappeared and Napier Gerard emerged. Jacques was surprised and delighted to find that his pupil was not only far more intelligent than he had at first thought but had also developed a thirst for knowledge that matched his own. Jacques believed in a disciplined and regulated lifestyle. Hard work and punctuality had always been his watchwords, and these were the virtues he now set out to instil in Napier.

Napier for his part loved his new life. In the past he had not had the time to stop and think or look around him at the rest of the world going about its business. Life to him had been a constant search for food and shelter and the bare basics of life, the acquisition of which had been a full-time and all-consuming occupation. Now for the first time he could sit back and study something other than the desperate need to stay alive. Now he no longer suffered from the constant pangs of hunger brought on by a perpetually empty stomach. He now knew the hunger of a mind long starved of knowledge crying out with a frantic need to be fed with information.

Jacques, now more than satisfied with his pupil's progress, began to plan out a curriculum for the boy; a course of study covering a range of subjects, interspersed by exercises and training in the use of the sword. At first Napier was kept well away from the rest of the household, Jacques restricted him to the Salle and his own quarters, allowing him the use of the Salle only when his employer and his son had finished and were unlikely to return. If he went out into the surrounding countryside Jacques always accompanied him, not through any fear of him running off – Jacques knew he would not do that and if he did it was his own free choice, he was not a prisoner. His reasons were those of caution. He did not want the boy falling foul of the duke, or anyone else for that matter, until he had given him a more sophisticated outlook and a more socially acceptable manner.

Eventually Napier's education progressed and his swordsmanship improved to the point where Jacques was able to introduce him into the training programme set out for the duke's son, this was done progressively and in so subtle a manner that neither the duke or his son questioned the change. In fact, using Napier as a training partner proved to be so successful that even the duke congratulated Jacques on a job well done. If appearances were anything to go by neither he or his son seemed to have any recollection of the day a ragged urchin burst out of the undergrowth and attacked the boy with a sword. At least if they did they gave no indication of it. They treated Napier in exactly the same way as they treated any of the other servants. This of course meant he should speak only when spoken to and even then it should be in a respectful manner. He was ignored when he was not needed and when he was he should perform the task allocated instantly and efficiently. Jacques was aware that this was the normal relationship between aristocrat and servant and was quietly pleased he had succeeded in getting the boy accepted into the household. Now he knew it was safe to get him fully integrated into the general working life of the manor house. With this acceptance Napier was now free to go where he wished at any time, providing he obeyed the rules applicable to any of the servants and Jacques could continue with his plans for the boy's education.

As the years rolled by the relationship between the fencing master and his pupil developed. They became as close as any natural father and son, so much so that Jacques had instructed his friend Françoise Faubert, a well-known Parisian lawyer, to draw up adoption papers naming Napier officially his son and heir.

Despite the fact they were training partners, the aristocrat and Napier were never more than master and servant, and Napier was looked upon as a piece of training equipment. The boy would use him and leave him with less interest than he would have in an old sword. Napier for his part knew his position in life and accepted it without resentment; if he did resent it he certainly did not admit it, showing no more interest in the lad than the aristocrat showed in him. Jacques, however, was not fooled by this charade. He could sense the rivalry simmering just below the surface and took great pains to ensure that it did not erupt into something more serious. He kept a careful eye on them both. Immediately as he sensed an edge of resentment creeping into the training, Napier would find himself with another job to do and his opponent would have another exercise to perform.

Throughout their teenage years there was no change in the pecking order or in their attitude to each other. Jacques was able to keep them apart and now with both of them approaching their nineteenth birthdays, he was justly proud of both his pupils. Napier was now a fine, happy-go-lucky young man, knowledgeable and articulate, accustomed to speaking French with Jacques and English with everyone else. He could read and write not only in English, but also in French and Latin with equal fluency.

Napier's academic abilities were not general knowledge.

Jacques did not think it wise for the masters of the house to know that a mere servant was better educated than they were. It was not that the duke's son lacked intelligence; in fact, he was a very able student if he wished to be so – the opportunities to learn had been readably available to him, as his father had provided him with the best tutors money could buy. However he was surly and lazy with academic subjects and achieved far less then he was capable of attaining; only with Jacques fencing lessons did he make strenuous efforts to learn. Now, as he approached manhood, Jacques believed he was a match for any swordsman he had ever seen, with one possible exception: his own adopted son Napier. Jacques could never make up his mind which of the two were the better: the duke's son was certainly the most stylish and the better technical swordsman, but Napier was more fluent in his movements and had a natural talent as a fighter. Privately Jacques suspected that even though they were equals in swordsmanship, if the unthinkable were to happen, and a duel took place to the death, their different personalities would give the aristocrat a slight edge. He had a cruel and sadistic streak and would undoubtedly kill without hesitation any opponent who gave him the opportunity. Napier on the other hand was compassionate and understanding. He would seek to wound rather than kill, and it was that slight hesitation would be his undoing.

The duke was immensely proud of his son, the swordsman, putting a far higher value on his ability than any academic achievement. After all, a gentleman did not have to be knowledgeable – when you are rich and powerful you can pay someone else to do the thinking – but as far as the duke was concerned a gentleman most certainly had to know how to defend himself.

The duke's heir had inherited his father's temper. He had not as yet taken part in a duel, but it was only a matter of time before he did so. His quarrels with his friends had been frequent. Only his position in life and his much-vaunted ability with a sword had prevented a challenge being made. Eventually the inevitable would happen – someone would find his honour slighted beyond endurance and the challenge would come. The duke could hardly wait for the moment he would be able to boast to his friends of his son, the duellist. At every social event he would look eagerly for the sound of raised voices in anticipation of the moment of challenge.

It was this waiting period in expectation of the first duel that was fast becoming a bone of contention between the duke and Jacques. The duke was keen for Jacques to remain in his service to see his son through his first duel, then he would consider the contract completed; Jacques on the other hand believed he had discharged his commitment to the full. Jacques, now well into his seventies, was becoming increasingly homesick for his native land, a very fit man for his age, his one overwhelming desire was to return to his beloved Paris, taking his adopted son with him, and settle down to retirement and a peaceful life in the city he considered home.

He had sent his money to France at regular intervals where Françoise Faubert had made some shrewd investments to ensure a reasonably affluent retirement. On this subject he had recently received a letter from Françoise confirming the purchase of a house close to his fencing Salle, the intention being that he and Napier should live there. Napier would run the Salle for him, his adopted son despite his youth being imminently qualified for the task. Jacques, having completed his plans for a return to Paris had no wish to wait over an uncertain period for the expected duel to manifest itself, after all he reasoned it could be weeks or it could be years, indeed who could tell. Therefore he had made up his mind at the first available opportunity he would approach his employer the duke on the subject, to inform him he considered his contract completed and intended to leave for Paris immediately.

The following morning the duke's son had not as yet arrived for his practice. Jacques and Napier were alone in the Salle, when the door opened and the duke popped his head in and looked round for his son. Jacques immediately seized the opportunity to broach the subject of his return to Paris, but the words fell on deaf ears. The man categorically refused to involve himself in any discussion of the subject whatsoever. He turned on his heel and cut Jacques short with a curt retort.

"I do not wish to hear any more on the subject. I have told you before and now I am telling you for the final time, no one leaves my employment until I am good and ready to allow them to go."

So saying, he strode out of the Salle and into the dining hall.

Jacque's eye flashed with anger, he was not about to allow himself to be dismissed in this manner, without pausing to even to allow himself the time to put down the sword he had been holding, he followed the duke angrily into the dining room, within seconds the two men were arguing furiously. Napier walked to the doorway, but he did not follow Jacques into the dining room; he thought it more prudent to remain in the Salle, as his presence would only aggravate the situation. In any case it was not his quarrel; Jacques could usually manage these matters perfectly well on his own. From where he stood in the half open doorway he had a clear view of the hall, the two men and the dramatic events that followed.

The dining hall was an impressive high vaulted room, its oak beams and stained glass windows gave it a distinctly medieval look. It was part of the original house before the re-building and alterations were carried out by the duke's predecessors. The oak-panelled walls were hung with tapestries and symbols of heraldry; standards from ancient battles hung alongside weapons of all types, some of them dating back to the middle ages. Dominating the far end of the room with carved stone columns and massive stone mantle was an enormously impressive fireplace, with roaring log fire kept well stoked by the servants who acted on the direct orders of the duke. He preferred this room to any in the house and liked it to be warm as he spent much of his time in it. The door, which gave access to the narrow stone stairway leading to the kitchens, was at the far end of the room, during the formal dinners that were frequently held; a large folding screen would shield this doorway from view. The food would be ferried from the kitchens and placed on the long mahogany sideboard situated along the adjacent wall. Contained in this sideboard were all the family silver and cutlery required for the functions and dinners held at the manor. He was partial to a drop of brandy, so much so that at his insistence a wooden cask of the spirit at all times stood on the sideboard. It looked very much out of place on the polished surface, where it stood alongside the solid silver wine coolers, inlayed trays and jugs that were its more elegant companions. The dining table itself would be better described as substantial rather than elegant. As far as anyone knew it had been there since the hall was first built, made entirely of English oak. A whole wood must have been felled to obtain the massive blocks used in its construction. Sixty guests could be sat round it, on chairs that were in direct contrast to its solid, square, unyielding appearance. These chairs had been recently delivered from a London workshop where furniture was now being made from imported woods to delicate designs almost fragile in their elegant appearance.

The duke had sat down with his back to the fire; from his viewpoint behind the door Napier could see his face clearly. He was sitting slouched low in his chair with his face cupped in one hand. His eyes glared at Jacques, glittering out of a thunderous expression that would have sent a lesser man scuttling for the nearest bolt hole. Napier could not see Jacques' face but he knew that the good eye, alongside the black patch, would be flashing right back at the man. Jacques was a person who whatever the situation or mood would never fail to look a man in the eye.

He stood with his back to the door he had just walked through, the sword he was carrying laying flat on the table before him. Leaning forward with his face thrust towards the duke, he stood almost on his toes, holding the weight of his body on his arms spread out before him, his palms face downwards on the table.

Standing as he was inside the Salle with the door between himself and the dining room, Napier could hear the raised voices and could distinguish the note of anger in them, but apart from the odd word pitched higher that the others he could not make out what was being said. As he watched he became more and more concerned that the argument was getting out of hand. Suddenly the duke jumped to his feet, livid with rage. With one sweep of his hand he scatted crockery and cutlery off the table, expensive china crashed to the floor, as well as the remains of his breakfast, not cleared since he had not given his servants any time to do their work. Now with the sound of angry voices echoing down to the kitchen none would dare to show their faces until all was peaceful again.

This sudden outburst of physical anger gave Jacques the chance to make some jibe conjured up from his rapier-like wit. The duke stepped back with an abrupt jerking movement, almost as though he had been physically struck. Then, without any prior warning, he reached out and grabbed a two-pronged pickle fork from the table. With his face contorted out of all recognition in a mask of demonic rage, his eyes bulging out of their sockets flashing hate and looking almost like the devil himself, he lunged with all his strength at the fencing master's unprotected face.

To Napier it felt as if he had suddenly gone deaf: the angry voices stopped abruptly and through the silence his sensitivities seemed to feel as well as hear, the sound of his father's agonised scream. Jacques had turned towards him with his body contorted with pain, his head thrown back and his hands held up right in front of him with the fingers spread wide, almost as though he wanted to clasp his head but dared not. Napier stood transfixed unable to move or even think as he gazed in stupefied horror at the stag-horned handle of the fork protruding from his father's one good eye. The blood pouring down his face and was staining the front of his shirt, spreading over the white fabric in a crimson blotch. Napier hurled himself into the room unaware that he was screaming with rage, unaware and uncaring that the target of his hatred was one of the richest and most powerful men in the country. Oblivious to everything, feeling and seeing nothing but this monster who had just blinded the man who was the only father he had ever known.

He hurled himself at him like a demented wildcat, desperately his opponent tried to fight off the spitting, snarling demon who had every intention of ripping him to pieces, but he had no chance against the strong fit youngster whose strength was increased tenfold by the searing hatred and boiling anger that surged through his brain in a torrent of maniacal vengeance. Napier kicked, scratched and punched his victim, venting his anger in any way he knew how. He had no control, no thought of what he was about, just something inside of him telling him to inflict pain and hurt upon this most hated of enemies. Suddenly he did not want to touch this man. He felt he wanted to throw him from him, see him splattered against the wall broken into a thousand pieces. Pulling the duke to his feet he grabbed him by the arm and, using his full weight, he pulled him towards him and threw him, using his arm like a whip. Taking him completely off balance, he flew uncontrollably headfirst into the open fireplace, downwards on the burning logs.

Still seething with blind fury, Napier picked up the first available item to hurl at his opponent. Seizing the cask of brandy from the sideboard, his anger gave him the strength to lift the heavy barrel above his head. With superhuman power, he hurled the heavy missile at the figure in the fireplace, who was struggling and shouting in pain desperately trying to extricate himself from the flames burning into his scorched flesh.

The cask sailed across the room, smashing itself against the stone mantle of the fireplace. The combination of its own weight and the force by which it was thrown was too much for its construction: the wooden sides caved in, the two steel hoops holding it together came off the ends and the staves fell apart, cascading the volatile spirit onto the open fire. The whole front of the fireplace erupted into a fireball, hiding the unit and the man behind a wall of flames, it seemed an absolute certainty that nothing could live within that inferno. Then, like a phoenix emerging from the fire, came a grotesque mannequin of flame. Burning from head to toe it blundered wildly about the room, flapping its arms and kicking out wildly with its legs. It jerked around in a horrifying parody of dance, quite oblivious to everything but the searing agony within it, the thing that appeared no longer human spun furiously about the room, setting light to every combustible item it stumbled into.

Napier stood open-mouthed. He, the author of this tableau from Hades, stood rooted to the spot and frozen into immobility by the sudden and horrifying consequences of his actions. A movement seen out of the corner of his eye jerked him out of his stupefied state; the duke's son had entered the room and was reaching across the table about to pick up the sword placed there by Jacques only minutes before. Napier had to act quickly. This was potentially the finest swordsman in England; if he were to arm himself with that sword, Napier would be dead. If he were armed himself then maybe it would be a different story, but unarmed he stood no chance whatsoever. Desperately looking for a weapon, his eye fell on the display of ancient weapons on the wall. The nearest to hand was a flail-like club called a 'morning star', a heavy steel ball set with a number of steel spikes attached to a short shaft by a length of chain. Ripping this implement of warfare from its mountings, with fear and desperation adding speed to his movements, he swung the flail in a deadly arc bringing it down with all his might on the extended hand about to pick up the sword from the table.

The sound of the heavy ball crushing bones and flesh as its steel spikes bit through the human tissue and embedded itself into the solid oak of the table mingled with the crackling flames and the scream of agony from the youth, with his mutilated hand crucified to the table, stuck there as securely as a butterfly pinned to a board. All this ferocious action, from the moment Napier had hurled himself onto the duke to the instant of dealing with his son, had appeared to have lasted for hours, whereas it had, in fact, taken place in a matter of seconds.

Almost as thought he were seeing it for the first time Napier looked around and surveyed the scene. The fire had taken a firm hold, tapestries and wall panels were alight all round the room, the fireplace end, right up to the roof beams was an inferno. At the far end was a charred smoking heap, unrecognisable as a human being, and which was all that remained of the IV duke of Mulgrove. On the table as yet untouched by the flames lay a figure squirming and writhing. At the end of its arm, anchoring it to the table, was a spiked ball chained to a shaft that was surrounded by a mass of bloodied pulp that had once been a human hand.

Suddenly through the turmoil a voice calling his name penetrated his confused senses, interrupting his horrified understanding that he had been the perpetrator of this scene of destruction. Jacques, the fork still sticking out of his eye, was feeling his way along the line of chairs and calling to him; he had managed to conquer his pain and, despite the fact he had been deprived of his sight, he was now thinking rationally. In fact Jacques was now more in control of his senses than Napier. Once he was able to grasp the younger man's arm his strong personality came to the fore. Thus he was able to force him to think clearly and to control his trembling limbs. At Jacques request he quickly explained the events of the last few minutes. The old man had heard the noise and felt the heat from the flames; he was aware there had been conflict about him, but because of the agonising pain and the consequent blindness, he had been unaware of the full extent of the horrors Napier had inflicted on the house of Mulgrove.

Now he knew exactly what must be done.

"Quickly," he said to Napier, "take my arm lead me to my quarters, you must escape from here before they catch you."

Without so much as a backward glance at the duke's son, who lay moaning and whimpering on the table, Napier half carried the stumbling, bloodstained Jacques out of the dining room and into the Salle. Locking the dividing door behind him he was surprised to find how quiet and peaceful the Salle was, almost as though shutting the door and blocking out the sound of the crackling flames had transferred them to another world. This he knew to be just an illusion of safety, the door would hold for a while but it would only be a matter of time before the flames consumed the rest of the house.

Wasting no time he half carried and half pushed the old man across the Salle and into his book-lined room within the tower, pausing only to help Jacques to slump into his chair at the desk. He hastily locked the door and started to pile furniture against it to use as a barricade.

"Never mind that!" shouted the fencing master. Once again Jacques had taken control of the situation.

"Quickly, boy, load my pistol!"

Napier rummaged in the cupboards and found the wooden case. Taking out the flintlock he took powder ball and wad; spilling more powder than he was putting into the weapon, he managed to get the pistol loaded. While Napier was thus occupied Jacques had been feeling about in the drawers of the desk and produced a soft leather bag of coins and a sealed envelope, these he put into a leather pouch, which he now thrust at Napier.

"Here, boy, take these and go quickly! In this bag is enough money to get you to France and see you settled, the envelope contains my Will. Take it to Paris, find my friend Françoise Faubert. He, as my executor, will see that its terms are carried out. I have left you everything – my money, my house, my fencing school, they are all yours now!"

At first Napier did not comprehend the implications of his father's words; he started to argue.

"But what about you? We must find bandages. You need medical treatment. We must escape together!"

Jacques interrupted him, "No, boy, it is impossible. We cannot escape together. Alone you have a chance, I would only slow you down. We would be caught before we had gone a kilometre. My time has come, give me the pistol and go quickly."

Suddenly the whole horrifying realisation of what the old man intended to do hit Napier with stunning impact. His blood ran cold and the colour drained from his face. His father intended to end his own life here in this room. Blow out his brains with the pistol.

"No, you cannot," he almost screamed at him. "You must not do this. There must be a way we can escape together. We will take our chances and meet our fate side by side."

The old man held out his hand; he was speaking quietly now almost gently but with authoritative conviction.

"My boy, you are not my blood relative but you are as much a son to me as anyone ever could be. I am grateful for the years we have shared, but now our lives must part. Do not grieve for what fate has inflicted upon us, we can do little but accept the course of our lives. I have had a good life without regrets, now it is over and yours is just beginning. Do not throw it away before it starts. I have prepared you to the best of my ability for the years to come; use the knowledge wisely and live your life with honour. Now go, quickly. Do not throw your life away before it begins. I made up my mind years ago that if I lost my other eye I would not live out the rest of my life in darkness. Give me the pistol, the pain is almost unbearable, do this as your last act of kindness to me. You would do no less for a dog if he were in pain!"

Napier protested; his whole being rebelled against the very thought. How could he allow this to happen and yet deep inside he knew the old man was right. He knew that burdened with an old man, severely wounded and blind, they would stand no chance of outrunning the mounted men and dogs who would be scouring the countryside in pursuit. In his mind's eye Napier could see this proud man captured and humiliated. They could expect no mercy nor would they receive it, even if they escaped being ripped to pieces by the hounds. The prospects of being beaten to death or hung on the spot were high, allowing for the possibilities of being taken alive they would fare little better. There would be no judicial mercy for men who had killed a duke and burned his son alive. To see his father broken by imprisonment and humiliated by a farcical trial, followed by the inevitable death by hanging, this was more than Napier could stomach.

He became very calm and clearly in his mind he knew what he must do. Steadily and very quietly to avoid the slightest click he drew back the hammer and cocked the flintlock. Swiftly and silently he moved to the desk; without hesitation he pointed the weapon and shot his father through the forehead. Jacques slumped back in the chair, his head thrown backwards by the force of the ball; he had died instantly without knowledge of what was happening. Napier broke into a cold sweat and swallowed hard. He had done what he knew he must do, however hard the act had been for him to carry out. He had saved his father from the trauma of having to take his own life; he had taken away his pain and agony and given him a swift and merciful end.

There are those who would condemn Napier for what he had done. There are those who would say that where there is life there is hope, that you must struggle on no matter what the odds or the consequences. Napier however had no conscience stricken doubts or regrets about what he had done. He knew with absolute certainty that Jacques would prefer to end his life this way. This was Jacques' personal code, the code by which he had lived all his life, the code he had striven to instil into Napier throughout the years of companionship and education they had shared together. Consequently the code had given Napier the strength to commit the act he and Jacques would consider to be the kindest and most unselfish act that any one human being could do for another.

Napier struggled to surmount the sense of grief and overwhelming sadness that was threatening to overcome him; he had to shrug off the desire to throw himself into a corner and weep. With tears blurring his vision, he pulled the fork out of his father's eye. Gently he laid the arms in position o the desk with the palms downwards he pushed the body forwards and laid the head on them looking almost as though he had gone to sleep.

Instinctively he would have liked to go back into the house and fight his way out, killing as many people as he possibly could in retribution for the death of his father, but common sense and plain humanity told him he would be fighting against paid servants who had done him no harm and had played no part in the tragic events leading to his present predicament. The people responsible had already been dealt with and to dally now with pointless heroics would only lead to his capture and make a mockery of the sacrifice made by Jacques. There was only one course of action now and that was to make good his escape while he could.

Picking up the pouch containing the money and the documents he slung the strap over his head and picked up the pistol. A moment's thought decided him that it would be of little use, he had never been much of a hand with firearms; with its accompanying powder and shot the weapon was far too heavy for a man on the run who was trying to move swiftly over rough terrain. Besides what good would a single shot be against a pack of mastiffs? Flinging the pistol from him he moved over to the wall and took down Jacques' sword from its rack. This magnificent weapon had been Jacques pride and joy and it would be a much truer companion against the odds he must face. Slipping the hanger strap over his head he adjusted the sword on one hip and the pouch on the other, he was now ready to go. However before he went there was one last task he must perform, one last duty to his adopted father.

Taking the flask of gunpowder he scattered the contents around the room, next he unscrewed the base of the lamp and poured the oil everywhere until it was empty. The other lamp stood on the window ledge; luckily he did not have to search for a tinder- box. It was there where it always was, kept by the lamp. Hurriedly he struck flint to steel after several tries he was successful in producing flame with which to light the lamp. Throwing open the window, he sat with his legs astride the sill, the lamp held in one hand. The window was small and sitting as he was with his body blocking out the sunlight, the room appeared dark with the yellow light of the lamp casting shadows into the dim corners. The interior was a shambles, as the feverish activity of the last few minutes had resulted in all the familiar objects being scattered about the floor. In his haste to spread the volatile fuel about the room, he had pulled down shelves and furniture; Jacques' treasured books and belongings were laying in heaps alongside the upturned furnishings. In the middle of it all, the desk remained undisturbed with the body sitting in the chair, appearing to have fallen asleep over one of his books, as Napier had seen him do so often in the past. This scene would be etched forever on the inner eye of Napier's memory in the years to come. He sat looking almost afraid to commence the final act, until voices in the Salle brought him to his senses with the realisation that he must close the final chapter and go quickly if he was to make good his escape. He could not stay to bury Jacques, yet he did not want to leave the task to others who would do the job without mourning and with less feeling or ceremony than they would give to a farm animal. All he could do for Jacques now was to give him a Viking funeral, consumed by the flames amongst his treasured books and belongings so no one else would have them. Jacques would like the poetic irony of that.

With this thought in mind he flung the lamp with all his strength at the far wall. The resulting explosion and rush of air from the erupting flames nearly ended his escape before it had started. Napier had been totally unprepared for the results of his actions, and he was blown backwards through the window with a twenty-foot drop to the ground below. More by luck than deliberate intention, his foot still inside the room, caught under the window frame, and this halted his fall sufficiently for him to twist round and grab the bottom sill. For a split second he felt a sickening wrench as his arms took the full weight of his falling body, halting its plunge for a moment before his tortured fingers gave way and he plummeted to the ground. The jolt as he hit the ground jarred through his whole body; he lay on the ground gasping great gulps of air, his shocked lungs desperately trying to pull back in the oxygen that had been forced out of them.

For precious minutes he lay there, then his brain started to sound the warning signals. 'Get on your feet and start moving,' he told himself. Struggling to his feet trying to ignore the pain in his legs where it felt as if his bones had been pushed up into his body. With a wry smile he imagined himself with legs about six inches long, but this was not time for humour misplaced or otherwise, so casting a quick glance around to see if anyone had seen him he hobbled across the grass and disappeared into the shrubbery. Keeping his head down and using as much cover as was available to avoid being seen from the house, he crossed the kitchen garden and scaled the perimeter wall without too much difficulty. Having recovered completely from his fall he was relieved to find he had not sustained any serious injuries.

Now that he was out of sight from the house and had reached the cover of the woods, he took to his heels and ran as if the devil himself was after him.

3

Run with Your Brains or the Dogs Will Have You

Young and fit as he undoubtedly was, Napier could not continue the flat-out pace he had set himself. His mindless headlong flight took him for approximately three miles before he collapsed on the ground, gasping for air like a landed fish. He was angry with himself for his thoughtless panic. He now knew his only hope was to think clearly and to pace himself if he were to stand any chance of out-running the inevitable pursuit. As soon as his pounding heart and pumping lungs had settled and he was able to comfortably sit up and wipe the sweat from his brow, he looked around and took stock of the situation and found himself on top of a hill. From here he could look back over the route he had taken and see in the valley the manor house he had just left.

As yet, there were no apparent signs of pursuit; indeed it was doubtful if anyone down there had the time to even think about it. Black smoke was pouring out of the house; rising in a column in the still air it hung in a great black cloud a dirty blotch in the blue sky, overhanging the trees and spreading across the green fields. The whole dining hall wing was ablaze the entire roof had fallen in fuelling the flames with its massive timbers. He could see clearly the stone tower that had been his home for so long; great tongues of red and yellow flame were licking out of the windows. In his mind's eye Napier could see the interior of the tower with the charred body sitting at the desk. Tears streamed down his face as he gazed at this his father's funeral bier. Men looking no bigger than ants were rushing to and fro, some winding water up from the well, others forming bucket chains in the forlorn hope that the pitiful drops of water they threw would quell the roaring flames threatening to engulf the entire area.

As Napier stood and watched the dramatic scenes below him, he began to formulate a plan of action. He realised for the first time that headlong flight was not going to be much help to him. It did not matter how quickly he ran or how far he travelled, men on horseback would move quicker, dogs would track him wherever he went and men would betray him for the reward that would undoubtedly be offered. He must use cunning and guile. He must use his head to outwit them. Another five miles and he would cross the Southampton road. They who knew him and Jacques would know perfectly well he would have every reason to make for France and then on to Paris. There were many people at the house who were familiar with both their histories and would have no problem in putting two and two together and thus work out his eventual destination. They would expect him to go to the Southampton road in the hope that once there he would be able to take ship for France, then, via Le Havre or Dieppe, he could move on to Paris. But he would confound them: he would turn north not south, then he would cut across eastwards until he found the Birmingham and the London road, only then would he turn south and head for London and continue his journey, eventually moving from the capital bound for Paris. It would be easier to remain anonymous whilst mingling amongst the crowds in the teeming streets. Once in the city he would be able to lose himself for a while, then he could move on to Dover and find a ship bound for Calais or Boulogne, before the final journey to Paris. This route would probably take months whereas if he went straight to Southampton he could be shipping out in a week. However he would stand a better chance taking the longer and less-expected route. The Southampton road would be watched every inch of the way and would be far too dangerous for him to take.

Turning his back for the last time on Mulgrove Manor, Napier squared his shoulders and set off on his journey. This time, however, there was a difference in his flight, and he no longer ran mindlessly without thought of direction or energy expended. He set off at a brisk trot, knowing if he kept a steady pace he would be able to cover many miles without stopping and more importantly if an emergency did arrive he would have a clear head to cope.

Napier did not realise it but he had matured in the last hour. All the training and education Jacques had given him was now his most valuable asset. He had risen this morning a youth and now, at the commencement of his journey, he was a man. As he ran Napier placed his hand on the hilt of his sword to steady it – Jacques' sword, the one he had carried since his early days as a mercenary. He remembered the story Jacques often told of how he had acquired it in the Holy Land. He had saved the life of an elderly craftsman, who was being beaten and robbed by thieves. He had driven them away and helped the old man back to his home. He was staying in the area for a while and because of this he was able to visit him again and they became friends. The old man had been an armourer skilled in the manufacture of weapons. Retired, with his sons operating his workshop, he apparently made the occasional weapon whenever he felt the need to do so. The elderly craftsman, being grateful for Jacques' help and his subsequent friendship, insisted on manufacturing a sword as a present. He claimed to possess the long forgotten secret of Damascus steel and had hidden away sufficient material to manufacture one more blade waiting for the ideal occasion to use it.

'A blade made of this material,' he boasted, 'would be unique in all the world!' The eventual completion of the weapon proved that this was no idle boast. The sword was unique and all he claimed it to be. A practical weapon made to be used and not simply displayed; it had none of the elaborate ornamental work inlaid with gold and precious jewels that were the hallmark of most presentation swords. Modelled on the design of the European small sword, the designs were decidedly of the East. The pommel was solid silver and fashioned in the form of a snake's head, its jaws open with forked tongue and fangs ready to strike. The body of the snake came down the back of the handle and would itself around the base. The handle itself was superbly carved from ivory. The guard was also made in the shape of an intertwining serpent and was made of steel for durability. Magnificent as the craftsmanship and conception of the handle might be, it was eclipsed by the appearance of the blade – highly polished and engraved for three quarters of its length, it gave off a slightly blue sheen. This blade had been the topic of discussion and attempted duplication by many a well-known sword maker, but none could duplicate its cutting edge. It could be honed to the sharpness of a razor and many was the time that Jacques had used it in the field for that very purpose. The overall appearance of the sword, its design and faultless craftsmanship, the unique material with which it was made, coupled with the silver inlaid crocodile-skin scabbard and belt, made it a very outstanding weapon indeed. Even its maker, having seen the overall result, considered it his lifetime achievement, a masterpiece never to be bettered, and therefore never again did he make another sword.

This very fact was the worrying thought buzzing through Napier's brain now. It was a unique weapon, so unique that anyone who saw it remembered, Jacques on many occasions had been offered large sums of money for it. The possession of it could identify him as clearly as if he had his name stamped across his forehead. Only they who lived at the manor and its surrounding community could identify his face, but a circulated description of the sword would identify him to anyone who saw it. Reluctantly he made the decision that he must abandon it. This sword was the heritage he valued above all other but he knew he could not keep it, strapped to his side it would be a Judas that would betray him to anyone who saw it. Napier kept up his steady pace. He knew he was making good progress over rough ground, and although he had no means of telling time, when he came within sight of the road he guessed he had covered the five miles in less than an hour. Since his escape from the hall he had not sighted any people who would be able to tell his pursuers where he had gone, now as he approached the road there were signs of human activity.

In the distance, travelling south, a bullock cart heavily laden trundled slowly along. If he could catch that cart he would be able to lay a false trail. The road was muddy and deeply rutted with wagon tracks. This was obviously a busy highway. The tracks of drovers and their animals mixed and mingled with heavy bullock carts and the thinner tracks of coaches and carriages. Napier set off running at a steady pace in the direction of Southampton, with the absolute certainty he would be followed. He had a healthy respect for the nose of the bloodhound; in the past he had seen them work and discussed them with their handlers. He knew that despite the heavy activity and multiple tracks on the road, once they had his scent they would follow him with little difficulty. The bullocks were pulling the heavy cart very slowly at barely a walking pace, the driver sitting slumped sideways in his seat made no attempt to hurry them along. He dozed in the sunshine, lulled into sleep by the rumble of the wheels and the slow plod of the animals' hooves. Napier quickly caught up with the slow-moving vehicle and the situation was ideal for his purpose. The sound of turning wheels straining timbers and harnesses, the noise from the bullocks, their cloven hooves kicking at the ruts and loose stones in their path made it easy for him to approach the rear of the cart unseen; slipping the strap of the sword off his shoulders he took one last look at the beloved weapon, then reluctantly and with a conscious effort of will pushed the sword into the sacks on the back of the cart. This was a deliberately thought out ploy to deceive his pursuers. If he could not keep the sword then at least he would use it to send the hunt of him in the wrong direction.

Hopefully there would be sufficient time to carry out his plan by the time the fire had been dealt with and the authorities informed. Many hours would have passed before the order for the hunt to begin could be given, with the duke and his son both dead, the servants – leaderless and without a clear direction, with no one to instruct them – could not be expected to instigate a hue and cry without orders from a magistrate and this, therefore, gave Napier the valuable time he needed to make good his escape.

His intention now was to follow the road south until he found a suitable hiding place where he could wait for a vehicle going north, if he could approach unseen from the rear and climb aboard, then his feet would be off the ground and the dogs would lose the scent. He would be moving north while the hunt followed his trail south, once the dogs lost the scent they would assume he had been on the bullock cart, with any luck the sword would be identified and handed in for a possible reward. Thus the pursuers would have physical proof of the direction he was heading. All this was conjecture of course and based on his assumption that the hunt was in possession of the necessary knowledge and would take the expected action, but it was worth the risk and the waste of precious time to set the ploy up if it worked, and sent the hunt off on a false trail while he continued on his journey unhindered.

Having disposed of the conspicuous sword, he sat down at the side of the road and considered his next move, he felt sure he was safe for the moment, there was time to review his position and plan carefully. The manhunt would not start until the morning, he was sure of that. It would take until the evening to put the fire out. Every man available would be needed for that. Then they would have to identify the bodies before they could know fully what had happened, even then they would not know he was on the run until they had made a head count. Only then would they be able to mobilise the officers of the manorial court. Yes, he was happy; in his mind he had until at least daybreak before the hunt began. By then he would be well on his way in the opposite direction.

He gave the cart carrying his sword an hour to disappear from sight then set off to follow it on its journey south, he travelled on down the road walking out of the mud wherever possible in order to lay a good scent for the dogs to follow. He had covered something in the region of three to four miles, and was beginning to have doubts about the wisdom of his plan, when he saw ahead the patch of road seemingly ideal for his purpose. He had been looking for a badly worn, deeply rutted and difficult stretch, running through trees or bushes where he could conceal himself; hopefully, he would be able to climb aboard a vehicle slowing down to negotiate the tricky terrain.

Stopping and considering the stretch of road, he saw it to be exactly what he had in mind. The bushes were thick and wild, growing close up to the edge of the track; once a driver had his wheels in those deep ruts he would have no choice but to drive almost touching the bushes. Fear of breaking a wheel would fix his attention firmly on the control of his animals. Providing the load was high enough and given sufficient space at the rear, there should be no problems in sneaking aboard for the ride. However he was not so naive that he did not realise a coach or wagon travelling through open country might well have a guard on board armed with a blunderbuss. On difficult stretches such as this they would have every reason to be afraid of highwaymen. One glimpse of someone skulking in the bushes would certainly result in their opening fire with possibly disastrous results.

Therefore it was not without a certain anxiety and trepidation that Napier concealed himself and waited for the next vehicle on its way north. Lying concealed in the bushes, he well knew that precious hours were slipping away. He could see by the position of the sun that it was well into the afternoon.

Earlier on he had watched a train of pack horses go by, and two men with heavy packs had stumbled past, cursing the uneven state of the road, but of the type of vehicle he had been looking for there had been none. Gradually he became more and more agitated and began to fall prey to his own fears and anxieties. He knew that he must get aboard a vehicle otherwise his plans would fall about his ears. If he was still there at nightfall his chance would have gone, the day wasted laying there waiting for his pursuers.

In the distance he could see a narrow strip of road winding over the brow of the hill and going down into the valley where it disappeared into the trees to finally appear again not half a mile from where he lay waiting. His eyes were tired and strained from staring at that narrow ribbon in the distance, hoping to see something moving on its surface, but, apart from the pack horses and the two men walking, there had been nothing. Finally he got to his feet there seemed little point in waiting any longer, and very real danger if he did so, his plan to deceive the hunt had been a good one but it had depended on luck and apparently fate was not going to allow him to implement it.

He must move quickly now, forget his intentions to move north and make a run for Southampton with all its attendant dangers, try to make up the time he had lost waiting for a non-existent vehicle to appear, now he must throw caution to the winds and attempt to outrun the dogs. Pushing aside the bushes, he glanced into the distance and there he saw it moving fast down the ribbon of road. He had almost missed it. A vehicle of some sort had disappeared into the valley. Slipping back into the bushes a tide of hope surged through him, this could be his chance, with any luck he would still deceive those dog teams, and implement his plan as originally intended.

Impatiently he waited for his first sight of the hoped-for transport, it came far more quickly than he had anticipated and he marvelled at the speed of modern day transport, a coach and team of six, carrying passengers. The horses strained at the traces as they galloped towards him – would the rutted road slow them sufficiently for his purpose? Climbing aboard would be impossible at their present speed, now it was close enough for him to see the oiled harnesses with their burnished embellishments and to see that the coach was of a modern design, well sprung and light for fast travel. A splendid sight under any other circumstances with the sun shining on its black polished coachwork and its freshly painted red wheels. Napier, however, was more interested in the people it carried. The driver leaned forward urging on his horses, a bunch of reins held firmly in both hands; the guard sitting beside him the sun shining on the brass barrel of a blunderbuss laid across his lap. Despite the heat of the afternoon both men wore tricorn hats and heavy greatcoats, however the thick clothing did not appear to make them drowsy; in fact, as Napier observed to himself, they were far too damned alert for his liking.

The driver was obviously familiar with the road for he was pulling back on the reins and slowing down the coach as it approached the rough stretch where Napier was concealed. The guard was also not lacking in his duty, and he had picked up his weapon and was holding it at the ready. They were now close enough for Napier to see him pull back the hammer and cock the flintlock. Peering through the foliage, Napier bit his lip apprehensively, not only because of the firearm – he knew the power of such a weapon at close range – but also because he had just noticed two passengers on the top sitting at the rear of the coach. True, they appeared to be dozing, but nevertheless as they were seated on top and at the rear they were an additional hazard to his sneaking on board unobserved. Still he did not have an option this would be his last chance; he knew he must try despite the dangers. Fortunately the coach had slowed to a crawl, the driver reined in the horses and allowed them to pick their own way over the badly churned up ground.

This was exactly what Napier had anticipated, now he must time his moves to the second. The wheels were in the ruts, the leafy branches were brushing against the sides of the coach; he must make his move the moment the rear wheels passed his hiding place. The driver and guard would not be able to see him because of the bushes, so the real danger was the two passengers: if they continued looking ahead he would be out of their line of vision, but if they looked back to the rear of the coach then he would be in full view. However, there was no time to worry about that; he knew that he must commit himself, regardless of the danger. Concealed in the foliage he watched the spokes of the rear wheel pass slowly by, inches from his face, at the crucial moment he broke cover and slipped in between the big wheels at the rear of the coach. He had got away with it! There was no challenging shout. Now that he was close up behind he was out of the line of vision of anyone on the coach, the only problem remaining was to get on board.

The baggage platform at the rear was piled up with trunks and valises tied down with rope, they were protected from the elements by a strip of canvas fixed at the top and tied down at the bottom. Pulling himself on to the rear, Napier was able to wriggle under the canvas, where he would be concealed from prying eyes. The coach lurched on its springs as the extra weight hung onto the rear, but the movement went unnoticed, masked by the natural swaying and bumping of the carriage as it pulled across the rutted uneven surface of the road. He had done it! He was on board and safe, but only just. The platform was full of baggage; clinging to the ropes Napier was precariously perched on a two-inch strip of free space protruding from the pile of luggage, fortunately the canvas strip gave him a little support, otherwise he would have been thrown off at the first bump.

Having negotiated the rough area the coachman laid on the whip and quickly had the horses pulling strongly; again unaware that he now had an extra passenger. He appeared determined to make up good time over the relatively smooth going ahead; meanwhile the stowaway was finding the going extremely rough indeed. Spread over the baggage on his precarious perch he felt every single bump. Jolting and swaying, the coach threatened to rip free his hold at every buried rock and hole in the road. Perched as he was with his feet barely lodged on the narrow ledge, his weight almost entirely suspended on his arms, he had managed to twist them through the bindings but the ropes were cutting into his arms as he hung on with all his strength. The coach ride, which had been his salvation, was now becoming his nightmare; however, nightmare or not it must be endured. If he were to fail, the consequences would be unthinkable.

The buffeting he was taking was bad and the discomfort extreme, but through it all – the noise of the speeding coach, rumbling wheels and drumming hooves – came another sound, a sound that cut through it all and struck terror into his already thumping heart: the baying of excited hounds on a scent. Pushing his head to one side he managed to look back along the road by peering through the side of the canvas. They had just passed the area where he had joined the road earlier in the day; there was the path he had travelled on his cross-country flight from the manor. Coming down the path and straining at the leash were two teams of dogs, the bloodhounds leading and the mastiffs bringing up the rear. Going by the excited behaviour of the dogs and the men holding them in check, there could be no doubt they had a scent. They had missed the coach by a hair's breath, another few seconds and they would have met them coming up the road. Without a doubt they would have flagged them down to check the passengers and to question the driver. He could not have hoped to avoid detection with those trained noses and dripping fangs merely feet from where he was concealed.

As the coach laboured on he went cold with fear that the men had stopped the teams at the road and were staring after the speeding vehicle; doubtless they were wondering whether or not they should follow it. He breathed a sigh of relief when he saw the dogs pulling away, anxious to continue down the road, the men allowed them their head, satisfied they were on to a strong scent. Sure in their own minds that ahead of them their quarry was running. His plan had worked brilliantly. They were on a false scent and he was travelling away from them in the opposite direction. He allowed himself a grim smile of satisfaction. Nevertheless it had been a close run thing. How could they have mobilised so quickly? He had totally underestimated the speed with which the magistrates were able to get men on his trail. There and then he made a mental vow that never again would he take such a risk. Because his plan had worked so well the hunt was now on a false trail. He had even been privileged to watch them follow it but it could have gone so desperately wrong. He was under no illusions. He knew that it was more by luck than good judgement that he was here now and not stranded down the road, a few pitiful miles in front of the dogs where he would, without doubt have been caught within hours. But it had worked. A miss is as good as a mile. If they find his sword they will put two and two together and conclude his direction lies south and onward to the coast, whereas he was going north, putting miles between himself and the pursuit with every turn of the wheels.

How long he remained in his self-inflicted torture at the rear of the coach he would never know. He had lost all sense of time and was oblivious to everything but the wracking pain in his arms and legs and the ache throughout his body buffeted and bruised by the swaying bouncing coach. Evening was fast approaching and darkness began to close in quickly. He felt he could no longer hang on; the swaying coach threatened to break his hold at any moment, only willpower was keeping him there now he had long ago lost the feeling in his hands and feet. His self-discipline alone allowed him to prolong his ordeal.

Suddenly through his semi-conscious senses he heard the sound of a coach horn. The guard was heralding their approach and arrival at their destination. He felt the motion of the coach ease and slow as the driver reined in the horses. Oblivious to the danger of being crushed by the rear wheels Napier released his hold and allowed himself to slip out from under the canvas screen. Completely exhausted, he dropped like a rag doll and lay in a crumpled heap on the roadway. Almost in a daze, he watched the rear of the coach disappear into the twilight. A warning voice in his head began to tell him he must find some cover. Staggering to his feet, he managed to cross the road and fell into a cornfield where he lay concealed, recovering his strength. Laying there, looking up at the clear sky, lulled by the smell of the growing corn, its slender stalks sheltering him from the cool evening breezes, there would have been no great hardship in spending the night there, but having lain there for a couple of hours Napier was now fully recovered. His muscles, stretched and strained by his recent ordeal as a stowaway, were now back to normal and he felt none the worse for his experience.

However there were now other urgent needs crying out to be satisfied. Not a morsel of food had passed his lips all day and despite his many exertions he had not taken any form of liquid either. This neglect of the inner man was beginning to catch up with him, his stomach felt as empty as a drum. The hunger he could have tolerated but his raging thirst was a torment and his mouth felt as dry as an old biscuit. Food he could manage without for a while, but he was desperate to find something to drink. He began to think about the coaching inn that he knew must be within walking distance. There would perhaps be no element of risk there at the moment, as the hunt would be concentrated on the roads going south and he was many miles north of the manor. Therefore he reasoned it most unlikely that he would be recognised. Rising to his feet he decided the risk was worth taking; he must have food and drink. Also it was important to obtain supplies for his coming journey, and there could be no denying that a comfortable bed would be most acceptable.

A few minutes walk brought him within sight of a small village: half a dozen houses dominated by a large inn, obviously a staging post as the stables covered a larger area than the inn itself. As he approached the village he gave himself a thorough dusting, beating the dirt from his clothes in an attempt to offer a more respectable appearance. Arriving alone and without transport would draw attention in itself, so anything he could do to be less conspicuous would be to his advantage. Most of the houses were in darkness, unlike the inn, which was well lit, the soft lights of the lamps streaming from every window sending a visual welcome to all who saw it.

As he entered the doorway Napier thought there could be no more comforting sight for a weary traveller than the interior of an inn. The smoky room was full of guests obviously passengers from coaches on an overnight stop, most of them sitting behind a pewter pot full of frothy ale. This was a good sign, the more crowded the bar the less chance of him being singled out and remembered. On each table there still remained plates containing the debris of their evening meal. Any doubts or fears that Napier may have had disappeared the moment the smell of ale and food wafted under his nostrils, his confidence restored he shut the door behind him and entered the room.

As was the custom of country inns everywhere the clientele stopped talking and turned to look at him as he entered. Most of them gave him a cursory glance, adjusted their wigs or puffed at their pipes then turned back to their friends and carried on talking. The innkeeper had been busy drawing ale from a line of barrels that stood on trestles over the far wall, he looked up as Napier entered and frowned at the dishevelled intruder, then looking away, continued with his task. Napier stood in the middle of the room wondering who to approach. He was about to call the innkeeper when the man stopped what he was doing and appeared to be mindful of his duties as a host. He came bustling over, threading his way through the tables and wiping his hands on his apron as he came. He was a large man, grossly overweight, and his bloated face and ruddy complexion gave clear evidence of the excessive consumption of his own ale.

Inexplicably his whole manner had changed. At first sight Napier had thought him to be quite a surly type of person, but then his whole manner had altered – he was jovial and hearty as a good host should be, lumbering across to great Napier like a long lost friend.

"Welcome, young sir, to my humble establishment. My house is at your disposal. Can I be of any service to you?"

Napier replied that he required food and drink, and also a bed for the night.

"Ha! Then you are in the right place. We have the best food, the finest ales and the most comfortable beds you will find in many a long day's march. Come this way, young sir!"

So saying, mine host took Napier by the arm and led him to a side door.

"No doubt you will want to have a wash and tidy up first." He said, "I will show you your room and send a wench up with a jug of hot water. Once you have completed your toilet, come down to the bar and my wife will have a hot supper on the table for you!"

Napier would have preferred his food and drink immediately and seen to his toiletry afterwards, but he knew he must observe the proprieties and not draw too much attention to himself; therefore, he followed his host through the side door and under the arched carriageway, which led into the courtyard at the rear of the inn. Being surrounded by buildings on all four sides the courtyard was very dark, lit only by two storm lanterns hanging there, they gave a little light but hardly enough to illuminate a large area such as the pitch dark courtyard. In the dim light from the lanterns Napier was just about able to make out the general layout, the three sides facing them were given over entirely to stable accommodation; above the stables on the left and right hand buildings a wooden balcony with a handrail ran the full length of both sides. Because of the darkness he could not see beyond the balconies, but guessed these would be the guest rooms. His assumptions were quickly confirmed when his host took one of the lanterns. Turning to his right he held up the lantern and revealed a set of wooden steps leading up to one of the balconies. Taking the steps with a great difficulty, heaving his bulk from one step to the other the innkeeper grunted and wheezed his way to the top. Napier followed impatiently, one step at a time, as he waited for the fat legs in front of him to move from step to step. Finally they reached the top where the man led him past door after door until they reached the end of the narrow balcony. Taking a bunch of keys from his belt he opened the last door and entered the room beyond. Setting the lamp down he produced a tinderbox, and fumbled with the flint, cursing the fickleness of modern devices. It took him a good five minutes before he was able to produce a flame and light the candle. Napier stood there and wondered petulantly about the possibilities of starving to death before the man got round to putting food on the table. Having got the candle burning to his satisfaction, mine host picked up his lantern. Once again he assured Napier of the qualities of his hostelry, confirmed that he would be sending up washing facilities and prevailed on him to make himself comfortable. Thus his duty discharged he went to the door and waddled off into the darkness.

Alone in the sparsely furnished room, Napier sat down on the bed and reviewed his position. He had to admit that since he had entered the inn he had thought of nothing else but his need for food and drink. Now in the quiet of the room his mind began to dwell once more on thoughts of his personal safety. All was not well. He had uneasy thoughts about this place. The innkeeper was far too jovial. True, innkeepers are supposed to be jovial – but with this fellow it did not come naturally. He was laying it on just a little bit too thick. There were unanswered questions that made Napier suspicious. His host had not asked where he was bound or where he had come from. He had not remarked on his dishevelled appearance nor had he queried the fact that he had no pack or other form of luggage. There was something about this man that did not quite add up, something about him that did not ring true. Now he came to think about it the innkeeper had been too damned keen to get him out of the bar and into the guest room. Another thing, why this room? At the far end of the balcony, why not one of the other rooms? Surely they were not all occupied?

Now that his suspicions were aroused, Napier moved swiftly. He might be wrong to doubt the innkeeper, but at this stage of the game he dared not take any chances. He did not bother to extinguish the candle but left it burning, quickly he slipped through the door and out onto the balcony, his intention being to put as many miles between himself and the inn as was humanly possible, he had been a fool to take such a risk so early on in the chase. Carefully shutting the door behind him he moved soundlessly over the wooden floor. Halfway along he became aware of loud whispers in the courtyard below him. Quietly dropping to his knees he felt along the boards and found they were not all closely fitted, he was able to place one ear to a gap and hear quite clearly the conversation being spoken in the courtyard below.

The first words confirmed his worst fears – they were obviously discussing him, he recognised the innkeeper's gruff tones saying:

"It *must* be him! The description fits exactly. No one travels without baggage unless they are on the run. You should see the state he is in, looking like that normally I would have thrown him out immediately if I had not suspected who he was."

His words were interrupted by a woman's voice, presumably his wife going by the tone and what she said.

"Shut up, you fool. Do you want the whole inn to hear you?"

Napier had to smile at this despite his predicament. The woman's voice was shrill and carried far further than her husband's.

"Have you locked him in?" she asked.

"No, my love," said the innkeeper timidly. "I forgot, but I put him in the end room. The door is thick and the window small!"

Once again the woman's voice interrupted him. She had obviously taken command now and was issuing orders, "Joseph, you are a good shot for a stable boy, take your carbine and stand below the window, if he tries to climb out, put a shot into the thatch, that will stop him. You go back and lock that door. No, wait a minute! By the time you have got your fat carcass up the stairs he will be out. Jeremiah! You are more nimble, you take the key – lock the door and stand guard until I tell you otherwise. You are the landlord, go back and amuse your customers; I will get one of the stable boys to ride to the manor. They will be here by the morning, if we all play our part, by this time tomorrow we will be sharing the reward!"

Napier could hear the rattle of keys as the innkeeper struggled to take them off his belt. All the time his wife harangued him for being a slow ox, making more noise than all of them put together. If he had been still in his room he would surely have heard them by now. The woman's voice was shrill and piercing. He had heard enough. Rising to his feet he crept quietly to the head of the stairs, but he was too late. Already he could hear Jeremiah's heavy boots on the wooden steps. He was trapped. He stepped backwards into one of the doorways in the vain hope that if he pressed himself into the darkness the man might go past without seeing him, as his hands pressed against the door it moved under his touch, he staggered rear first into the room. Fortunately he had the presence of mind to shut the door seconds before Jeremiah's boots went clumping past. No one in this place, however secretive they hoped to be, they didn't do things quietly. Napier crouched behind the door and could hear his footsteps thumping on the boards and the key rasping as it turned in the lock of the room he had just vacated.

Looking round to get his bearings, Napier had the shock of his life: a tall figure was standing looking at him. It was then that he became aware of the sound of snoring; the sound came from the bed where he could just make out a large bulk laying outlined in the darkness. The tall figure had not moved and he could now see that what he had taken to be the figure of a man was in fact a clothing stand, holding a dark-coloured cloak and a floppy felt hat on the top. Luck was once again on his side. Thinking to himself that the hat was not exactly his style, he quickly put it on and wrapped himself in the long cloak; then, moving to the door, he stepped out on to the balcony. Jeremiah was standing guard at the far end; Napier could see his dim outline leaning on the rail, trying to light a pipe, oblivious to the fact that he was guarding an empty room.

Napier did not hurry. He turned and bid Jeremiah a courteous good night. Jeremiah grunted, blew a puff of smoke down his nostrils then ignored the polite guest and continued with his pointless vigil. Steadily and with a calmness he did not feel, Napier descended the creaking steps to the courtyard below. He stopped short at the bottom and pulled back into the shadows. There, under the archway, his only exit to freedom, stood the woman he assumed to be the innkeeper's wife. She was holding a lantern and appeared to be giving instructions to a man on horseback. Napier did not have to know what she was saying. He was well aware of the contents of those instructions. This was the stable boy whose task it was to ride through the night and betray his presence to the authorities. He would have to wait until she went indoors, fooling dim-witted stable hands was one thing, but outwitting this woman would be quite another. He knew he would not walk past her so easily. Napier stood in the darkness with nerves at breaking point. At any moment he expected to hear a shout from above, the indication that Jeremiah had discovered the room he had been watching was empty. Eternity seemed to go by as he waited for the mounted man and the woman to move. Finally the man put spur to his horse and galloped off into the night. The woman watched him go, holding up the lantern in the vain hope the pitiful light would pierce the blackness. As the hoofbeats faded into silence the woman picked up her skirts and went back into the inn, leaving the carriageway in darkness. This was Napier's chance. Moving as quickly and as quietly as was possible, with the hat pulled well down on his head and enveloped in the cloak, he moved invisibly across the courtyard and under the archway, creeping past the side door, expecting it to open at any moment.

With a tremendous feeling of relief he ran away from the inn, an establishment that only an hour ago he had looked upon as a haven. Now he put it behind him, expecting at any moment to hear the sounds of pursuit as they discovered he was no longer in the room. He cursed his bad luck and naivety in taking such a risk. He should have known that the news of his flight would have travelled ahead of him. After all his careful planning, his ploy with the sword in the cart to send the hunt off in the wrong direction had all been in vain. By the morning the hunt would once again be on his tail and he was tired and without food or water would be in no state to outrun them. He had very little option but to keep going blindly, trusting to his wits and luck to protect him. Once he was out of sight and sound of the inn he threw off the hat and cloak, without any clear idea of the direction he was heading he ran off into the night.

4

A Fortress Built by Nature

Although he knew he must cover as much distance as possible during the few hours left to him before daylight, Napier was by now level-headed enough to control his running to a steady trot. That way he knew he would be able to maintain a steady pace throughout the night. As he ran the thoughts went through his head in a tangled mass. His brain was in a seething turmoil over the tumultuous and horrifying events of the last twenty-four hours, but he knew that he must try to think rationally if he were to stand any chance of survival. Those dogs would be very difficult to outwit. He cursed the evil luck that had placed him in the same position that he was in when he had first fled the manor, indeed, he knew his position was infinitely worse – then at least, he had a plan and had known the direction in which he had been heading and also his final destination. He had even succeeded in laying a false trail; but now he was running blind and with very little head start on the pursuit.

He had arrived at the inn in darkness; he was leaving it in darkness. Therefore he had no way of knowing in what direction he was heading and no clear plan to avoid the hunt. Despite the fact that he cursed his evil luck, deep down inside he knew that the fault was his. He had been tempted by the lure of creature comforts and, worse, he had totally underestimated the opposition a second time. It was clear now that not only had they mobilised far more quickly than he had thought possible, but they had been planning, and thinking ahead of him. They must have sent riders to all inns and villages within the radius of a day's march; his description and the temptation of a lucrative reward had travelled ahead of him.

Remaining on the road had not seemed a sensible proposition, he had lost all sense of direction and could well be heading back to the manor, and for all he knew, straight into the arms of they who were on their way to capture him. Having left the road he had been running for the last hour over open countryside and was much relieved to come across a fairly wide stream. His most immediate problem, that had reached desperation level, was his raging thirst. He had not taken any liquid in the last twenty-four hours and had been involved in the most intense physical exertions. In fact he was dehydrated and could not have carried on much further. Now he was gratified to lie down on his stomach and satisfy his craving for water. He lay there awhile, regaining his strength, then rising to his feet he set off running along the shallow bed of the stream. He was aware that this would not throw off the hunt completely. They would merely walk the dogs along the banks until they could again pick up the scent once he left the water, but it would slow them down and split their forces. Without a scent the dogs would not be in full cry, they would not know whether he had gone up or down stream, thus buying him valuable time.

Because the stream was shallow and the bed firm with small stones he was able to make relatively good progress, but the darkness was a handicap for, despite the moonlight, which gave him reasonable vision, he was unable to see where he was placing his feet. Consequently there was a grave danger of his taking a serious tumble, which was in fact what actually happened. The stream had been shallow and unobstructed for miles. He had been running easily, the shallow water giving little resistance when suddenly his foot hit an obstacle and he measured his length over a large boulder sticking up in the middle of the stream. He sat up soaked to the skin, the icy water rippling past his legs once again he cursed his evil luck. He had fallen across the boulder, now his scent was on the rock for the dogs to find; even if he splashed it with water he could not be certain those sensitive noses would not be able to pick it up. Suddenly, he brightened; he could use it to his advantage, if he doubled back down stream and left the boulder as a false scent. If luck was with him he would still be able to elude the dogs.

Having made up his mind that this ploy was worth trying, he turned back on his tracks and commenced to run as quickly as possible downstream. Now he was running with the current he began to make better progress, despite the fact that the surrounding countryside was comparatively flat he was running downhill with the flow of water. However he had grossly underestimated the distance initially run, also he had not realised how close it was to the hour of dawn. Over to his left there was a distinct lightening of the sky and he knew that within a short time the sun would be rising, to his dismay it also indicated that once again he was heading south straight back into the jaws of the dogs. Too late now to alter his plan, the die had been cast he must follow it through, come what may.

Very shortly the sun would be rising, no time now to consider the implications of the direction he was heading, his prime concern was to get past the spot where he had entered the stream. To his horror he realised he could not know the spot where he had stopped for a drink, as because of the darkness he had not seen the surrounding countryside, therefore he could not identify the spot where the dogs would lose the scent. All he could do was run and hope his luck would hold, and that he did not meet them head on. With that scenario all would be lost. He could now see the edge of the sun peeping over the horizon, the light was improving by the minute and he was tiring fast, his breath tearing out of his lungs in great gasps. Despite this he urged himself on to greater efforts, knowing his only chance was to get downstream before the dogs arrived. He could not hope for the hunt to arrive at the inn much later than dawn and therefore they would be on his tail at any minute now. Suffering agonies of anguished doubt he moved with a furious desperation, not knowing how far he had run. Had he in fact now passed the spot where he had first entered the stream, or was it still ahead and he running full tilt into the jaws of the dogs?

With the sun a glowing ball on the horizon, it was now fully daylight. Napier was full of apprehension that he had once again misjudged the situation: had he been too clever for his own good and run too far in the time available, trying to lay a false trail? Desperate for reassurance he looked eagerly around for any landmark that might tell him he was now covering fresh ground and that the hunt was behind him, not in front. But all the time there was this dreadful fear he would round a bend and see ahead the men and dogs that were his pursuers. Going by his own sense of time he thought he must have travelled far enough to be past the point where the false scent would give him a modicum of safety, but he could not be sure and therefore kept up his fast run despite the fact of his bursting lungs and his breath coming in harsh pumping gasps trying to feed oxygen into tired, flagging limbs.

He was running in broad daylight, only too aware that with the sun sparkling on the water splashed up by his pounding feet he must have been visible for miles. To his great delight he saw ahead the stream disappearing into a thickly wooded area, immediately he felt a profound sense of relief, not only because he knew that the trees would give him cover but also because he now knew for certain he was on fresh ground. The trees were the landmark he had looked for, and he knew with absolute certainty, despite the darkness, he had not passed through that wood during the night.

Throwing all caution to the wind, and regardless of the danger of broken limbs, running headlong along the rough bed of the stream he entered the wood and gratefully accepted the cover the foliage offered him. The anxiety drained from him to be followed by a feeling of security as he followed the stream into the dark green depths of the wood. The stream wound its way through a tunnel of foliage the trees became thicker and more dense as he penetrated deeper into the interior, Napier had never seen trees growing so close and tightly packed before. Mostly they were hawthorns. Their spiny shoots and trunks growing from a single stem packed together and interlaced with brambles, making a barrier so impenetrable it was doubtful that even a dog could squeeze through let alone a man, overhead the branches met above the water almost shutting out the light with the occasional shaft of sunlight penetrating the canopy, the trees grew close to the edge of the rippling stream leaving virtually no banks, just the water running through the living tunnel of vegetation.

Napier's confidence was returning now that he was no longer exposed to public view. He felt safe enough to stop for a short rest and to take a drink of the life-giving water. The sense of false security afforded him by the wood made him forget for a moment he was still a fugitive pursued by determined ruthless hunters. Confidence in a quarry is short lived, however. It had been quiet in the wood, the heavy foliage blanketing out the natural sounds of the countryside, then almost imperceptibly above the sound of the rippling stream came the faint baying of hunting hounds.

That sound again. A cold chill penetrated his very soul when he heard it; they were on his trail and they were not far off. The thought galvanised him into action, running like a frightened rabbit he now saw his tunnel of vegetation in a different light, the impenetrable sides were a restricting trap, like thorny walls they confined him to the line of the stream. He could not push his way through the stout thorny barrier and even if he found an opening he could not take it for fear of leaving a scent for the dogs, supposing there is local knowledge with the hunt they would know of this living culvert of hawthorns, if that were the case they would send a dog team to the other end and he would be caught like a rat in a trap. Now he was really frightened. His fear almost a tangible thing he could practicably taste it as he realised the horror and hopelessness of his situation.

He began to look desperately for a way out of the position he was in. His every instinct telling him he was in the swiftly closing jaws of a trap, he looked at the canopy above him, if only he could get into the tops of those trees he might yet escape. An impossible wish, if ever there was one. He might just as well wish for the moon. The hawthorn branches above his head were well out of reach and much too thin for him to climb. They would bear his weight if he were on top but he would never be able to pull himself up from below into their thin bushy structure. Growing on the left bank was a sycamore tree standing in solitary splendour among the hawthorns. How easily he could have climbed it but one foot out of the water touch that smooth trunk and the hounds would have his scent the moment they arrived. He looked at the overhanging branches, there was safety tantalising close and yet so far away, if only he could reach them and pull himself up out of the stream he would squirm his way into the tops and hopefully the dogs would lose his scent.

Standing there looking up he realised he was wasting his time. If he had a rope maybe there was a possibility but without one it was hopeless, the lowest branch was a good fifteen feet above the water. The bloodcurdling cries of the hounds jerked him out of his daydream. They sounded closer now, much closer. He ran for his life, splashing through the stream, dodging rocks and broken branches. Suddenly he stopped his headlong flight; there in the centre of the stream was the very item that could mean his salvation. A broken branch, a single bough about ten feet long with a stout twig at the base broken off short and forming a sort of hook at the end, if he could hook that forked end over the lower branches of that sycamore up stream, there was a good possibility of him swarming up it to safety. At least it was worth a try. He picked up the branch and, turning back the way he had just come, he started to run upstream. At that moment he heard the sound he had dreaded: behind him, downstream, the baying of a bloodhound.

His worst fears were confirmed he was trapped between two dog teams. There was no time to lose, he had seen these dogs work before; the men handling them followed a set plan. Having lost his scent when he entered the water they would split up: one team doing downstream the other going upstream, the remaining teams would be taken by fast cart to get ahead of the fugitive, they would then work back thus trapping the prey between the two teams. Once the hounds picked up the scent again a horn would be sounded, all the dogs would converge on that spot from different directions. This method worked very successfully. Many a fugitive running from the hunt in panic thinking the dogs were behind him had run straight into the jaws of the dogs coming from the opposite direction. Napier could see this fate staring him in the face and well he knew it, he only had minutes to avoid the trap; even now running with his lifeline tucked under his arm, he could be meeting he dogs coming downstream. Thankfully he reached the sycamore and tried to hook the bough over the lowest branch, it was only just long enough in fact he could not catch it by merely extending his arms over his head, he had to jump reaching as high as he could. The fearful sounds of the hounds were frighteningly close, filling the air with a volume of sound so tangible it could almost be cut with a knife. In fact the dogs were almost upon him. He had tried two or three standing jumps and not been able to hook the branch, now in desperation he took a few steps backward and tried a running jump, it was difficult – handicapped by the water but the extra acceleration gave him the few inches he required and he saw the forked end of the bough hook itself over the branch. Napier was left swinging like a pendulum with his feet above the surface of the stream. He remained for a second clinging on to the slippery surface fearful that at any moment his grip would slip or the forked end he could see moving backwards and forwards above his head would give way and send him crashing into the water. Thankfully it held, he began to pull himself up hand over hand towards the overhanging branch, expecting at any moment to lose his grip on the slippery wet bark. It seemed like an eternity with the sounds of the dogs getting closer all the time. Eventually he was on the branch and pulling the bough up after him. Quickly he swarmed along the branch, pushing his way into the tops of the hawthorns. The thorns tore into his flesh but he was oblivious to them, his only concern being to get out of sight of anyone approaching along the bed of the stream below him.

The bough that had been his ladder now became his platform, pushing it ahead of him he was able to crawl along and use it for support, a slight protection against the thorny twigs barely holding his weight. At this moment of extreme danger it seemed odd his thoughts were straying to his father and the hours they had spend together in the Salle. He thanked God for the thoroughness with which Jacques had done his job, forcing him *sometimes against his will* to exercise daily. A monotonous routine and at times he had to admit he had resented it, but now because of it, he possessed the strength and agility of a fairground acrobat. At this moment he owed his very life to those abilities given to him by his father's wisdom and foresight, swarming up that bough and reaching the safety of these treetops had been a feat no ordinary man could have performed.

However his safety was not yet assured, the dogs were but yards away. He could hear the men's voices and the sound of their feet splashing through the stream. He lay still not daring to move deeper into the wood for fear of them hearing the breaking twigs. Laying there with the thorns pressing into his flesh, trying to control his breathing, fearful of making the slightest sound that might alert the dogs, Napier's mind was agitated beyond belief. His every instinct told him to push his way deeper into that wood, put as much distance between him and the hunters as was humanly possible but wracked as he was by doubts and apprehension some inner discipline controlled his fears and enabled him to stay still and wait for his pursuers to pass.

The voices were directly below him now. To his astonishment he recognised them as the duke's men, two men he had known for years, spoken to on many occasion. Strangely enough he had always thought of his pursuers as strangers – faceless men who he did not know and who did not know him; it had never crossed his mind that he would be chased by men whom he had recently thought of as friends. Now of course he realised it could not be otherwise. These were the men employed by the duke and trained by him to handle the dogs for this specific purpose. For the first time since he had been on the run his shocked mind grasped the reality of the situation: he was truly alone! Friendless and every man's hand turned against him, the duke's power would ensure he was seen publicly as an outlaw; as such no one would dare to help him. That without question was the grim unpalatable truth.

By now the woods were filled with the sound of barking dogs, human voices cursing the dogs and the rough bed of the stream, all the conglomeration of sound involved when men and animals join in the excitement of hunting a human quarry. Napier was in a fever of anxiety, just how safe was he? How good were the dogs' sense of smell? Could they detect his presence even in the treetops? He risked moving his arm so that he could look beneath it, through the green foliage he could see the men clearly and recognise those well-known faces, images that in better times would have provoked a smile and a cheery word

– now they were his bitter enemies who would do him harm. His world had changed so quickly to become a frighteningly dangerous place. A chill ran down his spine for he realised if he could see them then surely they had only to look up to see him.

Suddenly above the noise of the hunt came the clear note of a horn, it would only mean one thing. They had found the boulder he had fallen across. The blast on the horn was the signal to say the dogs had found his scent again. His ruse had worked and with any luck he had sent them off on a false trail. The effect on the men below was immediate, they urged on the dogs telling each other they must be there when the quarry was caught, otherwise they would not be in for a share of the reward. The man with the bloodhound warned the mastiff handler to keep a tight hold on his dog.

"He must not be killed," he said. "Remember the young duke is offering more money if we capture him alive than if we return him dead!"

So the young duke had survived the fire! They must have freed him from the table before the flames got to him. This was the explanation as to how they were able to mobilise the hunt so quickly. He had identified Napier as the miscreant the instant he was rescued from the fire. It did not require much imagination to understand why he wanted him caught alive. His reason would most certainly not be a humanitarian one.

Napier lay concealed in the treetops listening to the hunters splashing their way upstream. He was soaked in cold perspiration, emotionally desperately relieved by his escape but realistically he knew he had merely won a brief respite, they would not give up until they had him and now, if ever he doubted it, the knowledge had been forcibly driven home: he was running for his life! He lay there until he was convinced they had all gone. Now he could no longer hear the baying of the hounds and quietness again descended on the wood he was able to review his position and formulate a plan of action.

The obvious option would be to drop back into the stream and make a run for it in the opposite direction but that would gain him nothing but a few miles start. Eventually his pursuers would realise they were on the wrong track and retrace their steps which still left him with the problem of leaving the stream without laying a scent trail for the dogs. However on reflection he had already solved that problem, here he was with his feet off the ground and in the treetops where no dog could catch him. It made sense to stay where he was and push his way further into the wood. Maybe further on the vegetation would not be so dense. Once he had traversed the trees he could see the lay of the land on the other side, the situation could be reviewed again and a new plan of action formulated. This however was not an easy option. Moving across those trees was most difficult and painful. The upper structure was a sea of thin thorny twigs. They supported his weight without problem being so dense and growing tightly packed together, but his every movement sunk him deep into their thorny embrace. If there had been some solid structure to brace against he could have used it as a firm base to push himself forward, but because of the fragile nature of the individual twigs his limbs merely pushed them aside and found no solid purchase to give him forward motion. However he still had the trusty bough he had found in the stream, it had served him well as a ladder, now perhaps he could still make use of it.

With great difficulty he removed his jerkin, a sleeveless garment made from pigskin. Then pushing the bough ahead of him he placed the jerkin on the bough, pulling it over his face and head he was able to pull himself along an inch at a time, while the jerkin gave him a modicum of protection from the thorns. By this laborious process he was able to make slow and painful progress across the lush green canopy. Napier had hoped the hawthorn would give way to a more hospitable species of vegetation but they did not. Inch-by-inch the exhausting process went on, he did not realise just how tired and physically drained he was becoming. The last twenty-four hours were taking their toll. Twenty-four hours without sleep, most of it running over rough country, the strenuous ride clinging to the rear of the coach had also taxed his strength. Add to that the expenditure of nervous energy, the lack of food; it was hardly surprising he had come to the point where he could no longer carry on.

Barely conscious, hardly knowing what he was doing, his tired limbs refusing to obey the commands from his fatigued brain, he pulled the jerkin over his head and oblivious to the thorns he sank into the foliage and gave himself up to the deep sleep his weary body craved. He awoke to a sense of confusion. For a few seconds he did not know where he was, everywhere there was pitch darkness. Gradually his perplexed senses returned to normal, he must have slept the whole day and most of the night. What hour of the night it was he had no idea, thick clouds covered the moon and the wood was in total darkness. Not a breath of wind rustled the leaves, the eerie silence broken only by his own breathing, and the occasional scuffling of some small animal on the ground below him.

Whether it was the silence, the darkness or the gap in time caused by is unsolicited sleep, Napier would never know, but a nameless fear began to take him in its grip. Fear of the unknown or fear of the overgrown tangled ghostly wood itself invoking childhood fantasies, or just the fear he would fall into that tangled web of trunks and undergrowth to remain wedged there unable to move, growing weaker by the minute, until death finally claimed him, his bleached bones waiting to be found by some future generation. Naked fear without a recognised cause can be a compulsive driving force, making Napier push his way through the treetops in an uncontrolled panic, forcing his way through the foliage unmindful of the thorns tearing at his exposed flesh. On he went through the darkness unable to see his hand in front of his face. He had lost all sense of direction, for all he knew he might well be going back to where he had started or he could just be travelling in circles and still be a mere few yards from where he had first began to traverse the trees. Desperate to get away from this frightening place he pushed on and on, the sweat streaming from his body.

Suddenly there was nothing, no leaves no trees no thorns, just empty darkness as he pitched head foremost into the abyss – falling, falling, falling into the unknown. He seemed to be suspended forever in blackness, then, thud! The world exploded into a bright flash, galaxies of tiny lights spun round in his head then blackness as he lapsed into unconsciousness.

When he finally regained consciousness his world had changed again. He blinked round at the sunlight filtering through the broad green leaves, the chirping of birdsong all around him, the smell of ferns and fresh grasses, nothing but peace silence and solitude. He shook his head to clear it. It ached abominably as he struggled to gain his feet his body felt sore and bruised all over, he looked at his arms they were covered in blood and cross-crossed with deep scratches. Putting his hands to his head he winced as he felt the congealed blood and the pain from dozens of deep lacerations. He guessed that his face must be in a similar state to his arms, scratched by the thorns and with their broken points embedded in the flesh.

Still, things could be much worse. He was still alive and apparently safe for the moment, and of the hunt there was no sign or sound. Doubtless they were still searching the stream trying to find his exit point, hopefully they never would. By good fortune he seemed to have chanced by one of those areas that nature, when left to her own devices, conceals and develops for her own enjoyment hidden from the world of man and visited only by the creatures she considers her own, Napier hoped that he would be one of them. He had not fared well with his own wits over the last few days and desperately needed the good offices of nature and fortune. He was standing under the spreading branches of a huge chestnut tree, its massive trunk growing fissured and gnarled in the middle of a clearing, providing a roof for thick walls of hawthorn surrounding it, making an impenetrable barrier, the ramparts of a natural fortress of spiked vegetation.

There were ferns and grasses of all types growing around the edges of the clearing. Judging by their undisturbed appearance the feet of man had not trod this area for many a long year. To Napier's amazement and delight there at the far end of the clearing a small spring bubbled up out of the ground; clear and inviting he could not have asked for more. Stumbling unsteadily across the grass he drank gratefully at the spring. It had an earthy flavour, but was fresh and clean. No wine or ale could have tasted better to Napier at that moment. Having slaked his thirst he noticed some pale green spheres covered with short spikes in the grass – chestnuts! They had ripened early for mid-September, and the sight of them was salvation for a starving man. Napier pounced on them with an eagerness that only extreme hunger could produce, he ripped off the shells pushing the delicious nuts six at a time into his mouth, swallowing them almost whole in his haste.

Having satisfied his hunger he took another drink at the spring. He then pulled up some ferns and made a comfortable bed from the bracken, pulling more ferns over the top of himself he fell into the deep sleep of the exhausted. When he awoke again night had fallen and the wood was once again in darkness, guided by the sound of water he found his spring and lay down for a drink, feeling about in the grass he managed to find a few chestnuts which he chewed for a while before returning to his bed of bracken where he remained until morning.

Once again he awoke with the sun in his face and the sound of the birds singing in the trees; everywhere there was peace and all was well with the world. He stood up and stretched himself. He felt good and none the worse for his recent experiences.

The little spring bubbled up out of the ground, its waters cold and fresh as he washed off the dirt and congealed blood caked thickly on his skin. The scratches he had acquired in his struggle with the hawthorns looked angry and red but they had started to heal and had lost much of their soreness. He fingered his face and reflected ruefully that he must be a pretty gruesome sight but without a mirror he could only guess at the damage inflicted by the thorns. Still they would heal and were nothing as to the damage the dogs would have inflicted if they had got their fangs into him. All things considered he had been extremely lucky. However breakfast was his main priority at the moment. He opened the leather pouch that Jacques had given him and took out a large clasp knife. This was the first chance he had to think about the death of his father since he had stood looking back at the manor watching the tongues of flame licking out of the tower windows. Now as he took out the knife he was overwhelmed with sadness. Jacques had acquired it in Italy and it was one of the items he always kept in his desk. Napier marvelled at the courage and control of this man. Despite the horrendous pain he was suffering, he still had the presence of mind to pick up items he thought might be useful and place them in the pouch.

Apart from his Will and documents relating to his fencing school and house, the pouch contained a bag of gold coins, the clasp knife, a tinder box and quill pen, all items that had come readily to hand as, blinded and in pain from his wounds, Jacques had felt about in his desk drawer. Even in his last moments he had been seeking to help him with items he thought would be useful to a man on the run, Jacques knew only too well the hours of the chase would be desperate ones. The knife of course was a godsend and Napier mouthed a small prayer as he carved a piece of bark off the trunk of the chestnut tree.

Holding his improvised plate he gathered and peeled a dozen chestnuts, chopped and mixed with some plump blackberries and a handful of dandelion leaves they made a most acceptable salad, which he consumed with great relish. Sitting there with his back to the tree trunk he began to appraise his situation and make his future plans. There was no reason why he should leave this clearing; he was safe for the moment. His pursuers would have no reason to think he was here. The only scent the dogs would have found would indicate he was travelling up stream and they would not think it possible for a man to penetrate that thick barrier of thorns. They would have to cut their way in to get at him and he could not see anyone pushing their way through the treetops as he had done, unless they wee absolutely certain he was there. Yes, he was safe behind the thorny ramparts in his fortress of vegetation.

Glancing around the clearing there was no doubt he would be able to survive here for a couple of weeks, he had experienced far worse privations in the years before he had met Jacques – the life of a mud lark, travelling showman's lad and juvenile vagabond had not been an easy one by anyone's standards. The main requirements were there: food was growing on the trees and bushes and water he had in abundance in the spring. It bubbled up out of the ground and developed into a small brook, which trickled into the undergrowth. Napier had already decided this was his way out. He was sure he would be able to squeeze his way along the bed of the brook, pushing under the thorns until it finally left the wood. Certainly he would be able to last a while on what was here. Apart from chestnuts the brambles were thick with berries and dandelions with their edible leaves were everywhere. He would have no problem with shelter. The wind did not penetrate that thick tangled woodland and there were ferns and brushwood aplenty, he would be able to improvise a bivouac of sorts to provide a dry spot from the rain dripping off the trees.

One by one the days went by; Napier counted them off, a notch at a time on an old tree root. The first week went by quickly as he busied himself developing his campsite. He constructed a very serviceable hut, cutting and trimming the straight hawthorn branches for its frame and building a bed off the ground into one wall. By the time he had interlaced thinner branches and ferns into the walls and roof the rickety structure became surprisingly strong and sound. The finishing touches were applied with handfuls of dry grass interlaced with ferns to form a thatch for roof and wall, Napier was delighted by his handiwork which proved to be resistant to the heaviest rains. Once he had constructed a door by the same method he could pull it into place and was warm and cosy insulated from the increasingly colder nights that heralded the approaching autumn.

Having provided himself with food and shelter his next priority was to find out just where his haven lay in a geographical location of the area. Also he must formulate a plan for his escape once he was sure the hunt had been called off. After a couple of weeks they would surely assume he had made good his escape and be heading for the coast, then and only then it would be safe for him to leave his fortress. To this end he spent the entire day cutting down two large hawthorn trunks, he could have cut down both in an hour with an axe, but without one the wood proved to be hard and unyielding. The clasp knife, although strong and serviceable, was hardly the correct tool for such a task. However, he finally succeeded and spent the following day trimming the branches to handy lengths, then binding the trunks together in such a way that the shortened branches formed the rungs of a rickety ladder, this he laid against the trunk of the chestnut tree. Tomorrow at first light he would attempt to climb the tree and spy out the surrounding land.

The following day he was up with the dawn. It had been his custom to wash and eat breakfast before commencing the day's chores but today there was far too much suppressed excitement for him to bother with such mundane things. It had been more than a week since he had incarcerated himself in this, his self-imposed imprisonment, during that time all he had seen of the outside world were shafts of sunshine beaming down through the foliage. Hopefully, he was about to look out on the outside world again, and what was infinitely more important was to find out where he was and in what direction he would eventually be going.

Impatiently he positioned his improvised ladder beneath the lowest branch. It was very unstable but providing he placed his feet carefully and made certain his whole weight was distributed over the structure in such a way that no one part had to take too much strain, he was able to climb its length and straddle the lowest bough. At first he had nurtured doubts about his ability to climb the tree, but once he was into the upper branches they grew closer together and climbing became relatively easy. He reached the top without any great difficulty and concealing himself in the foliage he sat back to survey the surrounding countryside.

The landscape surrounding the wood was reasonably flat; therefore from his elevated vantage point Napier had a good panoramic view of the whole area. The sun was just on the horizon a large red half round disc rising in the east, silhouetted against the dawn light were the smoking chimneys of a small village, this would be a good landmark. His intention was to move east and try to find a London road. If he set out for that village he would be going in the right direction and maybe there would be a possibility of acquiring some food for the journey. Over to the southwest he recognised the coaching inn where he had been so near to capture, obviously he had not travelled as far as he had imagined, he had thought himself to be much further away. Of course he had spent a great deal of time doubling back on his tracks, which would mean he had covered twice the distance without covering the mileage.

Napier was shocked to find that this wood, whose impenetrable nature had afforded him such a feeling of security;

was by no means as large as he had imagined. He had spent so many hours struggling to fight his way through the treetops and had been convinced it covered many acres. But now perched up in the chestnut tree he could look down on the tops of the foliage and see they covered no more than a hundred yards wide and two hundred long, in reality no more than a copse. Looking back this in all probability was the fact that saved him, the hunt ignored it considering it too small a place for him to hide. If it had been a larger wood they would have taken steps to check it out.

Day after day went by and Napier became bored and weary with his own company. At first he had been busily occupied with constructing his camp and devising means of making his life as comfortable as possible, but now he had exhausted all the possibilities, he spent much of the time perched in his tree staring gloomily at the surrounding landscape. During the first couple of weeks of his vigil, there had been a great deal of activity around his little wood; he had watched with considerable amusement the progress of the manhunt. The men appeared to be using the coaching inn as a base. In the mornings he would watch them setting out in carts and on foot to comb the surrounding countryside. The carts would set of at a fast rate loaded with a team, in a short period of time they would return empty, leaving the dog teams to move across country on foot eventually meeting up with their counterparts hoping to trap the quarry between the two groups. Even from a distance Napier could see their dejection when, with darkness falling, they returned to the inn empty handed, the hoped-for reward still eluding them. There had been a traumatic and very anxious period when they appeared to suspect his presence, the dogs had gone up and down the stream several times checking and rechecking the route they thought he might have taken, but the false trail he had left kept luring the dogs back upstream and the hunt would again concentrate back in that direction. The most nerve-wracking times for Napier were when they checked the wood, many times they returned almost as though they suspected he could not have vanished off the face of the earth so completely and must still be in the area somewhere. They would work all round the perimeter of the wood, teams travelling round to meet each other. Howling and sniffing the dogs would check every clump of grass and piece of shrub; Napier would sit frozen in his tree shrinking into the foliage, terrified that the wind might blow his scent to those sensitive noses. If that had happened the dogs would become excited, their handlers would read their body language and know he was there hidden in the wood.

His fears however proved to be unfounded. His hiding place was totally adequate. His false trail appeared to have worked like a dream. The hunt, frustrated by their lack of success, finally gave up and went away; obviously believing he had escaped completely. By this time he could count twenty notches on his tree root calendar. Three weeks he had lived in the clearing, three weeks on a diet of nuts and berries. They had tasted so good at first, now he could hardly chew them; to him they tasted like sawdust. He hated the thought of another meal of chestnuts. He sat with his back to the tree trunk listening to the cooing of the wood pigeons above his head, he had even contemplated catching them and to that end had constructed a bow and arrows spending many hours perfecting his marksmanship. Common sense however prevailed, he knew if he were to kill a pigeon or one of the rabbits that occasionally ran across the clearing he would have to cook it, and that would be out of the question. He had the means of producing fire with his tinderbox and there was no shortage of dry wood, but to light one would be foolishness of the highest order. One wisp of smoke rising from those trees would betray his presence instantly. Prudence dictated he be content with his dreams, of pigeon pie or rabbit stew with lots of fresh vegetables. Many an hour he spent staring across the fields at the village watching the smoke from the chimneys, torturing him self with thoughts of huge iron saucepans on the fires with their savoury smelling contents bubbling away ready for consumption.

He decided he would wait one more week, just one more week to make certain that the hunt would not return, that they had given up all hope of catching him here and believed he had left the area. It would be stupidity to be caught in the open at this stage when up to now he had fooled his pursuers so completely. Only a single week but it proved to be one of the longest weeks of his life. He pottered about the clearing trying to amuse him self. Always he would end up in his treetop watching the countryside. It was so quiet and peaceful now with just the odd cowman or farmhand working in the fields but so boring at least the hunt had been exciting for him to watch.

With no sign of man or beast who appeared to be part of a manhunt the temptation was strong to start out on his journey immediately, but he knew he must be certain the area was safe for him and was determined not to set off before the seventh day as per his pre-thought-out plan. He had consumed all of the available berries in the clearing. His diet was now mainly comprised of chestnuts. Desperately hungry but by now he had such revulsion for these nuts; he had to force himself to eat them. The seven days were an eternity of boredom but a week he had decided and a week it was going to be, and so it was that on the seventh night having seen no sight of anyone who appeared to be looking for him, he took one last look at the clearing, it had served him well and been his home and sanctuary for many weeks but now it was time to leave.

He checked the contents of his pouch before slinging it over his shoulder. All he had in the world was in that pouch; the money he would need to buy his way to France and the documents, the only proof he had of his inheritance, the other odds and ends apart from the sentimental value would be needed in his fight for survival on the journey. The light was beginning to fade quickly now as he lay down in the cold water of the brook and began to push and wriggle his way under the tangled thorns, there was barely room for him to squeeze through and many a time his clothes caught on a root forcing him to take his knife and cut himself free. For over an hour he forced and struggled his way down that claustrophobic tunnel of vegetation and water, an hour to cover no more than fifty yards, eventually he made it and stood up in the open with aching limbs. Strangely his feelings of elation and freedom were mixed with a fear that he was dreadfully exposed.

Standing in the pitch darkness he shivered in the cold wind, his clothes were soaking wet and he had no means of drying them, but he removed them and wrung them out as best he could. Dressing again in the damp garments was a miserable experience but he had no alternative, they would have to dry out on his body, he must start out on his journey as quickly as possible. He had hoped to be guided by the lights of the village but from where he stood there was only darkness, it did not matter too much he had a good idea of the correct way to go and wasted no time in setting off at a fast trot in an easterly direction and whatever the future might hold.

5

The Life of a Drover

From his treetop watchtower looking down on the countryside the area had appeared flat. He had not realised the wood was in fact in a slight hollow. Now at ground level he found himself running up a slight incline, it was hard going and he estimated at least a mile before he reached the top of the hollow. Having attained the higher ground he was rewarded with the sight of faint lights from the houses. His sense of direction had been accurate. He estimated a distance of roughly two miles and calculated it would take maybe twenty minutes to half an hour over the dark unfamiliar fields to reach the houses. He arrived at the village sweating profusely despite the biting cold wind, in fact the running had been quite enjoyable and he had pushed himself far harder than was necessary. There had been a great inner need to stretch his limbs after his constrictive confinement over the previous weeks. The exertion had dried out his clothes completely. He was feeling much more comfortable and relaxed, now that he was once again near human habitation, the thought of obtaining real food here made his gastric juices go wild with anticipation.

The village was a disappointment, he would not find the hoped for food here, as he approached he could see the houses were little more than thatched hovels, tiny wattle and daub boxes without windows. Those that did have them boasted a single unglazed gap with a piece of coarse woven fabric across, affording the only protection against the winter chills, dimly the light of burning rushes gave faint illumination into the darkness of the night. There would be no food to be had here. These people would be as hungry as he was. He had considered the possibility of stealing food, such action would undoubtedly be the safest option, but he could not in all conscience steal from they who obviously had so little. They would of course undoubtedly live off the land, as he had been doing over the last weeks. Rabbits and other wildlife would be their staple diet. Even so he had not as yet sunk so low. If the time came when he had to steal to stay alive then he would do it from they who could afford to lose it.

Without giving the village a second look he set off along the rough track he guessed to be heading east away from the cluster of hovels. He had not even considered the possibility of buying food. The money in his pouch would be useless in this situation. It would be ludicrous to expect people living in such poverty to give him change for a gold coin and gold coins were all he had. In fact he had in his pouch more money than these people would see in a lifetime. He would have gladly given a gold coin for a pan of rabbit stew but to do so would be to invite trouble. They who wish to travel incognito do not go throwing gold coins about. He was well aware of the existence of people who would slit his throat for a handful of gold coins. In fact the people he had known in his earlier life would have slit a throat for a pan of rabbit stew.

The track was well used and fairly smooth which made for easier going than the fields he had just crossed. His pace became easier now that he had got the frustration of confinement out of his system but despite this and the darkness he made good progress, knowing that he had covered a decent distance he ran for a couple more hours than found a sheltered hedgerow, burrowed his way in and curled up to sleep until the morning.

The following day he was up with the dawn and thinking about breakfast. However before he could eat it he would have to catch it and if he were to catch it he would require some form of hunting equipment. The obvious answer was a bow and arrows, using the skill developed and honed during his hiding in the hawthorn wood he selected and cut a springy bough from the hedgerow then, sat down to construct a crude but serviceable bow. To this aim his trusty jerkin had to be sacrificed, it had served him well in the thorns but they had taken their toll, the pigskin had been ripped and torn in so many places it was virtually unwearable anyway. As he drew out the thongs used to sew the seams, it fell apart; leaving it totally useless as a garment. He spent an hour plaiting together three of the thin leather thongs to make a clumsy but strong and useful bowstring, a few minutes work and he had strung his bow. All he now required were the arrows. These he made from ash tree shoots sharpened at one end and split at the other. He was glad he had not thrown the quill pen away; pushed into the split and whipped with the remaining thongs it became perfect flights for his arrows.

These labours had cost him a little time, but without a hunt on his tail he could afford to give a little thought to the practicalities; after all, he had to eat and to do that while keeping away from human habitation he would have to live off the land. Now with the bow over his shoulder and the arrows tucked into the flap of the pouch he set off at a fast trot keeping an eye open for rabbit burrows. He had not gone far when he spotted a small hillock dotted with shrubs. The telltale patch of sand under the shrubs told of the entrance to a warren. Now he would require stealth and, above all, patience. Concealing himself in the shrubs he sat down and waited for the first rabbit to make its appearance. Within a few minutes he was rewarded with the sight of three rabbits hopping about nibbling the vegetation. Taking careful aim he shot at the nearest animal but the arrow went wide. In the twinkling of an eye the animals disappeared down their burrows. When everything appeared quiet again they returned to their grazing as though nothing had happened. It took Napier several shots, and a few anxiety-ridden hours before he finally hit one. Having obtained his prey he immediately put flint to steel and kindled a small fire, once he had skinned cleaned and skewered his meal he placed it across two forked sticks turning it slowly over the heat from the flames. The smell of the cooking meat filled his nostrils, he could hardly prevent himself from grabbing the food and tearing it off the bones before it was fully cooked, but he was not that hungry that he would resort to eating raw, under-cooked meat. So in an agony of impatience he waited until he was sure the meat was fully cooked before taking it off the fire and eating it straight off the skewer. Napier had never tasted anything so wonderful in his life. He ate with gusto every single edible bit, after a prolonged diet of chestnuts and berries his first cooked meal in weeks tasted like something straight from the table of the Gods. The outer parts might well have been blackened and scorched by the fire but it was a meal Napier would remember for many a long year.

Living off the land is a skill not easily acquired and although Napier had the capability of covering at least twenty miles in a day, this distance was cut down considerably the excessive time taken up in hunting for food. Up to the moment there had been no positive direction to his flight, he had been heading roughly east in the hope of crossing a London road, but without maps or local knowledge he was to all practical purposes virtually lost. Since his experience at the inn he had shunned all human contact for fear of betrayal, a great deal of time had been wasted, either hiding from or skirting round people working in the fields or tending livestock grazing the common land. Whereas his present policy was undoubtedly the safest, the longer he took to get to London undetected the more chance there was of the hunt being abandoned in the belief he had made good his escape. Time, however, was running out on him; the autumn season was well advanced and the winter months were not far away and he was ill equipped for living rough during the bleak winter weather. He needed to get to a large town where he could buy clothing and personal items to change his appearance without arousing too much suspicion. It would be necessary to make human contact soon, either to ask directions or ideally to join some group of travellers who would show him the way. He was a little less conspicuous than he had been by the simple but larcenous procedure of stealing from a washing line he had managed to acquire a thick woollen shirt and a pair of knitted stockings also a warm grey blanket. This he rolled up and carried over his shoulder. He had seen the farmhouse on a clear moonlight night and had taken the risk of approaching from the rear with the intention of pulling up a few vegetables from the kitchen garden. While he was occupied with this task he had noticed the line of washing, although he had expected farm dogs to begin barking at any moment all remained silent, thus he was able to purloin the few items of clothing without a problem. Jacques had not brought him up to steal and in all conscience he found what he was doing distasteful. The though had crossed his mind to leave a coin in payment, but he discarded the idea. A gold coin for a few paltry items would point directly at him, a man on the run. Far better the owners believed the items had been taken by vagrants; and therefore not cause too much fuss. He had to be careful, he could not take the risk of the manhunt returning to the area.

His own shirt had quite literally been in ribbons and his socks so badly worn they were hardly worth wearing. His breeches had fared no better in the thorns but they would have to suffice until he could acquire another pair, at least now he had a warm shirt and socks that were more comfortable to walk in. After much soul searching he had made up his mind to take the risk and seek out human company, he had seen no sign of any man hunting activity and felt certain they had switched the hunt to the sea ports, therefore it would be safer for him to arrive at the coast in a conventional way alongside other people. Now that he had made up his mind he looked forward to the first meeting. He was by nature a gregarious sort of person and had not relished the loneliness of the past few weeks. It was now with anticipation and not with fear and suspicion that he looked for the sight and sound of people as he continued on his journey.

Despite his vigilance the first sight of human activity came unexpectedly. Up to that point he kept to rough ground, over the tops of hills and mountains through woods and wetlands, anywhere to avoid farm tracks or common land, places he might have met people who would know him as a stranger and suspect the truth of who he was. Once he had decided to seek out the help of his fellow man he started to follow a different type of countryside, keeping to the commons and the main tracks, where he knew there would be habitation. The previous day he had been successful in catching his food early, hardly able to believe his luck, he had cooked and consumed his catch quickly, with much of the day still to come, and not wishing to waste the day that providence and his increasing skill as a hunter had given him, he pushed himself hard and covered a great distance before darkness came. Finally completely exhausted he crept under a hedgerow, wrapped himself in his blanket and fell into a deep sleep. Normally he would have been awake with the dawn but because of the previous day's exertions, or maybe the comfort of the blanket, he slept on well into the morning. When he did awake it was to the sound of cattle surrounding his hedgerow, not only cattle, the noise of men and dogs mingling with the general din of a herd on the move.

Remaining where he was he peered through the foliage of the hedgerow. He could see the legs and feet of a great herd of cattle moving past his hiding place. These were not ordinary cattle their feet were shod, small rectangular plates of steel were nailed to their hooves, that could mean only one thing – drovers with a large herd travelling a great distance cross-country to sell their livestock, maybe at one of the country fairs. Napier remained concealed in the hedgerow until the herd had passed; once the dust had cleared he packed up his blanket then set out to follow in the wake of the herd.

By midday the cattle were approaching a pond where they stopped their forward movement and clustered round in a jostling, lowing mass, each one attempting to push its way through the throng to drink from the muddy water. At this point the drovers took the opportunity to sit down and grab a bite of lunch. This was Napier's chance to approach them and to enquire of the direction in which they were heading. They seemed an upright friendly bunch of fellows. Napier took a liking to them instantly. Apparently they were Welshmen taking the herd from Wales across-country, selling as they went. To Napier's delight they were heading to the south coast ending up in London where they hoped to sell the remainder of the herd before returning home.

When speaking to Napier the drovers spoke excellent English, although spoken with a lilting accent which betrayed their birthright. Conversations among themselves however were carried out in their native language. They had invited Napier to join them as they sat in a rough circle around a basket of fresh bread, beside the bread on a rough board was a delicious looking round cheese, each man had his knife and cut off a slice of cheese and a piece of bread as it took his fancy. Some of the men had onions which they ate raw biting into them as they would an apple, chewing the raw onion with great mouthfuls of bread and cheese. Napier looked on with his mouth watering. He had not tasted civilised food for weeks; even as he tried to keep up a conversation with the men he could not take his eyes off the bread and cheese. Some of the men saw his longing looks and invited him to join them in their lunch. This was something he had not expected. Although he had hoped to at least have travelled alongside the herd, he could hardly contain himself as he took out his knife and carved off a large chunk of bread and a piece of cheese. Soon he was chatting away like an old friend. Human company again, crusty baked bread and cheese – these were the commodities of human living sorely missed during his enforced exile of the previous weeks.

One of the men inquired where he had come from and where he was heading, he had anticipated this question and had been mentally concocting a story, which would give a convincing answer. He could see these men were not fools; they were shrewd businessmen well used to bargaining for cattle. Part of their trade would be to sum up a man from his appearance. They would have noticed his rough shirt and socks strangely contrasting with the well worn but nevertheless genteel appearance of his shoes and breeches. They would also be puzzled by his unkempt appearance, so completely out of place alongside his cultured voice and manners. Therefore he explained that he came from Leicester where his father was a clergyman, bored and disillusioned by the scholarly life and its strictly rigid religious rules he had rebelled against it, quarrelled with his father and left home to seek his fortune in London, hoping to finance his journey by finding work along the way. This seemed to find an area of common ground among the drovers, many of whom had experienced religious intolerance in their own homeland. Some of the men offered words of comfort and encouragement, the leader of the group suggested Napier travelled along with them for a while. They were short-handed and in return for helping with the cattle they would feed him on the journey.

Napier accepted the offer gratefully. This was an incredible piece of good fortune, not only would he be shown the way to London, he would also be relieved of the difficult and time-consuming task of hunting for food. Most importantly while merging with this group of legitimate travellers no one would suspect he was in fact a fugitive. He could not have hoped for a better stroke of luck; the Gods at last appeared to be on his side.

Mingling anonymously with the drovers Napier felt far safer and more secure than he had ever been during the previous lonely weeks. However he had to suppress his frustrations and impatience at the slowness of the drive, the cattle were not inclined to do more than amble and had to be continually pushed and prodded to keep them on the move. The drovers for their part were no more inclined to move quickly than the cattle they tended. They appeared to have no clear ambition regarding seeing an end to their journey. The drive was their life, they were dealers who traded as they travelled and would quite happily put their herd to pasture for two or three days on the outskirts of a small town while they went into the community to trade.

They were not wealthy men in the accepted sense, but they always had money available for business whenever it came their way. Mostly they would deal in livestock, buying cattle to swell their herd, or selling their own beasts to local farmers. By the natural scheme of things these deals would be done over a tankard of ale at the local Inn but occasionally men would come from the town and sit at the drovers' campfire to complete their trading. Napier would never visit the town during these stopovers, he would always offer to stay and tend the herd while the others went in search of trade, even when the local guests came to sit at the fire he would slope off to the far end of the herd finding some excuse to stay out of sight until the visitors had gone. The drovers for their part accepted this; he had told them he was a runaway from his home and therefore they assumed he was being careful in case word of his whereabouts got back to his father and in their eyes it was none of their business.

However avoiding the attentions of strangers was not

always possible as Napier soon discovered, having spent a long tiring day tending the herd, chasing and retrieving stragglers who seemed to think the grass grew greener the further from the herd they strayed, as the dusk began to fall over the meadows and the herd began to settle he returned to the campfire, threw a few logs into the flames and settled comfortably with his back against a rock. The warmth of the fire and the crackle of the flames seemed to have a soothing effect and soon his head dropped and he started to doze. He awoke to the sound of voices and looking round saw that he was no longer alone, sitting around the fire were some of the drovers and two strangers who had returned with them from the town. All of them were in a jovial talkative frame of mind, having just made a hearty meal washed down with flagons of the local Inn's finest ale.

They had discussed the relative virtues of various breeds of cattle and their comparative prices at local and London markets, but business and a head full of strong ale, rarely mixes well. Therefore they moved on to more mundane matters, one of the drovers remarked on the town being a sleepy little hamlet and doubted the possibility of anything exciting happening there.

"Not at all," said one of the locals, stung by the drover implying his town appeared dull. "We have our fair share of excitement. Why, only the other week we had riders bringing news of the most unbelievable heinous crime committed no more than a few miles from here. Indeed we are most vigilant in the town if we were to capture the villain a huge reward would be paid."

When encouraged by the drovers to relate the nature of this crime the stranger told them this story:

"No more than a day's coach journey from here the town stood a large manor house owned by a great duke who employed many servants..." Napier reflected wryly to himself the man was shrinking the mileage considerably to make the events appear more local, he knew he had travelled more than one day's coach journey in the last few weeks. However he sat quietly and listened to the man's narrative.

"It appears that two of these servants, a fencing master and his assistant" – the assistant in question was gratified to hear himself described as a huge hulking brute of a man, the teller obviously enhancing his tale again for better effect – "had been dismissed from the duke's services and had returned to the manor to see what they could steal. The duke, entering his private apartments, had caught them in the act, whereupon he was overpowered by the two of them, and tortured with the purpose of making him reveal the hiding place of his money. The duke heroically refused to give in and was roasted to death over his own fire. While this was going on the duke's son had appeared on the scene and was also overpowered by the two who crushed his hand with a mace in an attempt to force him to reveal the whereabouts of valuables or money. Fortunately for him the servants had been alerted and a great battle took place with much shooting. During the discharge of firearms the son was able to make his escape and direct the siege of the two men who were trapped in the dining hall. In a desperate attempt to escape they set fire to the manor and made a run for it. During the escape the older of the two was shot dead, the other got away and eluded his pursuers. To the best of the villagers' knowledge he was still at large somewhere in the area, believed to be making for the coast. The servants paid a high price for their loyalty to the master. Four of them were killed and many injured during the battle, as a consequence of these actions there is a large reward offered for the felon, who is said to be highly dangerous and must be captured at any cost either dead or alive."

Napier felt a surge of anger rise inside himself as he listened to this tissue of lies. Even allowing for the fact that the story teller was adding to the story to make it appear more lurid, the duke's riders must have told a story concocted specifically to blacken the characters of Jacques and himself in order to present them as murders and common thieves. It was true he had killed the duke and maimed his son but under entirely different circumstances to the story now told and where the killing and wounding of servants came into the picture he could not imagine. He knew no one else had opposed them or been involved in the whole escapade. He desperately wanted to denounce these lies, to stand and tell the truth if only for his father's sake. It was wrong that he should be remembered as a murderous killer and the duke depicted as a hero when it had been he who was the aggressor. His instincts were to tell these people the whole story as it had happened but at the same time warning bells were ringing in his head. Certainly the townsfolk would not care to believe the truth if the alternative was to receive a large reward and how far could he trust the drovers? He looked upon them as his friends but that was when they had though him to be an innocent youth whose only crime was to run away from home. Could their friendship be counted on if they saw him as a criminal on the run or would they be seduced by the lure of a cash reward?

All Napier's fears and distrust of people returned as he considered the possibility that even now his companions might be putting two and two together and identifying him as the fugitive in the town man's story. Outwardly he remained calm sitting looking into the fire not daring to look directly at anyone, out of the corner of his eye he scanned the faces lit by the firelight, all the while imagining they were staring at him. His fears proved to be groundless. No one leapt upon him. No one denounced him or tried to restrain him. They just sat around the fire discussing the delights of spending the reward if it were to come their way. Eventually they tired of the subject, the last comment being, "It is most unlikely he is still here anyway. If I were he I would be long gone by now. Doubtless some lucky devil on the coast will get the reward." To this remark they all nodded their heads and agreed. With that the company parted and all went their separate ways to seek their beds.

This incident had set Napier's nerves a jangling; his every instinct of survival now came to the fore. True his assumed role had stood the test and people's natural propensity to exaggerate a tale had worked to his advantage. He was depicted as a far bigger, older and more aggressive looking individual than he actually was and fortunately no one appeared to suspect he was other than he appeared to be. However he now realised how others would perceive what he had done. He would be a reward and there would be those who would betray him to gain it, but he had not bargained for a prefabricated story and that every hand would be turned against him. Now he was truly alone he could trust no one and must be constantly vigilant.

Napier's first instinct was to leave the drovers, set out on his own, keeping well away from towns and villages. However this would not be logical or sensible. To leave now would be to create suspicion. One word in the wrong ear would start the manhunt all over again. He had gained much by becoming part of this group when the whole of England was looking for a stranger alone. It would not be sensible to become a lone traveller. Again the wisest council he could give himself would be to curb his impatience and remain with the herd, regardless of how long the journey might take. The towns man's tale had put him on his guard, made him ultra cautious, made him realise the depths his enemies were prepared to sink to in order to effect his capture. There would be no limit to the distance the hunt would extend to. Even now every port along the coast would be alerted and watched. He knew now there must be no more mistakes, the slightest indiscretion could be his undoing.

To all intents and purposes he remained a simple drover, tending the herd as gradually but so slowly the mass of cattle moved closer and closer to its destination, until eventually they became near enough to the city and therefore allowed him to slip away quietly and anonymously into the narrow streets. Napier was not idle during the drive. Gradually but without being too obvious he began to copy the accent of the Welshmen, even persuading them to teach him a little of their language. Eventually to the casual observer he appeared to be one of them, gaining himself great comfort and security, safe in the knowledge that he no longer resembled the description of the felon on the wanted posters.

Even slow-moving herds must eventually come to the end of the road and so it was that late one afternoon the drovers halted their cattle at convenient grazing and there in the distance were the buildings and smoke of a large city.

"Over yonder is London, your destination," one of the men told Napier. "We will camp here now. It will be dark by the time we reach there. Better for us if we are entering there in the daylight."

Napier made up his mind the time had come for him to leave the drive and the men who had been his companions. It had provided a haven and sanctuary for so long when he had sorely needed it, but it had served its purpose and now he must go. Explaining to the drovers he was impatient to see the city, he took their leave after thanking them profusely for their kindness and hospitality, then headed towards the strangely familiar skyline with the good wishes of his friends ringing in his ears. It seemed the wisest course to enter the city under the cover of darkness where he could slip into the narrow streets without alerting suspicion. Within a couple of hours steady walking he was within hailing distance of the houses on the outskirts of the city, aware of how imperative it was he remained constantly vigilant at all times. Recent events had shown how easy it would be for him to be identified and a hue and cry alerted. With these thoughts in mind he sat under some bushes hidden from the view of any passer by. Now would be the time to formulate a plan of action while he waited for darkness to fall upon the community.

Napier knew this city well. As a child he had roamed the waterfronts and alleys in a constant search for the basic commodities of life. Always cold, always hungry, he had known no other life but the squalid rags filth and deprivation of the street urchin, sifting the mud of the river at low tide in a desperate search for anything that would allow him to survive for one more day. Now all these half-forgotten images came flooding back to him. He shuddered at the memories they invoked, Napier the young man who looked upon this city now, is a world away from the emaciated creature who left it all those years ago. He now stood fit and strong, well educated and knowledgeable. Everything he now was he owed to his adopted father, Jacques Gerard who now lay dead back at the manor. All the painful memories came flooding back. There and then he swore an oath that somehow, someday he would avenge the death of the man who meant more to him than anyone he had ever known. Above these thoughts, in his mind's eye he could hear the voice of Jacques advising caution:

'Think before you move. Do not go in bull-headed. Use your wits; take care before you take action.' Despite himself he smiled as Jacques' favourite phrases flooded his mind and he remembered the man's wisdom.

Despite this wise council going through his head he approached the sleeping city without any clear idea of what he was going to do. True he had money but it was comprised entirely of gold coinage. He needed to convert it to small change. He could not risk paying for food and clothing with gold as that would clearly invite suspicion, particularly in view of the ragged unkempt figure he now presented. His appearance had been fine while on the road with the drovers as they were also dressed in well-worn travel stained clothing, but in the city one such as he trying to spend gold would be a rare sight indeed. The duke could have many spies here who would make the connection immediately.

With all this surging through his mind, his brain concentrating on the struggle to find an answer, he had not been paying too much attention to where he was going and he found himself in the heart of the city, walking down an unlit alley in total darkness, the overhanging houses shutting out even the faint light of a cloudy overcast sky. Napier was not over concerned with this situation, as he knew if he kept to the wall he would eventually come to a main street, where at least he would be able to make out dim shapes in the darkness of the night.

Suddenly his blood ran cold. Just ahead he had seen, so quickly to appear and go, that he was not even certain it had been there, a tiny sliver of light ahead of him, even though it was there and gone in a flash his instincts told him exactly what it was. As a child he had seen this ploy used many times. Almost certainly waiting for him in some dark alcove was a footpad armed with a knife or cudgel. He would be holding a lantern with a sliding door or plate to cut off the light. Luckily for him this plate must have moved slightly allowing a chink of light to escape, warning him of what lay ahead. Now he was forewarned he knew what to expect. As he came alongside the concealed robber the hatch would be slid back and the light shone full in his eyes, temporarily blinding him with the sudden light. At the same time a swift blow with the knife or cudgel would put him out of action. Within seconds he would be relieved of all his valuables and left bleeding in the gutter while the thief made his get away. What to do? He had not weapon. Oh, for a good sword! He would show this footpad his victim had teeth but without a weapon he was vulnerable. Nevertheless he continued to edge forward, knowing that to turn and run could be fatal. The cobbles were so rough and uneven he would certainly trip and fall, the thief would be on him in a trice. Best to face the danger forewarned, trust to luck and providence. There seemed little point in trying to move quietly for he knew his assailant was aware of his presence. Suddenly his way was barred by an object that seemed to rock under his touch, feeling carefully around it he found it to be some form of shallow stone trough loose on its plinth, if he could lift it he could deploy it as a shield. He managed to get his arms around it, as fortunately it was not too big. It seemed square in shape and quite shallow. With a prodigious heave he lifted it and though it was very heavy it was not fixed down and came away easily from its plinth. Unfortunately it contained some foul-smelling liquid which poured all down his front and made him gasp with the cold and the disgusting smell. Nevertheless he maintained his grip and staggered forward, tucking his head below the top to obtain maximum protection, now by dragging his shoulders against the wall he was able to guide himself blindly along the street.

He was aware that the waiting assailant would be totally blind in the pitch darkness, just as he was and hopefully the footpad having heard the noise would assume he had fallen and continue to wait patiently for his victim. The weight of the stone trough was becoming unbearably heavy, Napier had to summon up every ounce of willpower to keep his hold, but he began to feel his numb fingers could no longer retain their grip. He could feel the weight begin to slip; he could no longer hold on. Suddenly the expected attack came; his concentration in holding the trough had been so great he had almost forgotten the waiting footpad. The darkness was cut by a shaft of light from the unshielded lantern, at the same time a dagger was driven in a swift forceful arc straight at what should have been Napier's body, but the intended target was not there, instead the steel blade shattered as it hit the stone. It's owner cursed and gasped with pain at the shock of the impact. A howl of anguish followed immediately as Napier unable to hold the weight released his grip and the trough fell with a sickening crunch across the lower part of the man's legs. The street once again plunged into inky darkness; the falling lantern extinguished itself and was lost in the void.

The night once so quiet was now rent by the agonised moans of the man whose legs were probably broken, Napier had to silence him and silence him quickly. The last thing he wanted was to be the centre of attention even though it was obvious he was the victim. Acting quickly in the pitch darkness he lifted the trough and threw it to one side, feeling along the man's body he found the head and holding him with his left hand he hit him with all his strength into the face, he must have found the right spot because the struggling body sagged and quietness once again descended on the alley. Napier remained on his knees listening. There was no sound, no running footsteps, no shouts no indication the scuffle had been heard – just silence. No doubt in this city, people ignored what did not concern them directly and kept well away from that which was none of their business. The night watch if they were around would be old men; loath to get involved in something they could not handle.

The overwhelming instinct in such a situation is to run blindly and put as much distance between you and the traumatic event as is humanly possible, but Napier fought down this instinct, took a firm grip on his faculties and began to think clearly and calmly. Here was his chance to obtain a change of clothing. He could not see the man's apparel in the darkness – they might not fit, they might be worse rags than his own, but it would be stupid to leave them when they might be the answer to some of his problems. He felt no pity for the man on the floor who had not moved; most certainly he was badly injured, but seconds before this man would have left him – a perfect stranger – laying in the gutter, bleeding and possibly dead with all his possessions taken from him, with no more compassion than swatting a fly. No, this man did not deserve pity and Napier had his own problems to think about, quickly he removed the man's coat which he laid on the floor, the rest of his clothing and shoes he laid on the top then he made a bundle of them all, tying knots with the sleeves and tails of the coat. If there had been a hat it had gone in the struggle and feeling about in the darkness for something that might not be there would have been a pointless waste of time. Quickly and carefully carrying his newly acquired bundle he felt his way out of the inky darkness of the alley and emerged into a main street where at least he could see the cobbles and the shapes of the buildings under the night sky.

It seemed a good plan to walk for an hour to put a reasonable distance between himself and the attack. Being around when the morning light revealed the injured or dead body in the alley was not a preferred option. Apart from the difficulties imposed by the environment he had neither the time nor the inclination to check on the robber's state of health; therefore the question, did he leave him dead or alive? He had no idea. Once he was well into another area of the city he found a sheltered spot under one of the bridges that crossed the river and lay down to sleep for the rest of the night.

As dawn broke the life of the river was already beginning to stir, and Napier awoke to the sound of water slapping the bridge, stirred up by the movement of boats and barges already about their business. He could clearly hear the voices of the crews and the creaking of rigging being hoisted as all manner of craft jockeyed for position on the crowded river. Rested and relaxed he had slept well; his travels in the open air over the past months had accustomed him to sleeping rough. He could now make his bed wherever he laid his head. Now as he took in the sights and smells of the Thames he had the time to consider his next move, he was ravenously hungry and parched with thirst but first he must take stock of the clothing he had acquired last night. Undoing the mud stained bundle he was pleasantly surprised to find the clothing completely opposite to what he had expected. This was no ordinary thief. He was clever and successful: the clothing was of sombre cut and of good quality. A man dressed in such a manner would be perceived to be of the scholarly or clerical profession and certainly not seen as a footpad or common thief. This was luck indeed! Napier dressed quickly in his newly acquired clothing, then wrapping his old clothes in a stone he sunk them in the water, he watched the bundle sink slowly to the bottom of the muddy river then brushed off as much of the dirt as he was able and took stock of his appearance. The waistcoat and breeches had been made for a man of wider girth and hung a little loosely on him but overall he felt he looked respectable – accept from, of course, his unkempt hair and beard. He was well satisfied with the acquisitions fortune had bestowed upon him.

He had thought the coat to be somewhat heavy in weight but had not had the time to investigate it properly, but now as he slipped it on he found the arms to be a trifle short and the weight to be far in excess of what was expected of a normal top coat. As he checked the garment he found it had been modified to assist the man in his chosen profession. There were three leather pockets sewn into the inner lining. One was long and narrow and empty, obviously to sheath the knife he had tried to use in the alley. The other two were situated on the other side just below the armpits. These contained his illegally obtained gains – he had undoubtedly had a successful evening. They were full of coins, fobs and snuffboxes, the combined contents of his victims' pockets. Napier laid them on the ground, the coins he put into his own pockets. They were the answer to a prayer. He could buy food and lodgings, anything he required without arousing suspicion. Now he did not have to go through the risky business of trying to change the gold coins he carried. The personal items of the footpad's loot were a different proposition. They would convict him, unfairly it was true, but nevertheless convict him if they were recognised and he would have a difficult time explaining how he came to be in possession of them, so, wrapping them securely in a large spotted handkerchief he consigned them to the same watery grave that his old clothes went to.

Now in the early morning light as he emerged from where he had spent the night, Napier was able to take a look at the area and to figure out just where in the city he was located. As a child he had lived here and had roamed freely through all its streets and alleyways, but now in another age and another time his memory was dim. He knew he was close to Billingsgate, he could hear the cries of the boatmen and the smell of fish was unmistakable. He must have passed unknowingly through the slums of St Gile's Parish; that would be where the night's encounter with the footpad had taken place. Knowing the area from his childhood he realised how lucky he had been to have passed unscathed through there on a dark night. However his urgent priorities now were finding somewhere to buy food and tidy up his general appearance so that he looked like a respectable resident of the city.

St Paul's Cathedral was a landmark dominating the City and Napier knew if he kept walking towards it he would pass through Cheapside, which if his memory served him correctly was a main shopping area. There he would be able to serve all his needs. As a child he had watched the builders putting the finishing touches to the great dome of the Cathedral and now as it loomed over the City it was an ideal landmark to lead him to his destination.

It is curious how he had never before considered his feelings for this city. Perhaps it was his formative years spent in rural surroundings, but now he realised he disliked it intensely. Compare the countryside so clean fresh and wholesome to this foul-smelling and dirty city. Already the streets were becoming crowded with people and animals about their daily business. The noise was the first thing you noticed. The sound of people talking and shouting, their feet on the cobbles, goods being moved from one place to another, shopkeepers stacking wares outside their establishments, street vendors singing out their cries for custom and street entertainers already beginning a day's busking. Huge steel-shod hooves of the great shire horses slipping across the cobbles as they strove for grip to pull the heavy drays with their steel-rimmed wheels adding their rumbling sound to the general confusion. All manner of light carts jostled for position in the narrow crowded streets, many were porters supplying the shops with their goods drawn by a single horse, others were hand barrows loaded high and heavy, limited only by its owners' ability to push it. Perhaps a little early for customers were the light carriages, the drivers shouting and cracking their whips trying to force their way through the throng transporting the early travellers around the city.

Napier had not noticed the smell before. Perhaps as a child he had grown up with it and took it for granted, but now it offended his country-bred nostrils. True the country had its smells but they were more wholesome and not reminiscent of death and decay as these were. The main culprit was the central drain running down the middle of the street. People used it as a dumping ground for rubbish, decaying vegetables, offal; dead cats, dogs and rats lay festering down its length waiting to be swept away by the next rainstorm. Natural tempest appeared to be the only method of clearing these open drains. Personal hygiene did not appear to be a popular pastime with these people either, a fact made obvious by the overpowering smell of body odour and bad breath caused in many cases by a mouthful of decaying teeth, from which there was no escape when pushed into a group on the pavement by the crush of road traffic.

At times like these Napier was glad of the secret pocket sewn into the coat he was wearing. Pickpockets were at their most active when the crowds were thickest. He was greatly relieved when he saw ahead of him just what he had been looking for: the sign of a barbers shop swinging above the heads of the pedestrians. Concerned about his own safety he had been wary of some of these shop signs, many looked much the worse for wear and in such a poor state of repair they swung precariously above the heads of the people, if they were to fall they could inflict serious injury.

It was a great relief to enter the shop, a haven from the noisy jostling crowds in the street, the barber appeared to be a good natured jovial sort of chap who bade Napier a good morning and gestured him to a seat in one of the chairs set in the middle of the clean swept floor. With a much-practised sweep he tied a large cloth around the customer's neck and snipping his scissors inquired which of his services were required. Napier had already decided on a cover story. His disguise as a Welsh drover had already stood him in good stead and he saw no reason to change something that had worked well; therefore, adopting the accent of the drovers, he told the barber to cut his hair short and shave off his beard. The barber would expect someone newly arrived from Wales to be different to a Londoner and would not question his long hair and beard. Mud-covered clothes were not unusual on a London street, they would not be questioned either.

The barber quickly and expertly finished his task. Napier could barely recognise himself in the small mirror the man held up for his approval and was happy to pay the few pennies he asked for his labours.

"If I might make a suggestion," the man said, "most gentlemen in the City wear a wig. I could sell you one if you wish to be in fashion."

So saying he brought out a box containing a selection and offered them to Napier who tried a few on for size, finally selecting a brown one. He rejected the powdered variety as too messy for travelling. Their transactions concluded the barber produced a brush and cleaned the mud from Napier's clothing, after which they bid each other good day and he stepped back into the street feeling a new man.

There was every reason to be confident now. He had money and he was in London where he could merge into the crowds; in his sombre dress and understated wig he looked every inch a cleric or scholar. In fact this was the disguise he had decided to adopt when the barber had enquired the purpose of his visit to the City. The idea had just popped into his head. He was a Welshman who had completed his education and had been lucky enough to secure a post as a teacher at a school in Paris. Consequently he was now on his way to France to begin his new job. He had no doubts regarding his ability to act out his new identity which would give him the every reason to look out for a ship to take him to France and no one would ask any questions. To complete his disguise he would require baggage and possessions. With this in mind he entered a pawnbrokers where he was able to supply all his needs. The pawnbroker had a full range of second-hand goods on display. His first purchase was a leather travelling bag. This he filled with toiletries and spare clothes; all of the same sober cut as the clothes he now wore. To complete the picture a black triangular hat and a selection of learned books put the finishing touches to the image he now affected.

Safe with his new image he had no need to hide in dark corners or keep a low profile. He could do as other travellers did. Rather than walk the crowded muddy streets he hailed a sedan chair and asked to be taken to a good inn. This was without doubt the best way to travel about the City. These men were licensed, and had the right to travel on the pavement, as they were in fact pedestrians even though they carried a passenger. They moved very quickly and with their heavy load could not stop easily. Therefore anyone hearing their cry of "By your leave, sir!" would be wise to get out of their way or be knocked into the gutter. Their progress across the City was swift and very soon they arrived at a large coaching inn where they entered through the main door and Napier was able to step out straight into the parlour of the inn. He paid the sedan men with thanks and sat down in front of a roaring log fire. There was just time to look round at the low oak beams and the welcoming atmosphere when the landlord arrived with a tankard of ale. He introduced himself as 'mine host', took Napier's order for food and a bed for the night then bidding him to take advantage of the comforts of his establishment bustled off to see to the order. The food took about half an hour to arrive but to a ravenous man it seemed an eternity, after all he had not eaten since the previous day. When it did arrive, carried on a steaming platter by a homely servant girl, he thought it to be the best food he had eaten in his life.

He spent the day pottering about in his room, reading the books he had bought and enjoying the comforts of civilisation he had done without for so long, going out sightseeing did not seem a sensible option because of the possibility of being unluckily sighted by someone who knew him. After all he must never lose sight of the fact he was still a fugitive. Keeping out of sight appeared to be the best plan; Never-the-less he did go down for meals and chatted to people who came in for a drink. One of the drinkers, who happened to be a water man, advised him to go down to Billingsgate where he could board a ferry for Gravesend. It was there that most of the sea-going ships were docked. That was where he would be most likely to get a passage to France. Encouraged by this information Napier decided to turn in early to his bed, have a good nights' sleep, rise early in the morning and set about seeking a berth on a ship. He would feel safer once he had crossed the Channel.

6

France and Dangerous Roads

Napier did not sleep as well as he had expected. The luxury of a bed was something he had not experienced for many months. It took him quite some time to become accustomed to its comfort again. When finally he did sleep he slept like a log and awoke far later than he had intended. Dressing quickly he packed his bag and hurried downstairs to a hasty breakfast where he informed the landlord he would be leaving that day. While he was eating the landlord obligingly despatched one of the kitchen boys to call a sedan chair, which arrived just as he was chewing the last morsel. They came as before: through the front door, setting the chair down in the parlour. Napier paid his bill and said goodbye to his landlord who wished him a safe journey. Then, settling back in his seat, he was taken to his destination without so much as putting a foot in the street. The two men set the chair on the dockside and Napier paid them the standard tariff. Without so much as a by your leave they picked up their chair and set off at a fast trot, looking for their nest customer, leaving him looking around trying to get his bearings.

This was a crowded, bustling and busy area. There was hardly an inch of dockside not taken up by stacks of boxes, bales and sacks. Porters were pushing barrows and carrying loads on their heads and backs in hasty organised confusion as they unloaded coal, fish and vegetables from the colliers, fishing boats, and merchant vessels lining up at the quayside. Further along the quay the ferryboats waited. Their owners shouting out their fees, touting for custom as they prepared to row passengers to the other side of the river. Just beyond were the wherries and large barges, their crews resting on their oars, sitting and making no attempt to assist the passengers who stepped precariously off the quay whilst holding their luggage and belongings, stepping uncertainly as they walked along the unsteady boat to find their seats. Napier joined the queue and finally managed to find a seat. It was then from the conversation going on around him that he learned he had been lucky to arrive on time. The heavily laden wherries, with their passengers and cargo, could only pass under London Bridge at high tide and therefore had to leave at the exact time.

At the appointed time they cast off and the rowers fitted their oars into the rowlocks and headed for the middle of the river where they would be in a good position for the difficult business of negotiating the arches of the bridge. This feat of navigation was looked upon as a mere occupational hazard by the watermen, but for the passengers it was a nerve-racking experience. The tide rushed through the stone supports like a mill race and only at the turning of the tide did the water slow down sufficiently for the barge-like wherries to pass through safely, but in the skilled and practised hands of the watermen the boat passed through without incident. Soon they were passing the Tower of London and the boatmen were rigging a mast and raising a sail to help them on their journey.

This was always a gruelling journey for the passengers. Long hours to be spent on seats that were little more than a plank, or trying to keep out of the way of the crew who worked non-stop, constantly resetting the sail or taking their turns on the oars. The wind was cold and cut like a knife. The passengers, huddled in their coats and cloaks, were constantly soaked by the spray every time the boat changed tack to take advantage of the wind or to avoid the many other craft on the river. However they made good progress and very soon the wharfs and warehouses of the City gave way to open countryside – flat featureless fields with little of interest.

Napier huddled into his heavy travelling coat, turned the collar up and pulled his hat down well over his eyes for fear of the wind blowing it off. He was glad of this, for it helped to keep him anonymous – not that any of his fellow travellers had attempted to strike up a conversation. They were all too busy huddled up in their own little worlds, trying to cope with the miseries of river travel. On the other hand, the trip was not totally unpleasant. There was a good side. The air was fresh on the river; the fetid smells of the City had gone. The smells of tar, hemp, rope and wooden decking were not in themselves unpleasant. The noise too was more acceptable. The general clatter and bustle of the City had been deafening at times, but here the shouts of the watermen were picked up and blown away by the wind, while the creak of the boat and the rigging, merged with the sound of the flapping sail, could be quite soothing if you closed your eyes and listened.

It was early evening when they finally hove to off Gravesend and the sail was brought down and stowed away. The boatmen were busy setting about their task of bringing the vessel alongside the quay to be moored for disembarking. Napier had intended to set about finding a passage immediately they had docked but as he waited for his turn to climb the ladder to the quayside, once again unaided by the crew, no doubt they were exhausted by the trip. He decided to find lodgings for the night. The rigours and privations of the trip had taken their toll, and with the lateness of the hour it seemed more sensible to seek food and lodgings now and to seek a passage on the morrow. It did not take long to find a place. Wherever there are people in transit there are always establishments ready to supply their needs and Gravesend was no exception. Napier found a small but welcoming inn where he was able to dry out his wet clothes and thaw out his cold bones in front of a roaring log fire. He made a hearty supper of roast meat and vegetables washed down with ale and retired to bed, falling asleep the instant his head touched the pillow.

The following morning, just after dawn, found him in high spirits. Fed and watered, he walked along the quayside searching for a ship. This proved to be none too easy a task. The forest of masts moored along the docks gave an enormous choice of vessels, but how was he to tell which would be going to France? French ships did not advertise their presence in British ports: the two nations were not at war and there was a flourishing trade going on. But colonial squabbles about the world made for an uneasy peace and an undercurrent of anti-French, anti-British feeling was always just below the surface. Napier was just about to choose a ship and make enquiries on board when he heard voices on the deck above him. They were conversing in Welsh. Suddenly he saw a flaw in his adopted disguise. If he were to join a ship with Welsh men in the crew, then he as a Welshman would be expected to converse with them. This he could not do. He had learnt a few phrases from the drovers, enough to fool a non-Welsh speaker, but he was far from fluent in the language. His disguise would be easily penetrated. Obviously his cover story required a re-think. After a moment's thought, he formulated another plan: he would keep the part about a job in Paris, but now he would become a French national, educated in England, travelling back to his nation of birth. This he could do easily. His French was perfect; Jacques had taught him well. They had often spent many hours conversing in the language. Any flaws in his accent would be blamed on his English education.

And so it was that as Napier, the Frenchman, he approached two important-looking gentlemen who were checking the cargo being loaded into a square-rigged corvette. They informed him that its destination was Spain and it was due to sail on the evening tide, but as luck would have it, they had on board some equipment used in the fishing industry to be delivered to the port of Dieppe. They did not normally take passengers, but if Napier wished they would stretch a point; he could go along as a fare-paying passenger and go ashore at Dieppe with the equipment when they loaded it. Napier did wish; in fact he was delighted. This was far better than he had hoped. There would be no other passengers to ask awkward questions. If his enemies suspected he was making for France they would be watching ports such as Calais and Boulogne where he would be expected to enter. He accepted the offer eagerly and paid the men the fare they asked. He noted they did not enter his presence in the directory, but quietly slipped the gold coins into their own pockets and nodded him aboard. This was even better because officially he was not on the ship. At the back of his mind had always been the worry that he did not have any papers or means of identification. If asked, his plan was to claim they had been stolen – a very dubious claim as well as a very thin cover story, one he was unlikely to get away with. One of the men came aboard with him and introduced him to the captain, a weather-beaten old mariner, who showed no surprise at his extra cargo, which made Napier suspect that this was not by any means an unusual occurrence. Perhaps the three between them made a tidy little extra profit from passengers that the owners were unaware of. Still, the arrangement suited Napier. It was none of his business. He was just happy to stay in the tiny cabin allocated to him, keeping out of the way until the ship sailed.

It was not really a cabin, just a store locker filled with coils of rope and rigging blocks, but there was a hammock, which he unrolled and slung from the bulkhead. It was not easy to get into, but after falling out a couple of times he mastered the technique and found it most comfortable and did not find it a problem to remain there, dozing, until the ship got under way. How long he lay there he did not know; he must have fallen into a deep sleep, as he woke with a start to look at his surroundings, at first he wondering where he was. With the customary confusion of a sleeper who awakes in a strange bed, he gradually became aware that the sound and the feel of the ship had changed; the bumps and bangs of cargo being carried up the gangplank and stored in the hold were now replaced by the creaks and groans of woodwork, as the ship responded to the pressures of wind and water. He could hear above his head the running feet, the shouted orders followed by the crisp replies of the crew responding instantly to the demands of the ship. It was a strange and alien world to Napier, who emerged onto the deck more then a little curious at the activity he saw before him. It was astonishing how much the ship had changed from the time he had come aboard. Then it had been an inanimate object just floating on the water, everything hung loose and all the activity came from the stevedores loading the ship and the crew preparing to sail, but now the ship was a vibrant master and the crew were its servants tending to its needs.

As a traveller new to the sea, he looked up at the taut rigging and the bulging canvas. The vessel had become one with the wind. The bows pushed the water aside contemptuously. One could almost believe it was a living thing, with nerves, muscles and sinews tensed and flexing as though it actually felt its control of the elements it used so effectively. An old mariner he had once spoken to had told him he believed a ship was a living entity. Napier had never fully grasped his meaning, but now, as he watched the Kent coastline slip away and the ship now clear of the sandbars of the Thames estuary heading for the open sea, he fully understood what the old man was trying to say.

An hour slipped by quickly as he walked the deck, watching the sea and marvelling at the skill and knowledge of the crew as they worked the bewildering network of ropes, pulleys and canvas above his head. So engrossed was he, looking up at the rigging and the agile sailors aloft, he almost bumped into the captain, who ignoring the clumsy naivety of landlubbers invited him to join his table for supper. Napier was grateful for his offer and readily followed him to the stern cabin. This was the main cabin of the ship and although large in area, it had very little headroom. A tall man would find his head in eminent danger from the heavy beams and the two brass lanterns hanging from them, swinging freely to the movement of the ship.

In contrast to the neat and tidy decks, the cabin itself had a confused and disorderly appearance. A large table stood in the centre, covered with charts and navigation instruments. Stacked around the walls were barrels, boxes and packages; books lay open and personal items were scattered about indiscriminately after use. The captain swept the charts and gear into a pile and dumped them *en bloc* on top of a brass-bound sea chest, with a gruff, "Sit ye down, lad."

He waved Napier to a chair and sat himself down at the head of the table. Almost as though this was a signal, there was a knock on the door and a man entered. He was about the same age as the captain with the same rough, weather-beaten nautical appearance. Eventually the captain would introduce him as the first mate. He sat down at the table and together they began to discuss the details of the ship's progress, ignoring Napier as though he did not exist. While they were thus engaged, a young boy of little more than twelve years of age came in and silently laid out tankards and plates on the table. His bare feet padded quickly about the cabin, his none too clean hands taking bread and knives out of a cupboard, placing them with a keg of rum and a jug of water in front of the diners. The first mate poured a liberal quantity of rum into the tankards and topped them up with water, handing one each to Napier and the captain. In the meantime the boy returned with a steaming copper pot containing a stew, which he then ladled into each plate. This task he performed silently and respectfully, taking great care not to spill as he did so. Then, without making eye contact or uttering a word, he moved from the table and stood, almost as though he were part of the furniture, in a far corner of the cabin.

Once the meal had begun the pair proved to be rough but amiable companions. They ate their food with chunks of bread and a knife. No other cutlery seemed necessary or available. Manners and etiquette were not the seaman's way. The stew contained a type of meat, but it was difficult to determine from what animal it came from, possibly a salt beef or pork. The bread was coarse and hard, but washed down with the rum and water was reasonably palatable. No doubt after weeks at sea the fresh provisions would deteriorate considerably and this present fare was as good as it was liable to get.

The company, however, was excellent. After initial introductions and a few questions regarding his eventual destination, they did not appear to be overly curious and quickly turned to more general conversation. Although their manners and language reflected the roughness of their calling, they kept Napier entertained with tales of the sea and seamen.

While they were eating, the brass lamps had started to sway alarmingly. The plates and tankards began to slide across the table and Napier began to feel he was about to lose his seat at any moment; however none of the other occupants of the cabin appeared to be affected. The captain, without fuss or hurry, calmly finished his rum and rose to his feet.

"Time we were on deck, mate. Looks like we are in for a bit of a blow. Better got those lubbers into the rigging and shorten sail. I'll bid you goodnight, lad," he said to Napier. With that he took his hat and went up on deck, followed by the first mate.

'A bit of a blow,' he said. By the time Napier had reached the deck the sails were coming down and the ship was rolling heavily in the tempestuous spume-topped sea. He looked up at the three stark masts whipped by the wind across the dark overcast night sky, saw the waves and spray flying across the open decks and decided the best place for him was his little rope locker of a cabin. To get there was easier said than done. Napier's landman's legs could not keep their footing on the slippery, heaving decks. He hung on with both hands to every rope and tenuous handhold he could find. To make matters worse, he was violently seasick by the time he reached his cabin. All of the supper he had just consumed had gone. The movement of the ship virtually flung him into the cabin. Picking himself up he struggled with the door and, with great difficulty, managed to close it. Getting into the hammock had been difficult while the ship was moored; in the gale it was downright impossible. Every time he tried he was thrown out, but eventually the feat was accomplished. He lay there, too ill with the seasickness to notice his wet clothes and the bruising he had taken from being flung from side to side trying to cross the violently mobile decks.

The short voyage to Dieppe took a full three days, most of the time being battered by the gale. Napier spent the days in his hammock, venturing out only when he felt he should try to eat and drink – only to bring it all up again while being sick in the scuppers, much to the amusement of the crew, who did not seem to share his belief that the ship was about to sink and that none of them ever see land again. Not that Napier gave a toss about the opinions of the crew or his eminent environment; he prayed only for dry land. Such were the effects of the misery of seasickness.

Thankfully even the worst gales came to an end eventually, and so it was with that one. In much calmer weather they finally dropped anchor off the port of Dieppe. Napier thought of solid ground under his feet and scrambled gratefully down the ladder into the cutter that had rowed out to unload the cargo the ship had brought. Bobbing about on the ocean swell and somewhat low in the water, the fully laden cutter turned its bow to the shore and the men pulled strongly on the oars, rowing away from the ship. Napier, sitting in the bows, waved to the crew before wrapping his coat around him against the chill of the offshore breeze. The crew, some leaning on the rail, others in the shrouds, gave him a hearty cheer. Napier suspected his popularity owed more to the amusement he had given them during his many visits to the bulwarks than to their admiration of his personality. Still they had got him here safe and sound. To his mind they had earned their moments of amusement and his admiration of them knew no bounds for the way they carried out their arduous and dangerous occupation.

As the cutter pulled for the shore he looked over the heads of the oarsmen and could see the ship he had just left already preparing to leave. Some men were straining at the windlass, others were climbing nimbly up the masts, shaking out the sails. A fresh breeze began to swell the stained white canvas, pushing the ship forwards as it moved before the wind. He watched it moving away, bound for Spain to deliver its main cargo. For him it had served its purpose. He was now across the channel, but that did not mean he was safe. There were many dangers still to be faced. Half turning in his seat he surveyed the approaching mainland. Who knows what awaited him there. The busy harbour was filled with fishing boats going about their trade. He wondered what he would find when he set foot ashore and started on the final stage of his journey to Paris.

Passing expertly between the many boats sailing in and out of the harbour, the rowers shipped their oars and the cutter slid alongside a stone jetty. Napier, having already picked up his bag, jumped out and climbed the steps. They were covered with algae and very slippery, smelling strongly of seaweed and salt water. Picking his way carefully he reached the top and stood surveying the waterfront.

Dieppe was much the same as any other fishing port, busy but without the frantic haste that had been London docks. Along the sea front were lines of small humble cottages presumably the homes of the men who worked the boats. Nets were everywhere – hanging up or laying on the shingle to dry. Here and there the fisher folk sat repairing them as fisher folk do the world over; Napier did not know what he had been expecting but somehow he drew comfort from this peaceful town and its almost familiar normality. Much to his relief there did not appear to be anyone in authority apart from a group of men unloading the cutter, one of whom he took to be the harbour master. They had walked straight past Napier without so much as a nod. His main worry had been the presence of customs men, but there did not appear to be anyone of that ilk around, possibly because the ship had not entered the harbour and they had deemed it not worth the trouble. Not wishing to push his luck he did not linger at the harbour looking for a waterfront inn. He preferred to walk further into the town, trying to ignore the pangs of hunger gnawing away at his insides. There had been plenty of good, coarse food on board the ship; but what he had managed to eat, he had not kept down – the motion of the ship had seen to that. Therefore, after three days without food, he imagined himself to be like a walking skeleton.

Inns seemed to be in short supply in Dieppe, but he did find a stall where he bought a loaf of bread and a small round cheese which he ate as he walked. Eventually he found a lodging house where he secured a room for the night. There he left his bag and set out to explore the town. Eventually during his wanderings through the streets he found a staging house. Subsequent inquiries revealed there would be a coach setting out on the three-day journey to Paris the following morning. Napier booked and paid for the last seat available and returned to his lodgings with a spring in his step. Things were looking up. There was hope for the future that at last his troubles would soon be over.

He arrived the following morning bright and early at the staging post to find the coach ready and waiting – a fine encouraging sight for any traveller. The bright clean paintwork of the vehicle and the horses standing in their oiled and polished harnesses were magnificent. The horses' coats were groomed and shining; they tossed their heads, snorting through their nostrils, and stamped their hooves on the cobbles in a show of impatience to be on the road and running. Napier threw his bag up to the guard, who caught it with a practice born of long experience stowed it with the rest of the luggage. He retained his small bundle of books to read on the journey and climbed into the coach to see two passengers already seated: a pretty young girl of approximately his own age and an older woman with a stern, frosty-faced appearance who was obviously her companion. He sat down opposite the girl and smiled a greeting; the girl looked away and blushed slightly, while the companion glared at Napier with a look that if it had been directed at the coach would have blistered the paint-work, making it obvious to him that conversation on the journey was gong to be strictly limited!

They sat in silence for a while, when suddenly the coach tilted sideways on its springs and a large overweight gentleman appeared in the doorway. He stood on the step trying to squeeze his bulk through the narrow gap. His actions were complicated by the fact he was wearing a court sword, which somehow had got itself wedged horizontally across the door posts, preventing his entry. He seemed unwilling or unable to relinquish his two-handed grip on the doorframe and was attempting to free the sword with strenuous wobbling movements of his stomach. Napier, trying to suppress his amusement, leaned forward and freed the weapon, thus allowing the man to pop into the coach like a cork from a bottle. He stumbled across, treading on feet as he went and flopped into the vacant seat, squeezing Napier against the far wall. Once safely seated he took off his tricorn hat and used it like a fan causing a small fall of white powder from his wig to settle on his shoulders. Next he took out a large handkerchief and mopped his perspiring brow. Only when this was done did he greet his fellow passengers and thank Napier for his assistance.

Napier had not handled a sword for months and for one who, before he had left the manor, had practised daily, the touch of the cold hard metal was comforting, yet strange but also familiar. Napier would have liked to also wear a sword, but he knew it would not be in keeping with his disguise as a scholar. He was about to lapse into memories of past happenings when his thoughts were interrupted by the sudden movement of the coach starting on its journey. It lurched from side to side, shaking the passengers and forcing them to hold on to anything they could to avoid being thrown from their seats, with a clatter of steel-shod hooves on the cobbles, the rumble of iron-rimmed wheels and the accompaniment of the guard blowing melodious notes on the coach horn, they were on their way to Paris.

Conversation on a coach drawn by six horses at a fast trot over rough roads is not easy, what with drumming hooves punctuated occasionally by the crack of the driver's whip. Then there was the coach itself, creaking and moaning as it lurched from side to side, rumbling over the uneven roads, sometimes dropping into ruts and potholes bouncing the occupants about on the hard seats. Certainly Napier considered it to be a far more uncomfortable mode of transport than a sea voyage; that is if you did not take into consideration the gale he had experienced crossing the channel. However, casting his mind back to his previous experiences of coach travel, hanging on to the luggage rack at the rear, he accepted beyond doubt that travelling as a paying passenger was far more comfortable a mode than clinging to the back as a stowaway.

The difficulties of coach journey conversation did not seem to worry the large overweight gentleman, who introduced himself as Monsieur Gaston Coural. He claimed to be the owner of a chandler store selling goods to the fishing industry. Apparently he was forced into making the tedious and uncomfortable journey in order to make contact with his Parisian suppliers. Napier had no choice but to return the courtesy and relate his cover story regarding a teaching job in Paris. His name he gave as Napier Feray, the surname Feray he had just seen in the book he was reading and gave it on the spur of the moment; a name was as good as any other when used as an alias. The stern-faced woman sniffed and gave a look which seemed to say, *Who I am and what I am is none of your business*, but perhaps thinking that it would be ill-mannered not to respond, she stated briefly her name was Madame Duvaux, travelling with her niece, Mademoiselle Marie Nattier, to see her brother who lived in Paris.

Having made the acquaintance of his fellow passengers, Monsieur Coural began to talk endlessly about the difficulties of running a business. He seemed to have little interest in any subject bar the buying and retailing of stock, of ropes that did not fray, pulley blocks that did not split and nets that did not rot. Madame Duvaux on the other hand seemed totally indifferent to his conversation and continually interrupted his narrative with moans and complaints regarding the discomfort of the journey. Napier sat and listened to these two most boring of travelling companions and amused himself by imagining either of them situated as he was on his last coach journey. *They would have had something to complain about then,* he thought with a private smile. Napier would liked to have engaged Marie in conversation and leave the other two to their tedium, but she refused to meet his eye and remained staring fixedly out of the window. Also he was afraid of attracting one of Madame Duvaux's icy stares threatening to turn him into a block of salt. Overall he was glad when the first day's journey was over; what with the general discomfort, the cramped conditions and the dullness of the company he was grateful to climb out of the coach and shake out his stiff, cramped limbs. Judging by the comments of his companions they also shared these views.

In comparison to the journey, the staging post was a haven, warm and bright with good food and comfortable beds. It was a welcome resting place for all the travellers. After dinner the ladies retired to their room and Napier settled in front of the fire, looked into the flames and thought how blissful it was to take a tankard of ale and cease travelling for a while. His pleasure, however, was short-lived when Gaston Coural joined him and continued his tales regarding the ups and downs of running a chandlers business. Within half an hour he was asleep and awoke to find Coural still prattling on, apparently unaware his listener was sleeping. Napier waited for a suitable moment to excuse himself, drained his tankard and, rising to his feet, he bid Coural 'goodnight' then retired gratefully to his bed. His companion, apparently not yet ready to retire, wandered off in search of another listener thirsty for knowledge of the chandler art.

The following morning found them all fully refreshed preparing to start on he second day of their journey. Napier suppressed a groan when Coural once again started on the never-ending saga of the chandler business and Madame Duvaux continued to bemoan her ordeal on the coach. He could understand her complaining, he just wished she would not do it so often; after all, she was not alone in her discomfort. He was pushed hard against the side by the bulk of Monsieur Coural and his legs were becoming cramped. He was just debating the possibility of stretching them out for a while without incurring the lash of Madame's sharp tongue, who might think he was trying to play footsie with her niece, when there was a dramatic change of events.

Over the general road noise a shouted command was heard: "Hold there!"

The driver was already reining in the horses. The block brakes screeched and there was a strong smell of burning wood as the driver applied them hard. The unprepared passengers were flung forward in a heap as the coach shuddered to a stop. Poor Madame Duvaux received the full weight of Monsieur Coural and the more fortunate Napier was thrown on top of Marie. In the confines of the coach, extricating themselves was difficult. While they were doing so, the crack of a pistol shot was heard and a blunderbuss fell past the window, followed instantly by the guard. There could be no question about it – this was the work of a highwayman.

The sudden turn of events had caused such confusion inside the coach it took time for the occupants to sort themselves out and gather their wits. By then the driver had climbed down from his seat and was opening the door. Then a well mannered, cultured voice made a polite request rather than an order.

"If you please, ladies and gentlemen, I would appreciate it if you would kindly step down from the coach and be my guests."

Coural was the first one to scramble clumsily out, followed by Napier who assisted the ladies to climb out one by one. Only when this task was completed did he turn round and survey the scene before him.

They were in an area of remote moorland. Thick clumps of rough gorse dotted about had no doubt given cover to the miscreant prior to the ambush. The driver stood on the turf at the edge of the road, his hands above his head, displaying the fact he had no intention of using a weapon. The body of the guard lay on his back in the red mud of the track a little distance away. He was obviously dead: a crimson patch spreading from his head indicated the ball had entered just above his eyes in the centre of his forehead. Napier had expected to see a group of ruffians and was surprised to see a lone figure on a perfectly groomed thoroughbred grey. He sat controlling his mount with his knees while in each hand he held a snaphaunce pistol. The most remarkable thing about him was his dress. Tales of highwaymen were common at that time and Napier had heard many, even though he had never met one; he had always perceived them as rough-living men dressed in dark travel-stained clothes and always with a black mask. This man was none of these. His clothes would not have disgraced a gentleman of the court, and were made of brightly coloured satins, silks and heavy brocade. They were immaculate. From his tricorn hat to his highly polished riding boots he cut the most elegant figure and the only indication of his infamous trade was the mask he wore. Made of red satin, it covered his entire face and hung down below his chin so that the whole face was covered; holes in the stitched and embroidered fabric allowed two glittering eyes to look out on the world, which he did with his head tilted well back, giving him an arrogant, haughty appearance.

Napier had by now recovered his wit, his mind racing to find a way out of this situation. He had no intention of allowing this man to take his money, sending him on his way to Paris penniless, but at the same time what to do? He had no weapon. The guard's blunderbuss was way back down the road; attacking a man on horseback was difficult enough, but with this man it would be suicidal, as he had already displayed his ability with a pistol. To hit a man on a moving coach in the head with a horse pistol held in one hand while on horseback displayed almost unbelievable accuracy. Without question he was completely ruthless. He had shown that by the way he had despatched the guard. Despite his dandified appearance, this man had to be feared. He would kill without compunction at the first wrong move.

He was still considering his options when the man did the most amazing thing. He placed one of his pistols into his saddle holster, obviously the discharged one used to kill the guard. Dismounting with a smoothness and grace born of long practice he draped the reins over a bush. Still holding the pistol, he uncocked it, rendering it unfireable until the hammer was re-cocked. He then pushed the firearm into his waistband, removed his hat and executed a deep courtly bow towards the ladies. Then taking Marie by the hand he led her a few paces away and address her thus:

"My dear Mademoiselle it would be ungracious of me to steal from a lady without giving some compensation in return; therefore, would you honour me with a dance before I rob you?"

So saying he began to dance, a skill he obviously performed frequently for he appeared to be very good at it. Marie had no option but to join him and complied with his request. At first Napier was taken by surprise at this bizarre scene he could not believe his eyes. This idiot was so cocksure of himself he actually believed the fear he instilled would keep them rooted to the spot, watching him dance, waiting meekly for him to finish then stand back and allow him to rob them. Well, that was his first mistake!

Gaston Coural was still wearing his sword, but clearly had no intention of using it. Napier reached over and deftly withdrew it from its scabbard. What a thrill it was to hold a sword again after all that time. There was a good chance he could reach his target before the man was able to withdraw and cock the loaded pistol. If he did not he knew he would be dead. This man proved himself to be an expert in its use and would not give a second opportunity. The highwayman, engaged in a stately minuet with the pretty Marie, looked up in surprise at the sudden movement; his eyes pierced through the holes in his mask and fixed on Napier. He did not, as expected, grab for the pistol; instead he drew out his own sword and faced Napier saying, "Well, well. At least one of you shows a little courage, but I must tell you, puppy, it is a mistake to draw a sword on Satin Jack!"

Napier took up the *en garde* position and sized the man up. If he was as good with a sword as he was with a pistol then he had the fight of his life on his hands. By the looks of him he did not appear to be an expert. His stance was unconventional and he held the weapon clumsily. It took only a couple of feints to convince Napier that this was no swordsman. His threatening boast about crossing swords did not appear to be backed by any trained ability. He did not think there would be a problem dispatching this braggart. Even so he knew he must not take any risks. This man must be disposed of cleanly and quickly. To wound him or convince him he was about to get the worst of the encounter would still leave him with the opportunity to use that pistol with possible fatal consequences. He knew without question that as a swordsman he was far superior to the highwayman, who clearly had little knowledge of the art. It would be easy to wound or disarm him but Napier had not been trained to take chances. He decided to keep it simple and direct; a tap on the man's sword with his own blade produced the desired result, the response being an instant parry, and Satin Jack fell for the oldest trick in the book. Napier avoided the blade and went in under the parry with a lunge that drove his sword straight through his opponent's neck, severing the jugular vein. He felt the jar as the blade hit the spinal column, glanced off and came out the other side. He pulled out the sword and Satin Jack sank to the ground, drowning in his own blood.

The victor looked down at the crumpled figure without sorrow or conscience. This man was a ruthless killer. He had shot the guard without compunction and gave no thought to the fact he might be depriving a family of a bread winner, or young children of a father, for no reason but his own selfish greed for booty. On the other hand had he succeeded in capturing him alive he would not have survived anyway, the penalty for highway robbery was death.

Once the danger had passed the others rushed over and surrounded Napier with excited enthusiastic euphoria. Coural grabbed his hand and pumped it as though he were never going to stop. Madame Duvaux thanked him a thousand times; declaring goodness knows what would have happened to poor Marie if Napier had not saved her. Marie for her part looked at him with hero worship on her face and never took her eyes off him. The driver kicked the body over with his foot.

"Good riddance to him," he said. "He killed my mate and for that he deserved all he got! I've heard of Satin Jack, he's terrorised this stretch of road for years. There will be a goodly reward waiting for you young sir!"

Napier assured him he would not accept a reward for himself, but asked if he would arrange for any reward to go to the guard's family. The driver thanked him profusely and said that this he would do, as he knew them very well. This apparent act of generosity prompted another round of back-slapping congratulations from the passengers who feted him as the hero of the hour. Coural said he had never seen a young man of such upright and praiseworthy character. Without doubt he had a glittering future ahead of him; Madame Duvaux agreed, declaring he was surely sent from heaven to help them – and Marie, she just looked.

No one was keen to hang around now the excitement was over. The driver had to make up lost time on his schedule and all of them feared the possibility of more highway robbers at this remote spot. After assisting the ladies back into the coach, the three men wrapped the bodies in travel rugs and tied them to the top luggage rack. They could not be left at the side of the road at the mercy of wild animals. Also the highwayman with a price on his head had to be handed over to the authorities, otherwise the reward could not be claimed for the family of the guard, whose body would be returned to them by the return coach.

The grim task completed, the journey continued with Napier seated beside the driver, taking it upon himself to perform the guard's duties. He was grateful for this change in his travelling status. Obviously it was essential to have armed protection for the vehicle on these dangerous roads, but mainly for reasons of personal privacy. He was still a fugitive and dreaded the thought of sitting confined in that box-like interior under the fierce glare of admiration from the other passengers who would undoubtedly bombard him with questions. They had already asked how he had become so proficient with the sword. He had managed to counter this question with the statement that an English school education always included fencing lessons. The answer seemed to satisfy their curiosity as they all remarked how lucky it was he had received such a complete education, and let the subject drop.

Now as he sat muffled against the wind, the guard's blunderbuss laid across his lap, his feet braced firmly against the footboard to prevent being thrown off the bucking swaying coach, flecks of foam off the sweating horses spattered his face as the unsparing driver whipped them into a gallop in an attempt to make up lost time. His thoughts were on his arrival at Paris where he had hoped to arrive anonymously and slip away quietly and unnoticed into the city, to merge into the population. This now appeared to be a forlorn hope. He certainly had not planned to arrive there a conquering hero in a blaze of publicity. The prospect was a frightening one. He had no means of knowing how far the duke's spy network was spread and someone who had despatched a notorious highwayman with a sword so effectively would undoubtedly attract attention in the wrong quarters. Still he would just have to wait for the future to unfold, with this thought he dismissed his worries and indulged himself with a smile as he imagined the scene in the coach. With the increased speed Madame would really have something to complain about!

7

Françoise Faubert and a Change of Plan

Napier's worries regarding his arrival in Paris were intensifying as the journey progressed. They were in the final stage of their travels and he had resumed his seat with the other passengers, his services were no longer required as a replacement guard sat on the top with the driver. The body of the highwayman had been handed over at the staging post. Much to Napier's relief this was situated in a small village where no one in authority was immediately at hand. The innkeeper, a pompous man with an officious manner saw the opportunity to pander to his self-importance and took control of the situation. He compiled written statements from the participants in the drama, placed them in an envelope and sealed it with wax impressed with his own seal. This, he explained, along with the body of the criminal and a written request for the transfer of the reward money to the guard's family, would be taken to the police authorities in Paris; a public service he promised to undertake personally. This task, he stated, was no less than his duty as a citizen of France.

It was with considerable relief that Napier, rising early the following morning looked out of his bedroom overlooking the yard. He could see the coach, with the horses already harnessed to it, standing beside a heavy cart with a large dray horse in the shafts. Two stable boys were busy loading a canvas-wrapped body. Obviously the landlord had decided it was too late to start his journey the previous evening and opted for an early start that morning. This was welcome news for him because without doubt the much faster stagecoach would arrive at the city well before the slow plodding dray horse. Therefore he stood a reasonable chance of slipping away before the authorities were advised of the highwayman's demise and the relevant publicity it would generate, publicity he as a fugitive could well do without.

The closer they came to Paris the more excited the passengers became; Monsieur Coural had forgotten all about his chandler's tales and was endlessly reliving the adventure claiming, without a hint of embarrassment, that he was about to draw his sword and dispatch the highwayman himself if Napier had not got there before him. Madame Duvaux, her discomfort quite forgotten, joined in the conversation, rehearsing the tale she would recount time after time in the drawing rooms of her friends in the years to come and Marie no longer looked out of the window avoiding Napier's eye. It was Napier who now looked away in embarrassment.

Eventually they reached their destination. The approach along the rough dirt road gave way to dwelling places and cobbles. The city was quite different in layout to London, and was more like an overgrown village. Large houses, occupied by merchants, were surrounded by narrow streets and alleys. It was one of these streets that gave Napier his opportunity. The driver reined in the horses and pulled to one side to allow a large, barrel-laden dray to rumble out of the side street he wished to enter. Napier seized his chance.

"This is the very street I have been told to look for," he said, and with that he jumped to his feet, opened the door and leapt out on to the cobbles. Swiftly he climbed the rear step, grabbed his bag from the luggage rack, a quick goodbye and thank you to the driver and he was away down a narrow alley before any of his travelling companions were aware of what was happening.

"Well!" said Madame Duvaux. "How very rude and ungrateful after all the friendly companionship we have given him."

"A truly modest and humble hero, madame," said Monsieur Coural, and they all nodded in agreement.

The streets of Paris were much the same as London: narrow, filthy and crowded. His shoes and stockings were soon coated in mud, so at the first opportunity he found himself a sedan chair and asked to be taken to the fencing academy near to the Pont Neuf where he knew the establishment was situated. In the comfort of the chair he was able to look about him. Above the heads of the crowds, oil lamps hung in every street. Without doubt Paris at night would be far better lit than the indifferent lighting of London. Also quite surprisingly there were very few beggars in the streets. He was later to find that the city had far fewer pickpockets and footpads than its English equivalent, a fact owed to the presence of a well-established military style police force and system of justice.

The sedan men knew their city well and before long he stood in front of his destination. He had waited a long time for this moment. Often he had sat and listened as Jacques talked of the school and described it in detail. In his minds eye he knew it intimately and had longed for the day when he would see it for himself, but not like this. He had always thought it would be with Jacques by his side and not as the circumstances were now, with Jacques dead and gone and himself as sole owner. Images of his past began to flood through his mind. He felt the dreadful sadness for the loss of a father and a fierce anger at the aristocratic family whose cruelty and arrogance had brought these events into being. What is done is done and cannot be undone. This school, however, would become Jacques' memorial. He would work night and day to make it the finest academy of fencing in the whole of Europe. With these thoughts he climbed the steps and entered the building.

It was then that he saw the name above the door, in large letters prominently displayed it read: 'The Françoise Faubert Academy of Fencing'. Strange, he knew Faubert to be his father's friend, he also knew him to be the lawyer who had dealt with all his father's business interests but he was not aware they had entered into any partnership together. This would require careful investigation without delay. Napier had never before entered a fencing school, although all his formative years had revolved around the use and study of the sword it had always been on a one-to-one basis. Now as he entered the hall he felt a thrill of excitement at the sights and sounds before him.

A group lesson was in progress. Two groups of men faced each other down the length of the hall. The practice movements they made were carried out with grace and precision, so together were they that their feet and the clash of blade on blade appeared as one sound echoing in the rafters of the hall. Two masters moved among them, their eagle eyes picking out faults and correcting them as they occurred. One did not require a detailed knowledge of the art to know that this was a very advanced class. Napier passed through the hall unchallenged and walked under an open archway to find him self in another hall, where pairs of fencers were practising their free play. Standing to one side two men stood waiting to find a place to practice; Napier approached and engaged them in conversation. He enquired of the quality of the school and remarked, that he had heard it was owned by a renowned master, one by the name of, Jacques Gerard. They replied this had been the case but he had died in England recently and the school had been sold to a new owner by the name of Faubert; a lawyer who was never seen at the school and hired masters to run it for him.

His worst fears confirmed. Napier enquired if they knew

the address of this Faubert, saying he had business with him. One of the men said he thought he had a house and an office in the Faubourgs, a district where rich merchants and nobles were building new houses. Napier left the school and walked awhile through the crowded narrow streets, lost in his own thoughts. He was angry at the apparent theft of his legacy. This man had without doubt heard of the death of Jacques and the events following it, seen his opportunity and signed the school over to himself, thinking that he Napier would be caught and no one would be left to challenge his ownership.

Now he knew what must be done. He would confront this so-called friend of his father's and demand the return of his rightful legacy. Looking about him he could see the twin towers of the cathedral called Notre Dame looming high above the houses with its position dominating the city. It would be a useful landmark. He was aware this building stood on an islet in the River Seine. Once on its banks he could find his way. The men at the school had told him the Faubourgs is a district on the outskirts of the city, situated alongside the river. He did not expect to have any difficulty in finding a boatman able to take him to that area. Once there he would eventually find the house he wanted. Shouldering his way through the crowds thronging the narrow streets using his twin tower landmark he eventually reached the river and realised he would have no difficulty in finding a ferry. They were plentiful, all willing and eager to take fare-paying passengers to any part of the waterway. The river without doubt was the life-blood of the city and a good percentage of the population earned their living there. The mere mention of the name Françoise Faubert was sufficient to prompt an affirmative reply. Apparently he was one of the best-known lawyers in the city; many of the watermen who plied their trade on the river had rowed clients to and from his house many times. The boatman who ferried Napier was able to take him right to the spot where the lawyer's house stood with its gardens running down to the banks of the river.

With a skill born of long practice the man brought his craft alongside the landing stage with scarcely a bump, shipped his oars and held it steady for Napier to climb out onto the riverbank where he found himself standing in a large garden surrounded by groves of freshly planted oleanders. Having paid off his transport he watched the man pulling away into the centre of the river then set off for the house – he had come here to confront a man and not to admire horticulture – but as he walked he could not help but notice the pleasant well-tended garden with flowerbeds and grassed areas sweeping down to the river. Here and there gardeners would stop their labours and cease tending the plants for a second in order to touch their caps in greeting as the visitor walked past. Now his feet crunched noisily on a gravel drive, which gave access to the imposing house still some distance away. No doubt carriages would use this drive when the residents wished to travel by boat. Beyond any question of doubt this was the house of a rich and influential man; the trappings of wealth were everywhere. There were numerous gardeners, fountains and statues; the house itself – a pale honey colour – stood gleaming in the sunlight. It was large and spacious, its many windows looking out onto manicured grounds, and the whole picture gave visual evidence of the success and importance of its owner.

It was not an old house; it gave the appearance of recent construction and modern design. Certainly the trees and shrubs in the garden had not yet reached maturity. At a guess it was not more than five or six years since it was built. Napier would have found the walk quite pleasant if it had not been for the anger he felt and his impatience to confront this man and demand an explanation for the apparent theft of his legacy. Now the crunching sound of his feet on the gravel started to irritate him. Loose and thickly spread, it tended to hinder his progress somewhat, adding to his mounting frustrations. He had expected the drive to give access to the rear of the house but it did not, rather it veered to the right and passed through a grove of broad-leafed trees, the remains of a forest cleared to build the residence. The contrast between open garden and woodland was intentional, for once the traveller was clear of the trees the full imposing splendour of the front of the house was revealed. No expense had been spared in its construction; the garden at the front was as well tended as the rear, with a drive coming up to the house turning and running parallel to the wide stone staircase before the main entrance, it then returned in the shape of a 'U.' Carriages approaching the house did not have to meet those going away.

Napier ran up the steps three at a time then paused to read the highly polished brass plate set on the wall. It proclaimed the owner as Françoise Faubert and stated his profession as a lawyer. In a room on the upper floor of the house with a window giving an unrestricted view of the grounds and the river, stood a large brass telescope on a polished wood tripod. Peering through the telescope, a short, thin, wiry-looking man had watched Napier's every move; this was Françoise Faubert. He was a man of complex character and conflicting attitudes. He possessed no personal vanity. His clothes were cheap and simple. In his dress and demeanour he could easily have been mistaken for a servant. Refusing to wear the peacock fashions of the day, he had no time for the brightly coloured cloths and silks favoured by other gentlemen of his class and scorned the fad of wearing powdered wigs favoured by rich and poor alike of that age, preferring to tie his thick grey-black hair in a tail at the back of his neck. Conversely his possessions were different. What he had, he flaunted. He could be both greedy and generous, the whole consuming aim of his life was to obtain more wealth and yet wealth itself had no meaning for him, only the means of acquiring it. This was a man who worshiped at the shrine of power and control. This was a man who despite having more money than he could ever spend, could not give up the pursuit of success that dominated his life. His character and the state of mind that drove him had been forged on the anvil of adversity. The secrets of his past life he kept a closed book, none of his contemporaries were aware of his humble beginnings.

Born in the slums of Versailles, where to obtain an education seemed impossible and to become a lawyer was then simply unthinkable, he had achieved both. Armed only with a natural intelligence and a ruthless nature, a complete workaholic, he had taught himself at first. Then, by the simple expedient of studying by day and stealing by night, he managed to attain the impossible and metamorphosed from slum boy to lawyer. Equipped with a business acumen bordering on genius, and a small capital accrued from his larcenous activities, he set about building the foundations of his wealth. Once he became affluent, he moved to Paris where he was unknown and very quickly became established among the wealthy merchants. Gradually his interests grew until there was very little that went on in the financial world of the city where he was not involved in one way or the other. Because of his ruthless nature and the need for accurate inside information, his network of spies was extremely extensive. Many of his enterprises verged on the illegal. Neither was he adverse to a little blackmail to further his own ends, secretly he was very influential in the cities underground crime activities. Nothing of any consequence escaped his controlling shadow. By trade he was a lawyer; by inclination he was a financier. In some activities he had no interest. The theatre, gambling or society balls had no appeal for him. When he needed to relax he would disappear into his workshop where he could indulge his interest in gadgets and mechanical inventions, making them to his own designs. His pride and joy were the tunnels he had built beneath the house to channel water from the Seine through wheels to provide power for machinery within the household.

This was the man Napier was about to meet, a man with a vast circle of acquaintances but very few friends. Strangely for such a ruthless man when he did make a friend he was very loyal to them. Jacques had been such a friend and had trusted him implicitly. Faubert watched Napier's progress through the garden until he disappeared through the trees, then, with a knowing smile on his face, he moved to his desk and sat down. He had been expecting this visitor. Not for nothing did he have a network of spies throughout the whole of France. He picked up and rang a small silver hand bell. Within seconds a liveried footman appeared at the door.

Napier snorted in disgust when he read the brass nameplate. This man who owned so much would cheat a friend over a legacy, which to a man of his wealth must appear to be nothing but small change. He was about to kick the door rather than knock when it opened as he approached it, a liveried footman stood to one side and addressed him as Monsieur Gerard and invited him to enter, with a slight bow and gesture of the hand he informed the surprised guest that his master was expecting him. The total lack of surprise at his arrival and the spontaneous use of his name took Napier unawares and for the moment took the wind out of his sails, so much so that he followed the servant meekly without a word.

Walking slowly with his head held high, as though he were guiding an emperor the footman led the way up staircases and along corridors, all decorated in the same tasteful and wealth depicting manner designed to flaunt the social standing of the owner. Eventually they came to a door where the footman stopped, squared his shoulders, pulled himself up to his full height and knocked discreetly. He then waited for several seconds before entering and announcing the visitor in a loud, booming voice: "Monsieur Napier Gerard, sir."

He then backed out of the room, closing the door quietly behind him. Napier found himself facing the slight unimposing figure seated at the desk. Faubert did not rise to greet his visitor but remained in his seat. However his greeting was cordial enough. He addressed Napier in the manner you would an old friend;

"Napier, my boy, good to see you after all this time. It is good to put a face to someone whom I have heard so much about. How was your journey? Please, sit down, my boy!"

Napier by now had begun to recover his wits. He had expected to have to give an explanation of who he was and his presence there, but here was this man in full possession of all the information he had intended to surprise him with. Now looking at this lawyer sitting there so calm and controlled, even having the temerity to greet him like an old friend, the anger began to rise up again burning like a white hot flame, with eyes blazing he accused him of betraying Jacques and stealing his legacy, finally demanding to know how he came by the knowledge of who he was and how he came to be there.

Faubert sat leaning back in his chair, hands in front of him palms together with fingertips touching. He was a man who never lost his temper and who was always calm, always in control. No event or situation ever drove him to panic. Thus he remained quietly listening to this tirade waiting for the accusations to finish. Eventually Napier began to run out of steam. He had said all he wanted to say and the lack of response from the recipient of his anger gave him no fuel for further argument and just added to his frustrations. Events were not going as he had expected and he had the uneasy feeling he was not on the winning side. As he lapsed into momentary silence the man at the desk leaned forward, placing his arms in front of him, his right hand resting on a carved wooden protrusion like a rounded semi-circle set into the highly polished top.

"You will find, when you get to know me better," he said, "there is very little that goes on in France – or anywhere else, for that matter – that I do not know about. I know how Jacques died, I know of the events that led to your leaving England. Incidentally you must tell me your version sometime; I'm sure it will be more accurate than the official version. I knew you were on your way to Dieppe. Do you really believe the customs men would have allowed you to set foot ashore if I had not bribed them to do so? You blundered your way across France and I was informed of every step – your adventure with the highwayman was heroic but did nothing for your anonymity. Predictably you arrived at the school and your enquiries were reported to me directly. I merely had to wait for you to present yourself. So you see, Napier, I control your fencing school, I control your legacy and I control you!"

This was too much for Napier, he started to move forward, his frustrations and anger completely overwhelming him.

"How would your spy network help you if I wring your scrawny neck!" he snarled.

Faubert showed no emotion or fear, he merely moved his hand over the protrusion which was actually a wheel hidden in the desktop. A section of polished wood rotated downwards at one hundred and eighty degrees and Napier found himself looking into the muzzle of a small but deadly blunderbuss – but this was no ordinary blunderbuss. Its stock had been removed and replaced with a handle similar to that of a cast iron kettle or a flat iron. The weapon was mounted on a swivel stand, a copy of those on the fore deck of a ship, thus giving it a range of fire covering the whole room. The user merely had to hold the handle in his right hand and cock the flintlock with his left. Anyone standing in front of the desk would stand no chance whatsoever; such a weapon at short range would be devastating.

Faubert was never a man to take chances. He kept the gun trained on his target and his finger on the trigger as he spoke.

"My dear Napier," he said, "do you really think that I would rely on my spy network alone to protect me? Now sit down and I will explain it all to you!"

The angry youth glared and grumbled a little, but in the end he accepted the fact he had no choice but to collect a chair from the far corner of the room and sit down in front of the lawyer, who had by now released the hammer on the flintlock and rotated it back into it's hiding place, ready for instant use should it be required again.

"I am rather proud of my little toy. I made it myself to my own design, you know, and incidentally you are one of the few people who have seen it and survived," he said in a matter of fact tone of voice. The very basic manner in which he made the statement made Napier's blood run cold; he was beginning to realise that Françoise Faubert was not a man to be crossed lightly.

He decided he had best listen to what the man had to say; after all he had little alternative and nothing to lose. The lawyer was looking at him with a slight smile on his face and eyes that seemed to penetrate his very soul, almost as though he could read his every thought. When he began to speak his eyes never wavered but continued to look directly at him reading his body language and analysing his reaction to every word.

"First of all, I must tell you, your father – and I know for a fact that is how you think of him – was my friend and despite what you may think of me I did everything in my power to protect his investments. But as I told him at the time, the investments he made were unwise and risky; also he had many gambling debts to be paid off. A fencing school is not a particularly lucrative investment and depends heavily on the reputation of its master. Jacques had a reputation equal to any in France but he was not there when the school needed him. As a result the business deteriorated, I had to sell his house to keep it going. I will admit that a flourishing fencing school has a clientele of influential important people, or they who are connected to them and as such is a rich source of information if you know how to harvest it. That is why I personally support it financially."

He leaned forward in his seat, like a parent who advises a naughty child.

"Now look here, Napier, just think sensibly about this. Suppose I were to pass the school over to you and you ran it with your name over the door, just how long do you think you would last when the Duke of Mulgrove got to hear about it? Is he the man to turn a blind eye and let you get on with it? Of course not! He would have your hide within hours of his hearing the news and well you know it!"

He paused for a moment to let this statement sink in. Napier sat there and did not reply. He had to admit he had not taken this possibility into account and could see there was no denying the stark truth in what he said.

"I have given this problem a lot of thought," Faubert continued, having satisfied him self that Napier understood the point he had made. "I have come up with a plan of action which should solve the dilemma. You shall come to live here and will take on the role of my wife's nephew. We will use your old cover story regarding an English education. It seems to have worked well on your journey here and gives a satisfactory explanation of your slight English accent. The name you used, Napier Feray, is as good as any other so we will use that also. What is left of your father's money I have invested in my name and will be used to give you an allowance. Add to this a personal allowance I will give you out of my own pocket and you will be more than well provided for."

Napier felt a weight had been lifted from his shoulders and was much cheered by this offer. He had come here thinking he had been cheated but now it seems plans had already been made. He was to live in a luxurious house, be given an income and sanctuary from his pursuers. He was about to thank Faubert and accept his offer when the lawyer held up his hand to silence him.

"You have not yet heard the terms and conditions of our agreement. I can see you find them acceptable, but there are strings attached. First of all you become the pupil of my wife, who will instruct you in the ways and manners of a French gentleman. She will show you how to dress, teach you how to speak, and instruct you how to behave correctly in polite society. You will remain confined to this house until she, and only she, decides you are sufficiently groomed to take your place in the community, as befits the nephew of a French gentlewoman. When your training is complete you will be introduced to the social elite of Paris as a member of my household. You will pay regular visits to the fencing school and become one of its masters where you will listen out for any information that might be of interest to me. Your main job – and this is where you will be the most useful to me, for Jacques has told me you are one of the best swordsman he has ever seen – will be to act as a duellist. There are times when it is necessary for me to dispose of people who get in my way. This can be done legally if you challenge them to a duel."

Napier was appalled. Could he be hearing right? His natural reaction was to reject this offer out of hand and he said so in no uncertain manner.

"I cannot do that! You are asking me to pick a quarrel with anyone who offends you and kill them in a duel, just because you want them disposed of. No, I will not do it! What sort of murderous scoundrel do you think I am?"

Faubert's eyes glinted coldly.

"Do not make your decision hastily. Think of the alternatives. Within the hour you could be on the streets of Paris with nothing. A word in the wrong ear and your enemies would have you at their mercy, whereas here I am offering you a haven, and a comfortable lifestyle in return for performing the occasional small service. Think about it. A young man with your ability with a sword will end up duelling anyway. What's the difference if it is you who instigates the argument? You and I – all of us in this world – have to fight to be on the top, without effort you get nothing. Where do you want to be, on the top or on the bottom? Make your decision now because I have the capabilities of arranging your future either way."

Fate was conspiring against him yet again. Napier was stunned by his impotence in controlling events. The choices before him were stark and inflexible. He had to admit he was seduced by the luxury of the house, and the thought of being a society gentleman with a private income was very attractive. Set against that, the thought of being once again a hunted felon with everyone's hand against him filled him with trepidation but to become a murderer, for that is what he would be, despite the fancy conventions and etiquette of duelling, it would only cloak the main purpose of disposing of someone who had become a nuisance. Yet did he have any alternative? If he were exposed on the streets of Paris without the protection of a powerful man like Faubert he would be dead within a week and what little he had seen of him was enough to tell him he was quite ruthless enough to carry out his implied threat. Also he had a healthy respect for the duke's ability to inflict his revenge, once he knew where to find him. He would not find it easy to escape a second time. Napier considered his options then reluctantly with many doubts and reservations and because he had no alternative, agreed to the terms he was offered.

Faubert stood up and smiled. "I knew you would be sensible. All the arrangements have been made, but first you must meet my wife. I think you will get on splendidly with her."

He walked to the door and held it open for Napier, then led him down the maze of corridors and stairways, all decorated expensively in gold leaf and filled with elaborate furniture topped with tasteful ornaments. Obviously someone was a great patron of the arts, painting of all types were everywhere, hanging on walls covered with imported papers. All this affluence could easily have deteriorated into a vulgar display of wealth but there was none of this about this house. Everywhere was a tribute to elegance, good taste and sophistication. Napier was impressed, he had seen nothing like it before – Mulgrove Manor had been grand and imposing but it was old. It's oak beams and stonework appeared dowdy compared to this place. Faubert now became the perfect host; giving a running commentary of his home as they passed along, Napier found his tongue and complimented him on his good taste and knowledge of furnishings. His reply was an openly honest statement; that none of it was his doing. All the interior decorating was the responsibility of his wife. She it was who supervised it all from start to finish.

"When you get to know her," he said, "you will find her to be the most amazing woman."

By now they were back in the main hall approaching one of the drawing rooms. Faubert referred to it as Victoire's room. Apparently she preferred it to any other. A footman standing in the hall moved to open the door for them but he was waved away. This was another quirk of his character. He had many servants to run his home but rarely used them for his personal needs, preferring to perform most tasks himself. As they entered the room, a small, petite, middle aged lady sat at a desk writing; she was neither plain nor pretty but had a natural uncontrived elegance about her, an elegance that was not just about the fashionable clothes and expensive jewellery she wore – this lady would have appeared elegant if she were wearing sackcloth. When the two men entered she put down her quill and tripped daintily across the room with a rustle of heavily embroidered satin bedecked with silk bows, lace and muslin. She took Napier by both hands and held him at arms length.

"Well, Napier, so at last we meet. I am so pleased to see you; I have heard so much about you. I am so dreadfully sorry about Jacques, a charming man. He will be sorely missed."

Napier struggled for words. He was again taken by surprise. No one in this house seemed to need any introduction. They appeared to know everything without the need for explanation.

He had not known what to expect prior to meeting the lawyer's wife. She had been described as an amazing woman, but to be honest he was not impressed. If this woman was to train him in the coming months then he was not looking forward to it. He had seen many of these social butterflies visiting Mulgrove Manor. They were frivolous, empty headed and totally illiterate, apart that is from an encyclopaedic knowledge of the social graces. This woman was no exception, she twittered away talking nonsense but saying nothing of worth.

Françoise Faubert stood to one side and allowed his wife to monopolise their guest. On his lips was the faintest hint of a smile, a knowing smile, almost a permanent part of his facial expression. It seemed to say that the world was his and there was nothing he did not know. It was said about him that he could read minds and indeed many of his acquaintances believed he could do so, a rumour he did nothing to dispel. In fact he actively encouraged it. The real truth was he read bodies not minds, and could read body language as other men read books, a skill he found most useful in business dealings and other more nefarious activities. Now Napier's body was telling him of the impression formed regarding his wife's social butterfly-type character; he smiled because he knew this was the face she turned to the world, the real Madame Victoire Louise Faubert was a different person altogether and Napier was about to find she was not all that she seemed.

Victoire was the only child of a man born to a noble family, but being the youngest brother he had no claim to a title, which suited him rather well. He had no liking for a courtly life. He was the cleverest of the brothers and much-preferred books to social activities. Well educated and with a small allowance from his family, he was able to indulge in a quest for knowledge he pursued all his life. Subsequently he became one of the most respected scientists and mathematicians of his age. His daughter he educated in the same manner as all young ladies of good breeding, as was the current fashion, but as she matured he began to realise she had an intelligence the equal, if not superior to his own. He could not, as an enlightened man, allow this intellect to go to waste, and knowing the deep prejudices existing against the education of women, he decided to take on the task himself. This he did with great commitment but in total secrecy, for many people would have thought him mad to teach science and mathematics to a woman; in a way it could prove to be a pretty pointless exercise, for when Victoire's education was complete, she was a scientist and mathematician second to none, but because of the prejudices and rigid thinking of the age she lived in, there was no outlet for her abilities. This produced many problems in her life because of the frustrations it caused. It was only when she met Françoise Faubert – a man of similar intellect who understood the problem – that she began to form an outlet for her mental skills.

They married and she moved to Paris where her husband had his home. By now she had already adopted the frivolous, naïve character she used so effectively to camouflage her real abilities. She began to develop a liking for public life and was the life and soul of Parisian society, particularly enjoying the gaming establishments of the city, where her gambling was legendary. She always won, a fact everyone attributed to luck, none being aware of the sharp analytical mathematical mind being used behind the veneer of frivolity. Strangely enough her winning did not make her unpopular with the owners of the gaming rooms or the people who lost their money to her. She was always aware of the dangers of greed and was always careful not to win too much at any one time. The combination of her lively character and her apparent luck made her a very popular personage who was always welcomed enthusiastically at all the gaming homes, where the owners knew the crowds would follow and try to emulate her. On a more serious side she was the accountant for all her husband's business activities and kept the books with an accuracy and efficiency that none could better, but more importantly for Faubert, she acted as his eyes and ears on the social scene, a world he was loath to enter. Loose talk was rampant in the gaming houses and drawing rooms of Paris. Many were the secrets mouthed in front of Madame Faubert that would never have been exposed if Monsieur Faubert were present. Behind the charade of society gentlewoman Victoire affected, none suspected the sharp analytical mind that missed nothing and saw everything. Thus this remarkable woman was able to use her intellect in a way that would have been normally denied her by society and was an essential equal part of her husband's business empire.

So began Napier's transformation. He had been presented to the servants as Madame's nephew, a fact they accepted without question. If any had doubts they would not voice them. The Fauberts were good employers who treated their servants well, but all knew they demanded absolute loyalty. Any deviation from this rule would be punished severely. Crossing that line was not worth the risk. Employers like the Fauberts came only once in a lifetime. Every single employee guarded their job jealously, a fact of which their master was well aware. Of Françoise Faubert, Napier saw little. He had given a task to his wife and saw little need to interfere, as he knew she would perform it well. Napier for his part had always considered himself to be equal in manners and refinement to any of the nobility, but he quickly found when it came to Parisian high society, he was a mere yokel, but he was quick and keen to learn. Well aware that his freedom to move between house and city depended on how quickly he acquired the polish of gentility.

The weeks and months passed quickly enough, Madame Faubert was an amiable and entertaining companion, who once she found Napier to be an adept pupil began to teach him the mathematical secrets of her success at the gaming tables. The two, despite their differences in age and background, became the closest of friends. Victoire, who never had children, secretly envied the friends who had and began to see Napier as a son. Napier, who never had a mother, found she filled the role very easily. He came to admire her immensely and lived in awe of her towering intellect. He could see now why her husband had described her the way he had, for he too began to see her as a very remarkable woman.

Naturally after being confined for so long to the house and grounds Napier began to get bored with his self-imposed incarceration. It was a wonderful place to live and the garden was beautiful, but he often found himself wandering down to the river and gazing longingly at the city, impatient for the day when he could shake off the restrictions that bound him and walk freely through its streets.

Eventually the day came when Victoire looked him over and compared the fashionably dressed young man with his courtly manners, up to date witticisms and small talk, to the shabbily dressed somewhat unkempt figure with his rough country manners who had first appeared on her doorstep and pronounced him ready. It was not that Napier had changed, physically, his features and body shape were the same, but such was the change in his grooming, confidence and general aura, his overall appearance seemed different. Without question a person who had known him well previously would pass him by, unrecognisable as someone they had known.

Françoise, although he had appeared indifferent to his wife's efforts to create a new nephew, nevertheless had taken a keen interest in the transformation and had watched from afar all that was going on. He was pleased with the results of the exercise, after discussion with his wife it was decided the time had come for Napier's introduction to society. Having considered their options, they opted for riding out with the hunt as being the best form of introduction. Victoire hunted on a regular basis, riding side-saddle, as she was an accomplished horsewoman.

Françoise on the other hand rarely rode. He took no pleasure from the pastime, mainly because he was not a particularly good rider. However he did go along occasionally when he thought there would be good contacts to be made. Napier for his part had misgivings. For one thing he had not had any formal riding instructions, therefore he was by no means an expert horseman. He realised of course that this was one of the main reasons for choosing the hunt. It would not be wise to make too big an impact on his first appearance. Another more personal reason for his uneasiness was that he remembered only too clearly the time when he was the quarry for such a chase. It was not a pleasant thought. However, it was freedom and a chance to get out into the wide world at last.

Consequently it was with mixed feelings that he arrived at the meeting place on the edge of the forest where they joined the group of flamboyantly dressed riders and formal introductions were made. Most of the men gave cursory greeting then got on with the business of controlling mettlesome mounts, stamping with impatience to commence the gallop. The women took more interest, depending on their ages and temperament. Some flirted outrageously while others looked at Napier sideways through the corners of their eyes, weighing the possibilities of future conquest. This sort of attention embarrassed him. He felt uncomfortable in the presence of these people, who seemed to be intent on no other purpose than the pursuit of pleasure. Napier was glad when the hunt began. The newcomer in their midst forgotten, the riders streamed off through the trees in pursuit of the first quarry of the day. Galloping through a forest is a difficult pursuit for an inexperienced rider and he very quickly found himself well in the rear, but nevertheless he was enjoying his taste of freedom after being confined to the house for so long. He began to understand as he became more familiar with his mount, the pleasure to be derived from riding a good horse. Now he could feel the power of the animal under him, the wind in his face and the thudding hooves over the leaf-strewn ground, passing through the good air, breathing in the fresh earthy smell of the forest. He did not care that he lagged behind the hunt and had not seen so much as an antler, let alone a stag. After a while he reined in his horse and allowed it to trot slowly, eventually he came to a quiet leafy glade with sunlight filtering through the trees. Here he dismounted and sat on a bed of moss with his back against a tree enjoying the tranquillity of the bird song, the sweet notes filling the air around him as he savoured the sights and odours of the forest.

Time had no meaning as he sat enjoying the peaceful scene while his horse more mindful of baser needs stood nibbling the grass nearby. He looked up at a sudden rustling in the bushes to see a magnificent stag stepping into the glade; it stood and looked at Napier, who did not move but sat perfectly still. The stag remained immobile, wondering whether there was danger here; deciding there was not it strutted across the clearing and disappeared among the trees. Perhaps a little disloyally, he hoped this was the animal the hunt was pursuing, which had avoided them in some way and sent them off on a false scent. He had to admit, he had more empathy for the animal than the people who hoped to kill it.

He tarried a little longer, enjoying his freedom and solitude of the green wood then reluctantly rejoined the hunt to find that the Fauberts were well pleased with the low impact his first appearance in society had made. Victoire, now fully confident in his ability to merge, began to obtain him invites to house parties and introduced him to the gaming rooms and all the fashionable places Paris had to offer. Soon he became a familiar figure about the city joining in the endless pursuit of pleasure, apparently the sole aim of the members of the social elite.

8

The Duellist with Much to Learn

Napier never rode with the hunt again but that did not mean he stayed out of the saddle, far from it, riding became a passion he pursued at every opportunity, spending hours exploring the forests and countryside surrounding the city. He soon tired of the endless parties and social events that were the frivolous lifestyle of the social elite and, like Françoise, began to attend them only when he thought it necessary. The gaming houses were different; he enjoyed the challenge they represented. During his visits he would often escort Victoire, who continued to teach and guide him in the art of scientific gambling. She would council him to never play the games of chance where luck is the only requirement; 'games such as those that are played with dice are only for fools', she would say. Napier took heed of this advice and played only the card games where memory and mathematics, when applied properly, gave you an advantage. This ploy paid off handsomely not only financially but also with the satisfaction of being a winner by his own efforts. He enjoyed the gaming tables immensely when he became an expert and rarely lost. He would have loved to become as good as Victoire Faubert but he knew he would never achieve that status, Madame was a genius at what she did, and none could compare. Napier often watched her play a hand and heard that tinkling laugh as she proclaimed yet again how lucky she was. He would smile to himself because he alone in the room knew her secret and yet he could not help but wonder why no one she played with ever suspected her winning ways came from her intellectual abilities – luck had nothing to do with it. It was a tribute to her skill as an actress, the part she played, the role of the frivolous empty-headed woman whom luck never seemed to desert, people even placed bets on when her luck would run out, lose their money and still did not suspect, the true reason luck did not dessert her was that she did not rely on it in the first place.

The months went by and life was good for Napier Gerard – or Feray, as he was now known. The generous allowance he received from Faubert, supplemented by his regular gambling had made him a moderately wealthy man. He no longer lived at the Faubert house, having gathered together enough capital to purchase Jacques' old house next to the fencing school and set up residence there. It was small but perfectly adequate for his needs, and it had the advantage of being conveniently close to the school where he spent most of his days.

His arrival at the school made an instant impression. No one, not even the masters, could match his skill with a sword. He became an icon greatly admired by the pupils and much respected by the masters, who found it hard to believe the story he told of acquiring his skill as an essential part of an English school education. Most suspected he was not telling the truth, knowing only the touch of a great master could have given him such abilities. However he was Faubert's nephew, and as such if he wanted to keep his secret they would not argue. After all he was an excellent addition to the school and a much sought after master who drew in many pupils and as they all knew; it was not at all wise to cross or question Françoise Faubert.

As time went by the plan to integrate Napier into city life began to work perfectly. He became very much a Parisian accepted everywhere as Madame's nephew. No one suspected the fashionable socialite was a wanted felon and did not make the connection with the man who still had a price on his head. He had settled into an established routine and had begun to gather a circle of friends. Altogether he was very content with his comfortable lifestyle, a lifestyle comprising of daily visits to the school, maintaining and developing his skills as a swordsman; the evenings he spent socialising and gambling. In fact, so successful was he at the tables he hardly needed his monthly visits to Faubert's city office to collect his allowance. It was during one of these visits that the finger of Fate once again intervened in the life of Napier Gerard.

He had pocketed his allowance and engaged in the customary exchange of banter with the clerk whom he had got to know well and had established a friendly relationship since becoming a resident of the city. Still smiling as he left the offices and contemplating the possibilities of going for an afternoon ride he looked straight into the deepest warmest, most beautiful pair of brown eyes he had ever seen in his whole life. They belonged to a young lady – slim, elegant and attractive – her dark hair hanging in soft waves over her shoulders was topped by a small triangular hat which like the rest of her clothing was dark and rather severe for one so young. To wear such clothing even though it was well cut and of expensive material would have made most girls her age appear dowdy, but not so this girl. The overall effect was a sophisticated elegance that few could aspire to.

Napier was quite taken aback, he managed to lift his hat and stand to one side, but in his confusion he quite forgot to bow. The two ladies – for there were two, even though Napier only had eyes for one – sank brief curtsies as they passed and, pushing open the door, disappeared into the building. He was entranced. Who was this girl? She was not part of the social scene, he would surely have noticed. Cursing his confusion, he must have looked like a country yokel. Surely she must have thought him to be a halfwit. No matter, he was determined to find out who she was. To that end he waited across the street for their eventual exit. When they were gone he would be able to question his friend, the clerk who surely could give him some answers.

An hour went by before they reappeared, Napier slid behind a convenient carriage where they would not see him. Unfortunately the fickleness of Fate deemed this to be the carriage waiting for the two ladies; they had to walk around to enter. Once again he looked into those brown eyes and suffered the same state of tongue-tied confusion that had so embarrassed him previously, made more acute by the giggling of the two women as they climbed into the coach. He was so angry with himself. He had never claimed to be or thought of himself as a ladies' man; life at Mulgrove Manor had never presented the opportunity to be one. Since his arrival in France he had socialised with girls of his own age, and had flirted with consummate ease. The ladies liked him and he enjoyed their company. Embarrassment was not a problem that occurred; for some reason this girl was different. At first sight the impact she made had hit him like a thunderbolt. Never before in his life had he taken too much notice of how people perceived him as an individual. Now suddenly it became important, imperative even that he should make a good impression on her and here he was acting like a village idiot. He must get a hold on himself.

First things first, he must see his friend the clerk, find out who she is, where she lives, what places she frequents, where he can make contact with her. With Napier, to think was to do so. With determined step, looking at the office he was about to enter, he crossed the street straight into the path of the moving carriage. The driver hauled back on the reins. The horses reared up, snorting and whinnying in shock. Napier flung himself headlong out of the way, rolling in the mud and filth covering the roadway; steel-shod hooves crashed down on the cobbles, missing him by a hair's breadth. The colourful oaths of the driver cursing him for an idiotic clod mingled with the laughter of the crowd, but the amused look on the face of the girl looking through the carriage window as it passed him did nothing for his bruised ego. He stood there covered in mud and filth watching the vehicle disappear among the buildings, knowing the impression he had made could not have been a favourable one.

Continuing with his original plan, Napier entered the office and found his friend struggling to keep a straight face. He had witnessed all that had gone on through his window and had no need to question Napier's mud covered appearance. Being a young man who appreciated a pretty face and a well turned ankle, just the same as Napier did, he also had been notably impressed by the girl. Therefore there was no difficulty experienced in identifying the object of his enquiries. It seemed the girl and her companion had been ushered into the inner sanctum, a place where people who worked in the outer office were not privy to its workings, however as a personal favour and despite dire warnings and much protestation regarding it being more than his job was worth and the confidentiality of clients, he made enquiries and came back with the information. She was a visitor from Versailles, currently in Paris with her father who was here on business. He did not know where they were staying or for how long they would be here but he had managed to find out her name. She was Mademoiselle Alexandrine d'Amblimont, a name Napier burnt into his memory. He gave the clerk a few Louies, along with a promise that wild horses would not drag out from him the source of the information he had received. Leaving the office, he was obsessed with a burning desire to find this girl who had become a focal point of his thoughts.

It had been quite a while since he had last visited the Faubert house. Now would be a good time to do so. Victoire with her society contacts knew everyone on the social scene and was the obvious person to help him. No one of any social standing could arrive in the city without Madame being aware of it. All thoughts of an afternoon's riding now forgotten, he made his way home to change quickly into clean clothes. Afternoon tea with Victoire was an occasion of formality and etiquette. It would not do to go there smelling of horse dung and covered in street mud. Within the hour he was heading for the river, to be rowed there by the ferrymen was by far the quickest way to reach the house.

Wishing the ever-present gardeners a cheery 'good afternoon,' he walked through the trees and approached the familiar front door; where he was met by a footman who led him to the favoured drawing room. There a smiling Victoire greeted him enthusiastically. She sent for tea and coffee then sat him down by the fire.

"Now, Napier," she said, "you must tell me all that you have been up to. We will chat and you must tell me everything that is happening in your life."

Napier lost no time in telling her about the girl and how desperate he was to meet her, following this with a request for her help in affecting an introduction. To his surprise, however, Victoire showed little enthusiasm. He had expected they would have put their heads together and started plotting; instead she continually tried to change the subject. This was unusual, Victoire Faubert, an incorrigible matchmaker, had many times attempted to push him on to girls of marriageable age, but only they whom she judged to be a suitable partner.

Usually he enjoyed his visits to the house, but now, walking back through the gardens on his way to the river and the waiting ferryman, he was puzzled. Victoire had not actually refused to help but her response was muted to say the least. It was fairly obvious she did not approve of the girl for some reason. Perhaps, matchmaker that she was, she had some other eligible lady in mind and saw the girl as an upset to her plans. But in truth that was not Victoire – she was nothing if not flexible. No matter, whatever the reason it was fairly obvious there would be no help forthcoming from that quarter. Therefore he resolved to engineer a meeting by his own efforts.

Parisian social life was of such far-reaching intensity that very few people of any standing who visited the city could avoid being drawn into it. All Napier had to do was to increase his social activities and eventually his path and that of the girl would cross. There was no doubt this was a sound plan, for within a few days Napier walked into a tea party at the Price de Conte's salon and there she was playing the clavichord for an appreciative crowd of socialites. Now she had been found he must take a firm hold on himself, none of the tongue-tied bumpkin rolling in the mud. Such an image must be dispelled and in its place the confident sophisticate must emerge. A bold frontal attack would be the best way of approaching her. In possession of a natural talent and expertly taught she played, extremely well, a popular piece by a young composer by the name of Mozart. Napier began to weave his way through the audience; he needed to be as close to the instrument as possible. Once in position he would be the first to congratulate her and by approaching would cut off anyone else attempting to engage her in conversation. Before the last notes had died away and while the crowd were still applauding he was standing by the clavichord and addressing her.

"You play very well, mademoiselle. Do you remember me? We have met before, I think."

Alexandrine turned those brown eyes on him and flashed the most beautiful smile, "I remember you very well, sir. You are the young man who frightens horses."

At that they both laughed, twin sounds that joined together – Napier's deep and masculine, hers soft and yet tinkling with a pure bell-like quality, sounds that shut out the chattering voices surrounding them. Just for a moment in that crowded room they were alone and isolated from the rest of humanity.

With the ice well and truly broken they found an instant mutual attraction and spent the rest of the evening in each other's company and, even though they mingled with the other guests, when engaged in conversation they would talk as a couple, reacting as though they had been together for years.

In the coming weeks the relationship developed. There being rarely a day went by when they were not in each other's company. Soon they were the talk of the city, the ladies of society who dabbled in the pairing of suitable couples and saw themselves as marriage brokers whispered behind their fans and predicted an eventual wedding. Only the Fauberts, of all Napier's circle of friends and acquaintances, seemed to be against the match. They did not attempt to prevent their meeting. Neither did they make any effort to encourage them; quite the opposite in fact. Victoire, on several occasions had hinted most strongly to Napier he would eventually have reason to regret the relationship and could do much better for himself. Napier resented what he saw as this unreasonably unfounded opposition. He loved this girl. She was his soul mate. There never was and never could be anyone else for him and as far as he could tell she felt the same way. He wished the Fauberts could have been more co-operative and understanding in their attitude. He was puzzled and hurt by it. Surely they could see that a union with Alexandrine was the key to his future happiness. No matter with or without their blessing he was determined to go on with the relationship regardless. He had the approval of everyone else he knew and was determined to seek the same from her father the instant he returned.

Despite the fact they had spent so much time together in the ensuing weeks he knew little of her background and as yet had not made the acquaintance of her father, who had returned to Versailles on business. He was expected to arrive back in Paris within a few days. The other woman, the one who had witnessed Napier's humiliation on the day they had first met, was her friend and companion who had been with her from an early age and was always by her side. She was a nice person who Napier liked and got on well with, in fact they also had become good friends. She had been employed as a companion to look after Alexandrine after her mother died, her charge had been very young at the time and barely remembered her mother, as a result her companion, although a paid servant, had taken her place and become very much a surrogate parent. The two women were inseparable apart from her father; she was her only family.

Those few weeks were the happiest of Napier's life. He had his health and although not a rich man, in comparison to the merchants and nobility of Paris, he also had his wealth. He had respect a position in society and best of all he had a woman whom he loved and who loved him. The only cloud on his horizon was Jacques Gerard. He missed his adopted father. How wonderful it would have been if Jacques were here to share his happiness and how happy he would have been to become the father-in-law of a girl like Alexandrine. Napier understood only too well the bond between the girl and her companion, after all had he not shared the same bond with his surrogate father.

Unknown to Napier there was a cloud forming on his horizon. He had forgotten his pact with Françoise Faubert. Time had passed and there had been no calls upon his services. He had drawn his allowance, developed his lifestyle, become part of the network of society that was the heart of Paris. Apart from the odd item of information gleaned from the school, which he passed on to Faubert, the lawyer had made no demand on their agreement. It was not Faubert's way to call in a debt just because it was owed to him. He much preferred to let it stand, sometimes for years, until the time came when he could use the payment to optimal effect. It suited his purpose to have many people who owed him either financial or emotional allegiance all locked away in his memory waiting for the time when their dependence could be exploited. Napier was different. He was kept waiting in the wings for a specific purpose. The reasons why he had not been called upon to perform his specialised services were twofold: one, disposing of people who opposed you under the guise of a legitimate duel had to be used sparingly, otherwise it became an obvious manoeuvre with dire consequences if exposed and, two, no problem had arisen important enough to be dealt with by this method.

Faubert was accustomed to sailing very close to the wind on many of his financial deals but his latest venture was beginning to worry him. He had invested a considerable amount of his available resources on a risky edge of the knife enterprise. If successful, the profits would be enormous and he was within a hair's breath of pulling it off. Without warning there had appeared a fly in the ointment. An entrepreneur of equal wealth and power had seen the potential and was exerting pressure to push him out. If this happened he would have to take considerable losses and even face the possibility of bankruptcy. Therefore he must be disposed of quickly before he could inflict serious financial damage. Fortunately for the lawyer, this man had made enemies of people at the highest level of government who were also anxious for his demise; Faubert had been called to a secret meeting with powerful men and was now under orders to destroy him by whatever method he chose. This of course meant that, within reason, he had a level of protection from government sources. Therefore because it was not possible to stop him legally using legitimate business methods, Napier with his specialist skills was the weapon he intended to use.

Napier received the note delivered by Faubert's most trusted servant, requesting him to meet the lawyer at a house party in the Rue de Richelieu the following evening. He knew when he read the note this might be the moment when he would have to earn his keep. It was rare for Faubert to make an appearance at a party and even rarer to invite Napier to join him. He never went anywhere for social reasons alone. If he required him as a companion it could mean only one thing – he had a job for him. Therefore, with feelings of unease, he entered the room and surveyed the scene of noisy gaiety, looking over the groups of laughing people and focussing on the sombre figure of Françoise Faubert. He was leaning on the far wall, an untouched glass of wine in his hand. He saw Napier instantly and greeted him cordially as he approached: "Napier, my boy. Glad to see you." Then his voice changed to a whisper and took on the note of a conspirator, "Look, I am not going to waste time chatting – I have a job for you. There is a man I want disposing of. I want you to involve him in a quarrel; in the ensuing duel he must die! This is important, do not just injure him. It is essential you make absolutely sure he is dead."

"To identify him I will cross the room and engage him in conversation. When I shake him by the hand that will be your man. I will then leave and go home, the rest will be up to you. Do not fail. It is important to all of us!"

Napier watched the lawyer crossing the room casually nodding to acquaintances as he did so. How he had dreaded this moment. True he had known it would come one day and to some extent he was prepared for it, but no amount of preparation could stop the cold shiver down his spine or the dryness of his throat. He wanted to run for the door, make a quick exit from this party that gave him no pleasure, but he knew he had no choice but to stay and stick it out to the bitter end.

Napier was not sure what type of person he had expected but the man who shook Faubert's hand, rather reluctantly it seemed, was certainly not the most imposing of figures. A much bigger man than the lawyer, taller and rather plump, a jovial rather rotund individual about fifty years of age, dressed rather flashily in a slightly old fashioned rather flamboyant style; he certainly did not appear to present any threat as an opponent in a duel. From Napier's point of view the man's appearance did not help matters. He was not a coward and whatever his fate might be, he would always face it with fortitude, but what he was expected to do went against all his instincts. He would have much preferred him to be young and fit and an expert with a sword – then at least he would have instigated a conflict with an opponent who stood a fair chance. Consequently if he dispatched him it would have been done with a certain degree of honour. To set a man up deliberately in order to kill him, knowing he had no chance, he despised himself for even thinking of it. He was not even certain he would be able to do it, and yet he had no choice. To refuse would result in his exposure and the return to a life of a hunted felon and eventually certain death. There was no option. Faubert had him snared like a rat in a trap. He had no choice but to comply.

With these thoughts in mind he began to move through the groups of chatting people, he could see his target clearly laughing and joking with his companions. He did not appear to be a man who deserved to die. Napier hesitated; surely he could make a run for it. He had money and a good horse, there were wild regions of France where he could hide – even move to other countries. Then into his mind flooded the image of Alexandrine. If he left now he would never see her again. She had become so inexorably linked with his future. The very thought was unbearable. The possibilities of such a loss hardened his attitude. He became calm, cold and controlled thinking only of the act he must do. To lose this girl now she was so much a part of his life was unthinkable. Now as he moved through the crowd he barely noticed or heard the people surrounding him, his whole sphere of vision focussed on his victim who totally unaware of his approach stood drinking and conversing amiably with his companions. Now he was close to his target and standing just behind him. Suddenly he moved sideways and knocked the man's drink all over him.

"You clumsy oaf!" Napier snarled, "Are you as ill-mannered

as you are clumsy? Apologise immediately!" The man looked startled for a moment; then regained his composure.

"Now just a minute, boy," he said. "You are the clumsy one. It was you who blundered into me."

Napier leaped onto this immediately. "Don't patronise me, you moron. I am no boy to be treated like a child."

The man responded instantly, "If you wish to be treated like an adult then behave like one. Go away and stop bothering me."

With this remark he turned his back and continued talking to his friends.

Napier grabbed him by his shoulder and spun him round. "You insult me, sir. I demand satisfaction!"

The man looked at him. This time there was a cold gleam in his eyes. His voice was calm and controlled, "Well, if that is your wish, my seconds will attend yours whenever they are available."

Napier retorted immediately. "My seconds, sir, are here. I have friends who will be delighted to assist me whenever yours are nominated."

His protagonist turned to his two companions. "Would you gentlemen be so kind as to act as my seconds?"

Having received an affirmative reply, he turned and, without so much as a glance at Napier, walked out of the room.

While all this was going on, the babble of speech had suddenly ceased. Total silence reigned in the room. No one there could have been unaware of the drams being out played before them. The closing of the door behind the gentleman leaving was the signal for the talking to begin again, this time with increased intensity. All mundane topics were forgotten; they now had far more exciting topics to amuse themselves with.

Napier, by now the centre of attention, had picked out some friends who he thought would be prepared to act as his seconds. They agreed readily enough, apart from one who, appearing more doubtful, remarked, "I hope you are as useful with a pistol as you are with a sword!"

The forthcoming duellist was puzzled and questioned the remark. His friend replied, "I know this man slightly; I spent a few months in Versailles recently where he is well known. He is considered to be an excellent marksman. To my certain knowledge he has taken part in duels twice in the past. On both occasions his opponents were shot dead. You were the one to make the challenge; therefore he has the right to the choice of weapons. A man such as he is unlikely to pick the sword as his weapon of choice."

Napier was stunned by this information. He did of course possess a full knowledge of the rules, etiquette, regulations and conditions of duelling. He knew as well as anyone, his friend was correct in what he said. He was however so steeped in the use of the sword that the possible choice of any other weapon had not entered his head. He had made a terrible mistake, one that could very well prove to be fatal. He had acted too quickly and without careful thought; he saw now only too plainly the course of action he ought to have taken. He should have antagonised the man to the point where he had no recourse but to issue a challenge. The right to the choice of weapons would then have been his; naturally his choice would have been the sword, where the odds would have been stacked considerably in his favour. It was too late now; the dice had been cast. He had put himself in the position of facing an experienced duellist who was a proven marksman, whereas he barely knew one end of a pistol from another. His chances of survival were remote to say the least. Only minutes before he had been worrying about the dishonourable act of killing a victim who had no chance. How dramatically the roles had been reversed.

The seconds wasted no time. They arranged for the duel to take place at dawn within twenty-four hours, a site being agreed outside the city, a commonly used clearing in the forest conveniently close to the main road. It was necessary to have somewhere discreet to avoid sightseers who would disrupt and cheapen the rituals governing a very serious business, but also because duelling, although not actually against the law, was frowned upon by officialdom. Indeed the king himself was known to disapprove of the practice and was thought by some to be considering laws that would make it illegal.

Sleep did not come easily to Napier the night before the duel. His intention had been to have a good night's sleep and wake up fresh and alert for the coming ordeal. He had no illusions regarding his inevitable fate and fully expected the following morning he would meet his death. He was realistic enough to accept his lack of ability with firearms made him the underdog and as such spent the day putting his affairs in order. He had no one to leave his worldly goods to, so apart from a small legacy to select friends he willed them to the poor of the city as a final act of atonement.

The long hours of the night passed slowly between alternative bouts of fitful sleep and wakefulness. He was not a coward but in all honesty he could not say that he was unafraid. He kept thinking of what death would be like, how he would react. Would there be much pain when a lead shot tore into his body? He hoped to face it like a man and die with honour. Whatever he must face in the morning the alternative would be unthinkable. The dishonourable disgrace of cowardice could never be an option. Suppose he was not killed and only wounded, would Faubert betray him in revenge for his failure to dispose of the rival who threatened his financial empire? These and other thoughts flowed through his head during the restless night until an hour before dawn, when he dressed and prepared for the short ride to the site selected for whatever Fate had in mind.

Napier Gerard rode alone with his thoughts in the cold dark hour before the dawn. He chose to do so, having no wish for company, preferring the solitude of his own thoughts on what could well be the last ride of his life. The conventional method of travelling to a duel in a carriage accompanied by his seconds, he had rejected. Maybe it was silly, but he did not wish to be conveyed by others to a spot where he had every reason to believe he would be carried away from. All men are different in character and personality but they all face the same traumatic dilemma when confronted by their own mortality, be they a convicted criminal facing the gallows, or a heroic soldier surrounded by enemy hordes. The doubts and fears are the same. How they spend those last precious moments is a personal choice and Napier chose to spend them alone with his memories.

Once he was clear of the city he allowed the horse to dictate its own pace and sat hunched in the saddle, wrapped in his travelling coat, totally absorbed in his own thoughts. He had not seen Alexandrine since instigating the duel and had been unable to contact her to say his goodbyes. Would she miss him, he wondered, when he was gone? Would she grieve for him or dismiss him as someone who had entered her life then left as quickly as he had come. If that were the case he would not condemn her for that. After all they had barely known each other for more than a matter of weeks. He had no way of knowing whether her feelings for him were as deep as his were for her. Maybe she would find solace with some other suitor. There was no shortage of admirers, he was well aware of that. The young bloods of Paris flocked around her, competing avidly for her favours whenever she appeared. Only the fact he had got there first held them at bay. Once he was gone there would be many only too willing to step into his shoes.

All too soon he came to the worn track leading to the designated area. This was a well--known spot for picnic parties and hunting groups as well as the more serious activity of duelling it often hosted. The track led a short distance through the trees opening up into a wide grass covered clearing where the damp mist swirled in ghostly white patches over the dark ground. The first grey light of dawn was beginning to filter through the trees as Napier arrived; others in the group were there before him.

Two carriages stood at either end of the clearing, their wheels glistening wet from the dew-covered grass. Men and horses shivered in the damp atmosphere as the early morning mist created moisture to drip off the leaves where it condensed as it wreathed around the branches.

The first carriage he recognised as one belonging to a friend. Dismounting from his horse he tied it to a tree and climbed into the vehicle. There he gave a cheery 'good morning' to his two seconds. He did not feel cheery but he had to put on a display of indifference for appearance's sake. He sat down between the two men who returned his greeting without comment. Being a second is not the most rewarding service to give, particularly when you expect your man to lose. Getting up in the early hours too hang about in the cold wet countryside is not conducive or helpful to cheery conversation. Therefore all three sat in silence waiting for the light to improve sufficiently for the duel to take place. Napier sat there, apparently relaxed and confident while inside he was seething with nerves. He was beginning to think he could keep up the pretence not a moment longer when a face appeared at the carriage window, one of the opposing seconds had arrived to suggest the light was now good enough for the duel to commence.

The cold chill still hung about the clearing as the mist dispersed under the first weak rays of the early morning sun. The opposing groups of seconds sat about their convention dictated tasks, they had selected a level area long enough to allow the ten paces agreed by the individual duellists. This area had to be carefully checked to clear any debris, loose stones or branches that might cause the contestants to trip or lose their footing. It was important that the orientation chosen should run from north to south in order that it ran across the line of the rising sun. This way no one could claim to be at a disadvantage by facing into the light. The scene was now prepared for the duel to begin. Seconds and combatants approached a small table set to one side upon which was laid a wooden case containing the pistols. Each man selected a pistol and handed it to one of his seconds. They checked it carefully before handing it back to the duellist. These tasks completed, the seconds withdrew to a safe distance, leaving the two men standing back to back with one second remaining. He had been selected by agreement to conduct and dictate the final terms of the duel.

Napier barely heard the man's voice as he outlined the consequences of the dishonour incurred if the rules were flouted. In his mind he was reliving his past life, the clearing reminded him of a scene long ago when a ragged urchin had chanced upon a similar clearing in the grounds of an English manor and how his life had begun at that moment and here it was about to end among the trees of France.

He was awakened from his thoughts and brought back to reality when the presiding second was asking whether either man was prepared to apologise and, if so, the dispute could be brought to a honourable end. Immediately his opponent answered, "No, certainly not!" Napier, although he would have given anything to have walked away there and then, could do no other than to follow his example and say, "No, I will not!"

The second stood back and said, "Very well, gentlemen, if that is your wish, cock your pistols."

Napier touched the cold steel of the flintlock. He hoped his fingers were not trembling as he pulled back the cock and heard the click of the spring as it locked into position. He could feel the presence of his opponent standing behind him. Did he feel the same mixture of fear and apprehension? Perhaps not; his chances of survival were much better and he had done it all before. He would have liked to glance behind him to check his opponent for signs of nerves but he could not. Out of the corner of his eye he could see the blue-black muzzle and the brass bound wooden stock of the pistol he held pointing upwards, level with his right ear. It was heavy and he could see it shaking slightly. From that moment he made up his mind to go down fighting, try to get in the first shot and hope it hits the target.

The voice of the second interrupted his thoughts.

"Are you ready, gentlemen? Take ten places."

Napier counted off the steps one by one. This was it the final act. He glanced round at the surrounding forest. Was it all to end here in the early morning light on the cold wet grass of France? He thought of Alexandrine and what might have been. If only he had been able to see her one last time. If only he had been able to say his last goodbye. It was all too late now. The die had been cast and he must accept whatever Fate decreed. Almost at the tenth pace now when he must turn and look down that menacing barrel, a hole in a piece of metal capable of leaving death and destruction in its wake. There it was, the tenth pace; then he heard the voice of the second giving instructions. "Turn around, gentlemen." Napier turned to face his opponent, he could not detect any sign of nerves, the man stood erect staring straight at him the pistol held upright in front of him as steady as a rock. Again came the voice of the second, "Are you ready, gentlemen?" Both men gave the affirmative answer, "Then fire as you will." Napier, so inexperienced with firearms, did not realise the need for calm deliberation. Too quickly he straightened his arm to line up with the target, before he had a chance to aim his finger touched the trigger, set to a fine adjustment to enable it to operate at the slightest pressure, the weapon discharged itself with a bang and a puff of smoke as the powder in the pan exploded. Napier's heart almost stopped, he had squandered his last chance now he must stand and face a marksman who had every right to stand and take his time picking out the exact spot on the target he chose to hit. This was a man who had proved twice before that he did not shrink from inflicting the ultimate penalty. At least he would face it like a man. He would not give the satisfaction of the sight of him fleeing from the scene and taking a ball in the back – a coward's death.

Squaring his shoulders he looked directly at his opponent intending to look him in the eyes, but instead of the barrel of a pistol and the eyes of a killer taking careful aim, a different scene unfolded before him. His opponent stood with his arm holding the gun hanging limply by his side, his mouth hung open and a trickle of blood ran down the bridge of his nose starting to spread over the side of his cheek. He stood that way for a moment, almost as though he could not believe the small hole in the centre of his forehead taking away the last dying embers of his life. Slowly it seemed, like a collapsing puppet, his legs crumbled under him and he pitched forward onto his face. Napier could not believe it, feelings of relief exhilaration and sheer incredibility at the astounding luck that had delivered him from the very jaws of death. Somehow the shot he had accidentally discharged had found its target. Miraculously he had survived the final demise he had thought to be his fate. Truly the hand of Fate and his guardian angels had been by his side this day.

By now the doctor had rushed to the man's side, it took a second to make a diagnosis. The victor walked towards them and was in time to hear him say briefly and without ceremony. "I fear he is dead." Napier was engulfed in all sorts of emotions. There was relief to be alive, exhilaration but also sadness for the man he had killed. This was the third man to die by his hand; maybe four if the footpad had not survived. The duke he had no regrets about, he would have done it again cheerfully as he was a man who richly deserved his fate, and the highwayman, well, he was on borrowed time anyway. If he had not died by the sword the rope would have got him eventually. But this man was a stranger about whom he knew nothing. He did not even know his name but he was to blame for his death, and yet not totally. If Faubert had not forced him to act – this man would not be laying here now. He felt so angry with Faubert. How on earth had he allowed himself to fall into the clutches of such a man?

Suddenly he became aware of a carriage being driven at speed into the clearing. To the sounds of horses being reined in it lurched to a stop close to the body, the door was flung open and a woman flew out of the carriage and lay prostrate weeping over the body of the dead man. She was wearing a hooded cloak which enveloped her completely, making it impossible to tell whether she was young or old; all that could be seen was a spread of black velvet and all that could be heard were the sobs of a heartbroken woman lamenting the loss of a loved one. Until now Napier had taken a 'him or me' attitude and it had not occurred to him that the taking of life involved others. Now it was driven home to him. If you take a life you destroy not only that person but also you touch everyone within their sphere of influence; he could only guess at what he had done to this woman.

He could no longer bear to look upon this scene that gave him such feelings of guild and remorse. He turned and walked away, the sobs of the woman still sounding in his ears. He had taken but a few steps when the woman came running after him, her velvet cloak flowing out behind as she ran, Napier heard the running footsteps but continued to walk away. He had enough confrontation for one day; then a hand grabbed him by the shoulder and spun him round to receive the biggest shock of his life. There, glaring at him with hatred blazing from them with an intensity akin to the fires of hell, were the brown eyes that had so entranced him when first he saw her on the steps of Faubert's office. The woman in the black velvet cloak was Alexandrine d'Amblimont. Napier was so stunned he did not feel the tiny fists raining blow after blow on his unprotected face and body. He did not hear the words of hatred she screamed at him as she vented her fury born of the savage loss he had inflicted upon her. He stood there completely bemused unable to utter words of comfort or explanation. Yet in his mind it was all so horribly clear he could see it all now. In all its stark reality, this man was

Alexandrine's father and he had just killed him, the father she adored and he had never met. The business rival so threatened of Faubert's financial empire that he saw no alternative but to dispose of him. He was the reason for Alexandrine's visit to Paris and this was the reason for the Fauberts' reluctance to assist him in her courtship. Both of them knew he was becoming emotionally involved with the daughter of the very man he would eventually be expected to kill.

The drama ended as quickly as it had begun with the arrival of Alexandrine's companion. She gave Napier a look of loathing then, taking the young woman in her arms, with soothing words she led her away. Alexandrine, through her tears, cursed Napier then quietly and ominously vowed that if it took her the rest of her life she would make him pay for the deed he had done that day.

What on earth had he done? He was the victor and yet his world had crumbled about his ears. He would have been better off if it were he being taken to the morgue than for this to happen. He stood there rooted to the spot, surveying the scene before him: the two women climbing into their carriage; the two seconds, assisting the doctor to lift the corpse of his opponent into the other carriage; his own seconds, too embarrassed by the scene to approach him, stood by their own coach unsure of what they should do. Through the green foliage the first rays of the morning sun began to filter into the clearing, birds began to sing again and Nature took back possession of her own, indifferent to the tragedy enacted by man within her domain. Not only Nature, but mankind also showed an equal indifference. As the day wore on, pleasure seekers came to picnic in the clearing, unmindful and uncaring of the lives so cruelly destroyed by the events of the morning.

9

Faubert Still in Control

Consumed by a white-hot seething anger, Napier leapt into the saddle and whipped his horse into a gallop. His mind in a wild turmoil of emotion at the perceived destruction of his future happiness; Alexandrine would hate him for eternity and who could blame her? Certainly not Napier, who knew only too well the perpetrator responsible for the morning's tragic events. The stark truth was staring him in the face. He had lost forever the love of his life, the soul mate he had hopes of in his dreams of the future – now in tatters, irretrievably gone. He had barely escaped with his own life. Only the intervention of the hand of fate had saved him and to make matters worse he had killed a man who had done him no wrong.

How he wished he could turn back the clock but he could not. If only he were able to go to Alexandrine, explain it all and comfort her, but he could not. What is done is done and cannot be undone no matter how fervently we wish it were not so. At this moment the sole purpose of his life was revenge. Revenge on the man who was the perpetrator of his misfortune to inflict some hurt, some punishment on the man whose greed and financial avarice had destroyed his honour, compromised his integrity, taken away his future and turned him into a foul murderer. He whipped his horse to greater speed. The ground had been soft in the forest but now the dull thudding of it's hooves took on a harder note as the galloping animal left the moss covered grass and came on to the hard packed surface of the road. Ignoring the ruts and potholes threatening the very lives of horse and rider, Napier continued his madcap ride, indifferent to any danger in blinkered obsession to take revenge on the man who was the focal point of his anger, the lawyer Françoise Faubert.

Crouching low over the neck of the labouring steed he could see the house ahead of him. Urging the tiring mount to even greater speed he galloped up the familiar drive. Within seconds he was leaping out of the saddle and running up the front steps leaving his exhausted horse untethered, foam flecked and covered in sweat, snorting and blowing great clouds of steamy breath through it's distorted nostrils. Impatiently ignoring the doorbell, he hammered furiously on the door with both fists; pausing only when it was opened by a puzzled looking footman. In his present mood he had no time for the conventions of propriety nor did he feel the need for the observation of good manners, he pushed past the startled footman without a word of explanation and ran at top speed across the hall and up the stairs three at a time. He knew exactly where his quarry would be. Intent on surprising him in his den he ran through the maze of corridors and stairs leading to the top floor, trailing a team of anxious footman in his wake.

The study door was unlocked. He flung it open to reveal the slight figure of Faubert sitting at his desk; the lawyer gave no sign of surprise or anger at this intrusion. He merely looked up from his work, put down his quill and waved away the footman who were crowding into the room preparing to overpower the Napier before he could inflict any damage.

"Thank you for your concern," he said, "there is no problem here. I will deal with it. Please continue with your duties." Turning to his angry visitor he said, "Good morning, Napier, please come in and close the door. It would appear we have something to discuss."

Napier did as he was bid and without comment closed the door then walked swiftly across the room drawing his sword as he did so. He knew the secret of the carved wooden protrusion set in the top of the desk and to prevent it being used laid the point of his sword on it. He had no intention of allowing Faubert the opportunity of rotating into action the deadly flintlock concealed below it; the trick had worked against him once, he would not allow it to be used a second time. Somehow the man's calm, unruffled attitude added fuel to his anger. He had expected surprise consternation – fear even, but the man merely sat there with that slight smile playing around the corners of his mouth showing no more concern than he would if taking tea with a family friend. Was there nothing could upset the persona of this infuriating man? Napier pushed the tip of the sword into the carved wood, his eyes blazing with anger.

"Have you any idea what you have done to me?" he snarled. "Now it is your turn to be the victim. You have manipulated me for the last time; I have taken all I intend to take off you. The time has come for me to take my revenge. Don't think to use that flintlock, you made the mistake of showing me your little toy, if you make one move towards it I will slice your hand off!"

Faubert sat back in his chair and smiled, a cold smile, certainly not one of welcome, his lips and facial muscles went through the motions but his eyes remained hard and calculating.

"Napier, I have every respect for you as a swordsman and do not intend to try my luck against one as skilful as you. There can be no doubt you are capable of carrying out your threat, but do you really think I would be so unprepared as to be protected by one little toy alone?" So saying he pushed with his left foot a lever set into the floor under the desk. With a rumble of well-oiled machinery the whole floor under Napier's feet began to slide smoothly and swiftly into the wall. He had no time to leap to safety, taken completely by surprise, the totally unexpected movement of the very ground beneath his feet left him struggling to maintain his balance. His sword, made so familiar through constant practice it seemed to be an extension of is own arm, the very weapon that gave him confidence to stand against all comers, slipped from fingers shocked into releasing their grip, he could only watch in helpless frustration as it spiralled down into the abyss opening up before him. The shining blade, looking like a silver leaf catching the light as it fell, struck sparks against the dressed stone walls of the pit as it bounced from side to side before plunging into the maelstrom of foaming water rushing along its channel at the bottom of the shaft.

This was the ingenious system of water-power that ran the machinery within the house. Faubert, with his enthusiasm for invention, had drawn up the designs to harness a small tributary running into the Seine, building the tunnels into the foundations. Only he knew all the secrets contained in the powerful water-driven machinery and he alone maintained it. Some of the equipment was quite benign and used openly for domestic purposes. The servants of the house had good reason to be grateful to Faubert's engineering genius; much of their work became easier because of the gadgets he invented and encouraged them to use. However there were other devices with uses of a sinister nature. These, like the trap opening up beneath Napier's feet, he had installed alone and in secret; only he and his previous victims knew of their existence.

Napier looked desperately about him in the vain hope of finding an avenue of escape but there were none. The trap had been designed with great care and extreme cunning. The walls were smooth and without ornament. No pictures or artefacts adorned them, once the floor had disappeared into the wall there was nothing even the most agile of victims could hold on to. All he could do was to stand and await his fate of helplessly toppling into the maelstrom of water. If the fall did not kill him then he would surely drown through being swept through the tunnels by the roaring current – God knows what sort of cogs and wheels would crunch his bones to pulp, until finally spitting his mangled body into the Seine, to be found by some boatman as just another nameless corpse floating down the river, a silent witness keeping yet again one more of Faubert's little secrets. He cursed the inattention and lack of foresight leading to his being caught so easily. It was all so crystal clear now the trap was sprung. He had often wondered at the unusual arrangement of the furnishings in the study but had not given it too much thought, dismissing it as part of the man's eccentricity. Now that it was too late the reason became blatantly obvious. Between the door and the desk there was nothing, no furniture, no rugs or carpets, just smooth polished floorboards. Every item used to furnish the room was situated behind the desk. Across the gap the once familiar room had now taken on the appearance of a ledge perched on the edge of a pit. There was the telescope standing on its' tripod by the window, the chairs and cabinets lined along the walls behind the great desk, the huge bookcase filled with all manner of books covering a diversity of subjects and the desk itself dominating the scene. There sat Faubert, still with that smile playing about his lips, a man in complete control of the situation, his right hand resting on the flintlock, the weapon that only seconds ago Napier had sought to prevent him using.

Now here he was completely helpless, the floor beneath his feet nothing more than a triangular ledge moving relentlessly into the corner, soon it would be nothing and he would follow his sword into the depths if he tried to jump the gap, which was doubtful from a standing start. Even if against all the odds he succeeded, the blunderbuss would cut him to ribbons before he landed. It crossed his mind he could jump and grasp the door handle but even if he reached it, how long could he hold on before he lost his grip and once again there was always the ever-threatening flintlock. The facts were staring him in the face – he was hopelessly trapped, once again at the mercy of the implacable ruthless Faubert. It was time to make his peace with his maker and for the second time in the one day await his demise. Just as he was preparing for the inevitable fall the machinery stopped, leaving him standing on a triangle of floor no more than twice the length of his own feet.

"My dear Napier," said Faubert, "You are far too impetuous. Your feet go running on ahead of you while your brain comes trundling on well in the rear. Perhaps under the circumstances you are now prepared to listen to reason. I bring you into my house and treat you as one of the family, I teach you to be a gentleman, introduce you to society and give you a lifestyle you could never hope to aspire to. On top of all this I protect you and keep you out of the clutches of the Duke of Mulgrove and you repay me by attempting to kill me! I call that ingratitude, Napier. What have you to say for yourself that will prevent me from restarting the machinery and sending you to your death?"

Working on the premise that when all is lost the only recourse is total defiance, Napier answered him with brave words.

"Start up your malignant machinery and be damned, I am not afraid to die. You might well have taught me to live an affluent lifestyle but you have destroyed any chance of future happiness I ever hoped for. Why did you not tell me the man you sent me to kill was Alexandrine's father?"

Faubert regarded him thoughtfully for a while and the trace of a frown flickered across his face.

"Yes, I do truly regret that, Napier, but you will recall that both my wife and I did all we could to prevent you becoming involved with that girl. We both knew the outcome would be disastrous but you would not listen and went blundering on to your own destiny, I could do nothing to prevent it."

Napier standing on his precarious ledge had to shout to

make himself heard above the roar of the waters at the bottom of the pit.

"Of course you could have done something. You did not have to force me to challenge him, you could have taken your chances in the open market and fought him as any decent businessman would by using methods of honest commerce, but no, you with your greed and avarice wanted to make your obscene profits without fear of incurring a financial loss. I was the pawn who was deceived into using my skills to kill him for you. I wish now that I had aimed merely to wound him and left you to do your deals and protect your money the best way you can."

Napier was surprised to see Faubert was laughing, a cold merciless laugh. All the more shocking by its' spontaneous uncontrived nature, his voice laughed and his mouth laughed but the eyes remained cold and humourless, as a man might laugh at a joke about his own death.

"Napier, Napier, Napier," he said, repeating the name as though to stress the point he was about to make, "you know nothing about the realities of life! If I had left events to take their course you would be laying dead in the forest now, the man you so foolishly allowed to make the choice of weapons was so technically superior to you in the use of firearms you could not have hoped to defeat him. You talk of shooting to wound him, the shot you accidentally discharged before you had chance to aim, went harmlessly into the trees leaving you at the mercy of one of the best marksmen in France. He would have dispatched you with consummate ease and with as little compunction or conscience as he would show to a mad dog. You did not shoot him, Napier. It was my coachman! A remarkable marksman hidden in the trees with a silent gun, using compressed air, a very useful invention of my own you know. Amazing how much power you can obtain from compressed air. I must look further into its use." He said, looking into the distance in a dreamy sort of way, almost as though in his mind he was already in his workshop tinkering away.

"However, be that as it may," he said, returning to reality and running his finger along the top of the flintlock to adjust its' alignment slightly to cover more accurately the figure of his victim perched on his precarious ledge, "It was not you who sent your fellow duellist to his maker. You had no hand in it accept to set him up as a target for a far better marksman than you will ever be."

Napier was totally stunned by this revelation. There was no need to wonder about it. He knew without question it was true. The gun had discharged accidentally, even then he had found it difficult to believe the ball had found its mark so unerringly by sheer luck, but at no time had it crossed his mind there had been a second shot. It was obvious now the startling truth had been told, his shot could not possibly have gone anywhere near its target. Despite his perilous position, his mouth went dry with horror as the realisation hit him: he had been the accomplice to a murder, an unwitting one, maybe totally ignorant of the events he was abetting, but nevertheless a major player in the crime that was committed.

As always thoughts of Alexandrine were never far from the back of his mind and now her image came flooding into his brain. He had not killed her father but he could not tell her so. As things were, she might one day find it in her heart to forgive him. After all, to kill a man in a duel is a honourable thing – if killing another human being can be referred to as 'honourable' – at least both combatants face an equal risk. Would she have forgiven her father if he had killed him, the man who loved her? He could not answer that but it is certain if she knew the part he had played in her father's killing she would not believe him to be innocent and most certainly never forgive him. No doubt she would go directly to the authorities; they would arrest him for murder and how would he convince them he had no knowledge of the crime about to be committed? What of the coachman? Was he a cold-blooded paid assassin or was he, like Napier, coerced and blackmailed into doing a job he had no real stomach for? His mind reeled at the thought of the man in the tree with that lethal air gun. He felt dirty and dishonoured his pride and his integrity taken away from him never to return. So shocked was he by Faubert's revelations regarding his part in the duel, Napier had quite forgotten his perilous perch as all these thoughts flashed through his mind in a split second.

Now with the sound of the lawyer's voice, he came back to reality with a start, almost losing balance as he did so.

"Now, Napier, listen to me," Faubert's voice was firm and authoritative as he spoke. "You may think that you have been badly used and you make think of me as you will. I own there is much truth in your accusations but you do not know the full facts, I did not order d'Ambliment's death for my own personal gain. The order came from a far higher authority than you can imagine; in fact right from the heart of government. If I had failed to carry them out then my own life would have been forfeited. Why do you think we were so against your relationship with this girl?

She is nothing of what you think she is; she and her father are dangerous revolutionaries who would have used the money made to topple the very crown itself. It was not their money that financed the venture. It came from the organisation they belong to. It was to prevent such a disastrous revolt. I was ordered to act as I did. True, it was very profitable for me once the lynchpin of the deal had been removed but I also did a great service for my country into the bargain." Faubert's voice became quieter and more consolatory; he sat back in his chair and stroked his chin.

"Look, Napier," he said. "This should not be happening to us. Your father was my friend and for the sake of his memory we should be friends. I want to protect you, not kill you."

The lawyer knew he had defused the situation and as though to prove it he released the cock on the flintlock and rolled it smoothly back into its secret hiding place, then continued to talk almost as though he were talking to himself.

"If you only knew the intrigues and dangers of politics today. You are naïve in such things and have no idea of the happenings in the corridors of power. I warn you now, there are things to come that will terrify us all, I don't know when or how many years in the future the terror will come, but mark my words it will happen, and God help those of us who choose the wrong side. Enough of this nonsense." Faubert snapped himself out of his reflective mood as though he realised he had said too much.

"Give me your word you will behave and I will return you to safety and we can talk about this."

Napier, stuck on his precarious perch, had little option but to comply. He had to keep very still to maintain his balance, and was only too aware one false move would be his last. Much as he would have liked to maintain a proud defiant opposition, the risk was too great. This was not a man to trifle with. He knew one touch on the pedal and the remains of the floor would disappear and he would follow his sword into the depths unquestionably to his doom. He was trapped, out-foxed and beaten and well he knew it; also, the lawyer's words had made him think a little. He was still angry, but looking back he could see there had been some things that had puzzled him and now deep down he had to admit there was a ring of truth to what had been said, but even so he could not bring himself to believe Alexandrine was anything other than the sweet innocent girl he believed her to be. No way could he see her being involved in intrigues and shadowy plots involving high risks against a vengeful state only too willing to inflict terrible punishment against anyone who opposed it. Surely Faubert was mistaken and it was her father alone who was the revolutionary and Alexandrine involved only as an innocent relative – all this, however, was by the by. His first and most urgent priority was to get himself out of his present predicament and back on to safer, more solid ground; therefore he reluctantly agreed to the lawyer's terms and gave his word he would comply.

With his acquiescence there was a rumble of machinery and the well-oiled cogs started to move the floor back into position, Napier felt a great sense of relief despite himself. He had to admit he was frightened. His legs felt weak and he had to make a conscience effort to prevent himself from shivering, that pit had been terrifying. He knew only too well how close he had come to experiencing its horrors first hand. The threat had been very real; Faubert had not been bluffing, he had no illusions about that. With a slight thud the floor clicked back into position and all was normal, no one could have guessed the terrible secret that lay under that area of polished wooden floorboards, everything looked exactly as it did before with not a single item out of place and Napier found himself once more standing before the desk looking at Françoise Faubert, Attorney of Law.

10

Vengeance and Shadows in the Night

To some men, success comes easily; born to riches, they make no effort to try or strive yet still success and power come with consummate ease. Others make up their minds as to their goal in life and work, struggle, sweat and strain until they achieve their aim through strenuous efforts and sheer ability. Others less fortunate are forced to remain at the bottom of the pile regardless of their personal efforts; luck appears against them whether they are idle or able. Napier was none of these. He came into the category of men whom Fate had earmarked for a path of destiny to be travelled without deviation, regardless of his efforts or wishes. Life would always direct him back onto that path, however hard he tried to guide his life in other easier more comfortable directions.

From his early life scraping a living from the mud of the River Thames, roaming the streets of London as a ragged orphan, not knowing who he was or what lineage he came from, the Gods had gifted him with the mind reflexes and body of a natural fencer. Then through a series of chance encounters a boy, who in the normal scheme of things would have lived and died spending his life on the mean streets of the City, was guided by Fate to the door of the very man who had the training and ability to hone those gifts to a state of perfection. Thus the raw materials of a duellist were brought to manhood. Fate however had not finished with Napier Gerard. By intelligence, education and inclination he could have been a scholar, teacher or lawyer, anything other than what destiny decreed he should become. But cruel Fate has no respect for sensitivity and set about hardening his character by a series of devastating blows: the death of his father, followed by the blood-soaked vengeful escape from the manor, which culminated in the privations he was to suffer during the manhunt where he was the quarry. Eventually he had shaken off his pursuers and become affluent, happy and successful, a popular person with many friends and best of all he has met the love of his life. Then with its cruel smile fate struck again. Took it away in one devastating event; the girl he loves became his sworn enemy. He killed a man in a duel and those who were once his friends now fear him. They smile at him, but very carefully; in their eyes where once there was trust lurks the spectre of terror. When Destiny has you in its clutches it slams all the doors. In Napier's case Fate had barred his avenue of escape by putting him in the clutches of the man who had him in his complete control – the lawyer Françoise Faubert, a ruthless puppet master who would not be afraid to pull the strings whenever he thought it expedient to do so. Thus the ragged urchin in the fullness of time had become the reluctant professional duellist prepared to do his master's bidding however distasteful the task might be.

All this had been passing through Napier's mind as he stood before the desk trying to get back his composure after his frightening ordeal. Faubert had risen from his seat and had moved over to the window where he seated himself comfortably in a deep leather armchair and motioned to Napier to join him in a similar seat opposite. No one would have guessed from the lawyer's attitude that mere seconds before he had been balancing his guest on the brink of death. Therefore it was not surprising that Napier when he took his seat did so carefully, looking around the area in a timid manner for fear of any more traps. The reason for his careful actions was not lost on Faubert who smiled and said;

"There is no need to worry, I think we understand each other now. I think the time has come for us to put our cards on the table. Nothing has changed with our arrangement. You are a much wiser and I hope a much more experienced man. It is doubtful you will make the same mistake again. You were lucky to survive but fortunately it all turned out alright in the end. No, do not say anything, I know you do not agree with me on the outcome."

Napier was about to say it almost certainly had not turned out alright, thought better of it and sat looking resentfully at his tormentor.

The unflappable lawyer sat back in his chair and spread his arms out in a gesture meant to encompass his surrounds.

"Look around you; see the wealth and power I have. Do you think I achieved all this without effort or sacrifice? It does not come easily, Napier, you have to fight tooth and claw to gain it and once you have it you never stop looking over your shoulder. The conflict is never at an end. The higher you climb the harder the battle becomes. Do not labour under the illusion that the world owes you a living. It does not. You have to take what you want and hang on to it by whatever method comes to hand. Take my word for it, the meek and the timid do not rule the earth. The only way you can stay at the top is by treading on others before they tread on you. That is the way of the world. The only successful course is to go along with it. If you oppose that or show weakness you go under.

Look here, my boy, I am offering you wealth power and position but on my terms. You don't have to accept them but the alternative is to go away penniless and without friends into a cruel unyielding world and never forget you have powerful enemies. The Duke of Mulgrove would dearly love to know where he could lay his hands on you. He is incensed that you escaped his net; even now his spies are still scouring the towns and cities of two nations in an effort to apprehend you."

Napier leapt to his feet livid with anger. "Do you think I care about wealth and power? Don't judge me by your avaricious standards; I had other goals. Now all I had hoped for my future and my domestic happiness has been snatched from me. As for the duke and his spies, I can handle them if I have to. Besides they have no idea where to find me, I have eluded them up to now. If I were to leave the country and went abroad they would never find me!"

Faubert leant forward in his seat and shook his head, his face taking on a grim almost sad expression as he spoke.

"Really, my boy. You must try to look a little further than the end of your nose for the answers to your questions. I can tell you without fear of contradiction the duke's spy master has always known where you are, and your present identity, he just has not chosen to inform the duke – I am the duke's spy master! It was I he engaged to watch the French ports and scour the streets of Paris with my agents. He engaged me the instant he realised there was a possibility you had managed to cross the Channel. So long as I continue to take his retainer you are safe. Regardless of whether you choose to stay or go I will not betray you. I owe that to your father; he was my friend." Faubert looked thoughtful for a moment then rose quickly to his feet with the air of a man who has made up his mind and was about to take some decisive action.

"Come with me and I will show you something that will open your eyes and make you realise just how far reaching a spy master's network of knowledge can be. Did it ever cross your mind to wonder how I knew you had left England, while you were still at sea trying to cross the Channel? How I knew you would be disembarking at Dieppe in time to bribe the customs to turn a blind eye to your entry into the country? How could

I have known about your adventures en route to Paris and the instant you arrived in the city? Please follow me and all will be revealed. I show you this as a gesture of my faith in you. What you are about to see, only the most trusted of my employees have seen."

So saying he led the way from the room where Napier had so nearly met his untimely doom. Striding ahead he moved quickly down the corridor where he stopped in front of a small door but no ordinary door this. It had obviously been specially made and would not have looked out of place guarding a strong room; manufactured from stout oak, studded and banded with thick iron, its substantial lock gave evidence it was not made to be accessed easily. Faubert produced a key, fastened to a chain hanging from his belt. A single key so securely located it merited its own attachment by way of insurance against loss. After turning the well-oiled lock he very carefully and meticulously returned it to his pocket before opening the door to reveal a narrow set of stone steps leading through the door. Napier negotiated the steps finding them to be barely wide enough for a man to pass without scraping his shoulders against both walls. Upon reaching the top, strange sounds could be heard coming from the attic. Here Faubert paused possibly to regain his breath but more likely to tantalise his visitor's imagination and to create a theatrical effect. The smell of the place and the slow, continuous warbling cooing sound reminded Napier of the dove house at the manor, where occasionally he had helped the kitchen maids to collect eggs, when as a boy he had whiled away his spare time helping out the cooks in return for cakes and other delicacies. Jerking himself out of his nostalgic memories he followed his guide squeezing himself through the stone arched aperture; which gave access to the area beneath the roof. Knowing the lawyer as he did Napier had not been sure what to expect, his repertoire of tricks and surprises were such that he had been prepared for almost anything.

What he had not been expecting was a pigeon loft, but what a pigeon loft! It was enormous with row upon row of nesting boxes, each with its own door. On each door was a board with a district or area, coupled with a person's name, written on it in chalk. Down the centre of the room was a row of desks where men sat on stools writing carefully and painstakingly on tiny squares of paper. Occasionally one would walk over to the nesting boxes, tie something to the leg of a pigeon then carry it over to an area open to the elements with a balustrade built across for safety's sake and throw the bird up into the sky. Through the many holes in the roof the odd pigeon would poke its head and coo almost as though it were signalling its presence in an intelligent manner. Instantly one of the men would collect the bird, place it in a box after removing the message from its leg and chalk its place of origin on the board. Returning to his desk he then copies the message on the tiny piece of paper onto a readable sheet, rolling it up so that it would fit into a cylinder with a fitted cap, the whole lot dropped into a tube set into the wall where it disappeared from sight.

Faubert looked around at all this and beamed a proud justifiable smile.

"This, Napier," he said, "is my communications centre. Without this my spy network could not function in the supremely efficient manner in which it does, and for that matter my business empire would not be as successful either. I flatter myself that nowhere in the world does such a system exist, pigeons are used by many for communications but not taken to the extent that you see here. Look at the way my men write. They are all handpicked for their loyalty and their expertise. These men could inscribe the full page of a book on an area of rice paper no bigger than your thumbnail. Do you notice these?" He picked up a small leather pouch with ties attached, on the side a tiny metal disc with a number stamped on it. "Each number is coded to a given area and agent. Providing we are careful to attach this to the leg of a pigeon from that specific agent, messages can be sent back and forth within hours, even during storms and tempest from the other side of the sea. A man might travel for days and still I would know where he was and where he was going well before he finally arrived. Every single word arriving here is transcribed into a readable text and sent down the tube you see over there. It leads to a safe in my study. Only I read all of the messages sent to this loft. It is with good reason I pride myself on being the best-informed man in the country. Not the King, his ministers or government official know more of what goes on than I. So you see, my boy, this is why from the moment you were spotted at a British port I was able to follow your every move within hours of you making it, and could do so again whenever I choose to put the wheels into motion.

Now your answer, Napier, if you please?" There was a slight note of irritation in the lawyer's voice. He had become impatient with showing off his organisational abilities and was ready to get back to his work, although justifiably proud of what he had achieved he saw the results of his creation as more important than boasting about it.

"Do you choose to stay and enjoy the comforts of a lifestyle I can give you or do you choose to spend your life scratching a living and forever looking over your shoulder? The choice is yours."

Napier was in truth too dumbfounded to argue. He knew he had very little option but to agree the terms. In his wildest dreams he had never envisaged how far reaching and intricate the sphere of influence Faubert's organisation encompassed. Well aware as he was that he had only been shown the tip of the iceberg it was enough to tell him that if he chose the opposing option his lifespan would be limited; therefore much against his own personal wishes and finer feelings he shook the lawyer's hand and agreed to the terms he stipulated.

Trapped between the perils of his previous pursuit catching

up with him and the coils of Faubert's cunning he had no choice but to continue with the deception of his life, as Napier Feray, nephew of Victoire Faubert, but now after the traumatic events of the duel his lifestyle changed dramatically; no more the carefree laughing gambler cruising through the social areas of a frivolous Paris, he found that such a lifestyle no longer had an appeal. In part it was because it was an inherent part of his agreement with Faubert, but mainly because it was an inescapable part of his physiological make-up. Most of his time he spent at the Salle. Here he could lose himself for a while, forget his problems and immerse himself in the role of fencing master. But even here he was not immune from the all-embracing influence of the spy master. Now that he was completely part of the Faubert organisation, the true nature of the fencing school became obvious. The whole structure was a network of whispering galleries, listening tubes and secret observation areas. There was nowhere in the building that could not be overheard or over seen. To this end people were employed to listen observe and pass on any information gleaned to their master, who knew the school to be a valuable source of information. Even Napier who found this sort of thing distasteful and alien to his nature was expected to be part of this organised invasion of privacy. Faubert's greatest strength was his ability to instil loyalty and discretion in all his employees, partly because he paid them well and gave them loyalty and support in return and partly because they were afraid of him. Some he controlled by knowledge of a past indiscretion they did not want made public. Napier was one of these. Others knew a good thing when they had it and were well aware any deviation of trust would be instantly and severely dealt with, thus generosity and loyalty could be replaced by instant and savage action if the need arose. Therefore despite the large number of employees, many holding positions of the strictest confidence, it was rare indeed for any of Faubert's secrets to leak out.

Unsurprisingly Napier drifted into an aimless existence without purpose, structure or reason. He could not get Alexandrine out of his mind, her father's death or her reaction to him. She was the central figure in the drama; the expression of sheer hatred, her face displayed when she ran across the glade to pound him with her fists, all this in stark detail came flooding back in mental images haunting his daylight hours and invading his sleep at night, turning his normal sunny character into something withdrawn and morose.

He had seen her once since the duel and that only at a distance. Even though he had tried not to do so he found himself checking on the time of her father's funeral and despite his better judgement had positioned himself along the route to watch the cortege from a discreet distance, far enough away from the road so as not to be seen. *This is wrong. I who have no right am intruding on private grief,* he said to himself and had almost decided to leave when he saw the hearse drawn by a team of jet black horses, dressed in their funereal plumage, approaching at a slow walk followed by a small group of mourners that were led by two women walking arm-in-arm. One he recognised as Alexandrine's companion, the other, wrapped in an all-concealing velvet cloak, he knew without doubt to be Alexandrine herself. Now he really must go, turn away from this sight that depressed and saddened him, but he could not. Maybe it was a masochistic need to punish himself or possibly a sense of misplaced duty but he had to see it through to the end. Therefore he stepped quietly out of his hiding place and followed the cortege to its destination.

At the cemetery the small group of people split and stood apart, the girl and her companion, a lonely couple on their own as though they were not a part of the other mourners. Napier stood outside the graveyard, concealed by trees, and went through emotional agonies, torn apart by remorse as he watched the brief ceremonies; a shameful secret witness of the girl's grief, envious of the part played by the faithful companion comforting her during her time of sorrow. He would have given the world and all he had to have been there by her side just like the companion, giving her solace in her time of need, but it could not be, she would have spit in his face and well he knew it. So at last he succumbed to his better judgement and walked sadly away.

Following the mournful events of that day, Napier became more withdrawn. His friends, once willing companions in a search for pleasure, now avoided him – partly because he was no longer social towards them and partly because they now feared him. They had always respected his skill with a sword but the duel presented a new aspect of his personality. He was now incorrectly perceived to be a fine shot with a pistol, but more pertinently he was now considered to be prepared to use his skills ruthlessly to gain his own advantage, therefore a man to be treated with care and deference.

His relationship with the Fauberts did not help matters. He no longer visited the house and communicated with the lawyer by notes and letters only when it became necessary. The lawyer's wife he somewhat unreasonably blamed for not doing more to keep him informed regarding the girl's true status. In his mournful state of mind he thought she could have intervened and prevented him from fighting the duel. Therefore the one person who might have been able to help him through his troubles he avoided and shut her out of his life.

Lonely and depressed he shunned the social scene and took to spending long hours riding alone and exploring the surrounding countryside. His solitary journeys became longer and longer until one evening, returning late after having travelled much further than intended, he allowed his tired horse to walk slowly along his accustomed route back into the city. The night had grown cold with the bright moon lighting up the dark clouds, blown swiftly across the sky by a stiff breeze that appeared to be blowing up for a storm. Sitting slumped in the saddle Napier shivered and drew his riding coat more tightly about him; turned up his collar and pulled his tricorn hat more firmly down over his eyes. Lost in his thoughts he allowed his mount to pick its own route along the rough track leading through a small wood. Not a sound broke the stillness of the night, no bird call or animal moving in the undergrowth, just the wind rustling the leaves in a reminder that their dryness meant they would soon fall and carpet the woodland floor. In fact if Napier had been more aware he might have realised it was too quiet, with only the creaking of saddle leather and the slow plod of his horse's hooves breaking the silence.

Suddenly, without warning the scene erupted into chaos. Noisy bodies crashing through the trees snapping twigs and pushing aside branches, men shouting, the familiar rasping sound of metal as swords were drawn from scabbards and hands clutching and dragging, trying to pull him from the saddle. His musings forgotten, Napier's brain flicked into action; the sudden shock rather than confusing him had galvanised him into awareness. Realising he could not resist the hands that pulled at him in the darkness, he did the last thing his attackers would expect and threw himself from the horse. When he hit the ground he rolled in order to put distance between him and his adversaries and to give himself space to move. In one movement, as he unsheathed his sword, his whole body unfurling into the *on-guard* position. Without question he owed his life to this action, a movement perfected honed through years of training and constant practise. In the darkness of the wood he could not see his aggressors but thankfully they also would be inflicted with this handicap. He looked around him hoping to see something. There was noise of men all around him but where were they?

Suddenly there was the flash of polished metal in a patch of moonlight; he lunged in its direction and was rewarded with the feel of his blade sinking into flesh and an agonised cry – a good hard tug and the blade came out. Thank God it had not stuck or he would have been in trouble. Wonderful, he had got one of them in a vital spot by the feel of it. Now, where are the others? Almost instinctively he felt rather than saw a figure lunging at him, sweeping his sword in an arc in order to catch the blade he managed to parry the incoming thrust and riposted immediately. Eyesight played no part in the movement. Years of training guided the blade unerringly to its target and he was rewarded once again with the knowledge he had delivered a thrust to a vital area, almost certainly along the line of the arm entering the body below the shoulder, penetrating the top of the ribcage, piercing the lung and into the heart. *Jacques' lessons in anatomy had been very thorough.* Now, how many more and where are they? It was quieter; no shouting or crashing about just the groans of an injured man. Yet his senses told him it was not yet over. The clink of metal and the heavy breathing of a frightened man guided him in the right direction. There he was, a dark shadow against a tree. Napier moved swiftly to his target. The man raised his weapon in a half-hearted defence – a hopeless gesture. He stood no chance face to face against a fencing master's educated blade. His attacker, in no mood for clemency, swept it aside contemptuously and ran him through without a second thought. Napier withdrew his sword. It took a great deal of strength. The blade had penetrated with such force it had gone into the trunk of the tress behind the man and stuck firmly into the bark. No longer supported by the blade, the victim fell forward onto his face without a sound. Thereafter peace and quiet reigned over the scene of battle.

    Napier stood and listened, straining his eyes to see in the darkness, there was not a sound. Even the groaning had ceased. Having satisfied him self that all of the attackers had been accounted for he sheathed his sword and began to take stock of the situation. Who were these men? Were they robbers waiting for a traveller, hoping to steal whatever he had on his person? If that were the case they were unlucky, he never carried anything of value with him and had nothing worth stealing. One thing for certain, they had picked the wrong traveller and paid heavily for their crime.

Curiosity prompted him to drag the one he had pinned to the tree over to a patch of moonlight, turning him over he received a shock that made him doubt his own senses. There revealed was the face of a boy no more than fifteen or sixteen years of age, a face that told with absolute certainty the identity of his other assailants. He did not have to look. He knew there could be no doubt of their identified. The three were always together. Youths barely approaching manhood, born of wealthy influential families, wanting for nothing, with money to spend they wore expensive clothes, always up to date and the height of fashion, strutting through the social scene of the city, they squandered their time in a relentless pursuit of pleasure.

Napier had first noticed them when, much to the amusement of the social elite, they had taken a fancy to Alexandrine, hanging on to her every word and following her around like besotted puppies. He and Alexandrine in happier times had often amused themselves by inventing ways to see how far they would go to appease her slightest whim, an emotionally cruel ploy maybe. but at the time it had appeared to be little more than a joke to pass the time – but why this? Why attack him like a band of cutthroats? Surely they must have been aware of the dangers of attacking one such as he, a man equipped with deadly skills in weaponry? Even in the dark they must have known the potential peril they faced. They had no need of money, their parents supplied them with all they could ever want and he to the best of his knowledge had done them no real harm.

A quick check on the others confirmed his worst fears: they were all there. The three of them, dressed in their finery and all dead. His blade had done its work well. How could he have known? To him in the darkness they were an unknown band of robbers. He had no choice but to defend himself. If they had identified themselves he could have easily disarmed all three of them and sent them on their way, accompanied by a swipe across the backside with the flat of his sword. Circumstances, however, alter cases and when your fight is against faceless opponents of undetermined numbers in the darkness, mercy is a virtue you cannot afford. You have one option and that is to give no quarter, whether their rich and powerful parents would see it that way, he was certain they would not.

There was nothing he could do, he would have to leave them where they lay and hope their deaths would remain a mystery. Hopefully the blame would fall on highway robbers chancing on the boys during some nocturnal adventure. Such things were not unknown on the dangerous lonely roads of France. Somewhere his hat had fallen off, he must retrieve it and also any other evidence of is presence at the scene. Then no one could connect him to these events.

Suddenly he froze, the sound of a horse snorting through its nostrils – could it be someone else on the same errand, an extra attacker he had not seen? Hoof beats, a horse silhouetted against the moonlit sky rearing up as its rider jerked the reins savagely, pulling its head to one side in order to turn and ride away. A slight figure – obviously a woman – her velvet cloak billowing in the wind. She thrashed the animal with her whip and galloped away, disappearing into the night.

Napier could not see her features but he knew without a shadow of doubt the rider could only be Alexandrine d'Amblimont. With such an image clearly visible on the horizon, signalling her presence on the scene, all the answers to Napier's questions presented themselves with crystal clarity. She had used her influence over these besotted youths to take advantage of their naivety and lack of worldly sense, thus persuading them to wreak her vengeance for her, with a ruthless determination to punish a hated foe she had sent these boys unprepared – and without knowing the risks they took – to their deaths. This was the final proof if ever he needed it. Their relationship could never be retrieved and he had made a deadly enemy who would be always looking to punish him in whatever ways she could find.

One thing he knew with absolute certainty: she could never expose him over this episode without convicting herself out of her own mouth. Therefore, with a heavy heart and sorrow for an act forced upon him, which he had no control over, he checked the area to ensure he had left nothing to convict him and then left the bodies to be found in the morning and a mystery for the authorities to make of what they will.

11

The Lady Gambler's Weapon of Choice

Victoire Faubert was not in the best of moods. It was not that she was going somewhere she had no wish to go to – quite the reverse, in fact. An evening of cards at her favourite gaming house was normally her most pleasurable evening's entertainment, but tonight she had other things on her mind. She had certain niggling concerns regarding Napier; he had not been to see her since the duel. She was well aware, of course, that he blamed her over the perceived deceit over her attitude to Alexandrine. She had discussed it with her husband and his considered opinion was they should leave well alone. Napier would forgive and forget. Eventually things would settle down and in the fullness of time all would return to normal, but Victoire was not so sure. She missed Napier's company and had looked forward to his afternoon visits when they would sit drinking chocolate, talking and gossiping like the mother and son they had become.

There had been times when he would escort her to the gaming houses, standing behind her chair where he could watch her play. She particularly enjoyed his watching because now for the first time there was someone who understood her skills and realised her ability to win came from her knowledge and intellect and not from the phenomenal luck of a pleasant, popular, but seemingly frivolous, empty-headed personality.

The fact that people perceived her in this way was her own doing and she did all she could to foster this image, but it was nice to know that there was an appreciative watcher who understood and admired her system of play. Many a smile and knowing look would pass between them when a prodigious feat of memory over a sequence of cards would produce a win, applauded as sheer luck by other players and the watching company. Now, however she would have to play the life and soul of the party socialite despite the niggling worries at the back of her mind. Her friends would expect it of her because that was the only person they knew. She could not allow them to think there was something amiss as that would lead to suspicions being aroused with the possibility of creating a dangerous situation for Napier.

Victoire Faubert was an amazing woman in lots of ways and without question she was nobody's fool. Although she did not have the same complex ways of gathering information as her husband enjoyed, she had her own methods and was equally well informed – because of her social standing, she was on chattering terms with everyone who is anyone in the social elite of Paris. Therefore trading on her reputation as a frivolous woman with no ideas or opinions of her own, apart from fashion and enjoyment, it put her in a unique position where no one thought it necessary to put a guard on their tongue in her presence. Many a state secret would be leaked within her hearing in the belief it would be safe to do so because she did not have the wit to understand. A very big mistaken belief where a woman like Victoire was concerned. A slip of the tongue here, an overheard sentence there, her astute and keenly logical brain would put two and two together and, unfailingly, she would come up with four.

It was these very powers of reasoning that gave her cause to worry about Napier. The death of the three boys had been the talk of the city. The wealth and power of their families made it a major topic of gossip. The general consensus of opinion centred on them being set upon by thieves or had died when some sort of nocturnal adventure had gone wrong. Everyone knew they were always up to some form of mischief or other. However Victoire thought differently. She immediately rejected the being set on by thieves theory. Everything these boys possessed was expensive – clothes, weapons, personal effects, horses and saddles – thieves would have taken everything. All they had was saleable. After all what would be the point if not for profit? Thieves by definition would have striped it all and left nothing but the bodies. The bodies had been left intact; nothing had been taken. Also robbers rarely used swords. They required expert training and skill in their use – yet, without question, swords had been used. Each one of the boys had a sword in his hand trying to defend himself but each one had been efficiently disposed of, expertly run through with a single thrust. Whoever did this was a swordsman without doubt, which again effectively rules out thieves who would have done their work with cudgels making a much more clumsy job of their butchery. Plus they would have been careful not to damage clothing; which did not sell well with a sword thrust through it. Thus ran the reasoning of Victoire's razor keen logic. Additionally, there were two other factors which when put together came to a very obvious conclusion. One, she was well aware of Napier's long and lonely rides, and she was also aware his normal route home passed through the very wood where the boys were found; two, Alexandrine d'Amblimont had returned to Versailles the day the bodies were discovered – therefore all the points came together. Victoire ticked them off in her mind. Unquestionably, the killings had been carried out by an expert swordsman – Napier was such a one, arguably the best in Paris. Also he would have rode through the wood that very evening, Mademoiselle d'Amblimont was a dangerous and vindictive enemy who hated Napier and would stop at nothing to inflict her revenge on him and she was the one person who wielded a tremendous influence over the boys. Using her feminine wiles she was able to control the naïve youths, body and soul. Victoire had seen with her own eyes the way they hovered around her and how she had used them to do her slightest bidding. Possessed of this knowledge it did not take a genius to work out reason plot and eventual result. What worried her about the whole business was did anyone else have the information she had and would they be able to put two and two together and come up with the same answer. Napier had to be warned to be on his guard but there was little to do but wait. It would not be a good idea to leave. He must stay in the city and act normally, giving the appearance that all was well.; to disappear now would look very suspicious and could set tongues wagging.

Sitting back in her coach, shaking a little as it trundled over the cobbles, she reflected that she had not wanted to come out this evening but a commitment in the form of a large dressmaker's bill made it necessary. Not that she was short of money, Françoise was generous with her allowance and would have happily paid the bill if he had known, but Victoire liked to have a measure of independence and took a pride in the financing of her own bills, hence this evening's coach trip into the centre of Paris. Her thoughts were interrupted by the coach coming to a stop and the coachman opening the door and folding down the steps; she climbed out, assisted by the servant whom she told to wait with the coach as she expected to be no more than a couple of hours, just long enough to win sufficient funds to pay off her dressmaker.

The gaming house was warm and well lit and, as usual, fairly full. Victoire moved elegantly through the players in a rustle of silks and satin, greeting the odd friend as she passed. Eventually she found a place to sit at one of the tables, settled down and began to play. Almost immediately, as was her custom, she began to win steadily.

Presently, three strangers approached the table and stood watching. They were all young officers of German or Prussian nationality, slightly drunk and in full uniform. They were obviously part of a mercenary group attached to the French army training at the Ècole Royal Militaire, probably aristocrats, either impoverished or younger sons who were not in line for an inheritance and therefore earning their living via the military. Eventually their leader, the older of the three and their superior either by rank or by social standing, his station made rather obvious by the fawning servitude the others affected towards him, enquired quite courteously if he might join the table. As he did so one of the others, perhaps a little more drunk than his companion, spoke to him in German, reminding him they had not come to gamble but to savour the other delights of the city. The soldier replied in the same tongue: "Don't be too anxious to be away, a few minutes spent here at the table will be long enough for me to empty the contents of this silly old woman's purse. The bordellos will be open all night. We will not have to spend our own money and she will be paying for all of us – so be patient while I take her for all she has." He smiled politely as he sat down and Victoire for her part smiled back, simpering behind her fan, treating the soldier to that girlish laugh of hers. In no way did she indicate that she spoke fluent German and had understood every word as clearly as if he had spoken in fluent French. She folded her fan and used it to tap him playfully on his arm, and she fluttered her eyelids while bidding him to sit down.

"Welcome, my friend," she said, "I shall be delighted to play cards with a handsome young man such as you." The soldier gave a knowing wink to his companions who turned away to hide smug smiles, confident in their leader's ability to finance their debauchery. He clearly fancied himself as a card player and had no doubt that his opponent presented little opposition to a player of his stature.

Their smiles, however, quickly turned to grim scowls as the

pile of money in front of Victoire began to grow steadily, and the soldier, who was no match for her skilful play despite his initial confidence, began to lose more and more of their months' pay – money they had pooled to spend in the pursuit of pleasure squandering their leave in the flesh spots of the city. The more he lost, the more reckless he became and the more his conviction grew that his luck would change. Victoire at the start of the game very quickly came to the conclusion that her opponent had little or no skill with the cards, despite his apparent unshakeable belief in his own expertise. It was this stupidity plus his general attitude of arrogance, coupled with her own mood of depressed anxiety that decided her to break the self-imposed rule of a lifetime and take this overloud boastful braggart for every penny he had. Normally she would have deprived him of a little, laughingly state 'how lucky she had been', make her excuses then move on to another gaming house, thus preserving her reputation as a lucky but frivolous gambler. In all truth she knew without question she was his intellectual superior and would have little problem in teaching him the lesson he so richly deserved. He however appeared to have difficulty in grasping the fact that he was being financially stripped by a mere woman, obligingly continued to pour his own and his horrified colleagues' money into Victoire's waiting purse. Eventually the last Louie was pushed across the board with trembling fingers. Victoire rose from the table with her substantial winnings, giving the company one of her beaming smiles, she thanked them all for an interesting and most enjoyable evening and left the room giggling like a young girl.

The soldiers did not answer; their crestfallen hangdog attitudes told a story mirrored in their glazed eyes. They could not believe the fate they had intended for this helpless, fluffy, middle-aged woman had descended with a crash right on top of their own heads. Victoire exited the club into the chilly night air. The alley was dark and full of shadows regardless of the flickering glow of the streetlights. Everywhere was quiet and despite the proximity of the club the dark shadows could be quite threatening for a woman alone, so she was quite glad she had asked her coachman to wait and was pleased to see the outline of her coach standing in the road. Wrapping her cloak around her she hurried towards it, only to be surrounded by three figures rushing after her out of the night. Even in the dark she recognised her recent companions of the card table.

"Good evening, gentlemen," she said, affecting composure she did not feel. "Can I be of any assistance?"

"Don't give me any of that Parisian gentility nonsense!" said their leader, all pretence at politeness and manners abandoned, to be replaced with the rude coarse roughness of a soldier. "You know very well what we want, you old witch. We want our money back and quickly or it will be the worse for you."

Victoire could see her coachman start to climb down from his seat where he had sat wrapped up in his coat and scarf, his hat pulled well down against the cold. No doubt he had seen what was happening and was about to render assistance. Victoire pushed past the men and walked quickly to the coach, at the same time ordering her man to stay where he was. She was well aware he would stand little chance against the three soldiers, therefore it made sense for him to remain at his post. There he would be able to drive quickly away as soon as she was on board; however, the man, showing admirably courage but little sense, continued with his first action and approached the group saying, "Are these men troubling you, madame? Can I be of any assistance?"

The words were no sooner out of his mouth than one of the men stepped forward, drawing his sword and reversing the blade hit him on the side of the head with the heavy brass hilt. No one could withstand such a blow; the coachman fell to the ground not knowing what hit him. Totally ignoring the stricken man the trio bundled Victoire into the coach and the leader climbed up onto the box and whipped up the horses. She struggled at first but soon realised she was helpless sitting between the two powerful soldiers; one of them pushed her roughly back into the seat with a curse and a warning to behave. Having satisfied himself that his victim was now under control he informed her of their intention to rob her of her winnings, and in a tone of voice that implied a threat rather than a promise he stated that if she did not give them too much trouble they would leave her unharmed somewhere outside the city.

Victoire sat back in her seat and tried to think. She had no illusions regarding their intentions. Their actions might have been fuelled by drink and committed without thought on the spur of the moment but she knew, as they also must have known, that having done the deed they could not allow her to live and inform on them – military law would have them in front of a firing squad – but how could she escape from this one? The situation appeared hopeless. It was all she could do to remain in her seat: the coach was travelling so fast over the cobbles, swaying from side to side, the passengers were shaken like peas in a bucket. The noise made by the steel-rimmed wheels and the drumming hooves made thinking impossible, she could only hope that something would happen to give her a chance to escape. It was a forlorn hope. The situation was dire and well she knew it; her life hung by a thread. These men would drive out into the countryside, find an isolated spot, knock her over the head, bury her and return to their barracks as though nothing had happened and no one any the wiser. She would just become another missing person in a city of many mysteries.

Victoire had not been the only one with a troubled mind that evening. Napier also had much to occupy his troubled thoughts. His enforced despatching of the three youths had been totally unexpected and he regretted it deeply, but the certain knowledge that Alexandrine had sent them to kill him and that they had been laying in wait to carry out that very purpose had been flooding his mind since the event and he could not stop thinking about it. He did not blame himself. He had merely acted in self-defence in the dark with no knowledge of who his attackers were, but whether he could convince the authorities of his innocence was a different matter; given the power and influence of the parents, he doubted he would even get a trial. Alexandrine! How could she do that to him? Her hatred must be beyond reason and certainly within the realms of madness.

Sitting at home that evening, his mind in a turmoil, he could not settle and certainly did not want to socialise; therefore he decided a walk would be the best way to stabilise his troubled thoughts. Wandering aimlessly without plan or purpose his path took him through the deserted street where shadows thrown by lamps and lighted windows would normally have made him alert to the possible dangers lurking there. Tonight he was too wrapped up in himself to consider the perils skulking in the dark corners of a dangerous city.

Suddenly, having just turned a corner, he became aware of noises and a scuffle occurring down the far end of the street. In the darkness and at a distance the scene was not clear but instinctively he knew the coach was one owned by the Fauberts, and that the woman being handled so roughly was Victoire. He began to run; as he drew closer he could see the prone body of the coachman on the floor. Straining every muscle he hurled himself down the street but to no avail he was just too far away, by the time he had covered the distance the horses had been whipped up and the coach disappeared at a speed too fast for human legs to catch it. Napier paused just for long enough to check the groaning coachman. He was all right, and attempting to sit up, but without doubt he would end up with a very sore head for a few days. Napier's first priority now was Victoire; he must somehow get ahead of that coach. Fortunately he knew the road it had taken, and knew that it went round in a long loop. If he was quick, and ran swiftly down the back streets, there was a slim chance he could get ahead of it. Already an idea was forming in his mind. There was a section of the road where a low stone bridge carried a footpath between the houses and it formed a narrow archway which the coach would have to pass under. If he could be on top of that bridge before the coach arrived, he stood a chance of getting on board; a slim chance he had to take. It presented the only opportunity he had of saving Victoire from whatever fate had befallen her, but he would have to run as he had never run before, as though he had the very devil at his heels.

Fortunately he knew the area well and, throwing all caution to the winds, he ran like a man demented down the narrow, dark and cluttered alleys with no thought for his own safety; knowing his only chance to save Victoire was to reach the bridge before the coach passed under the archway. Running wildly and at full pelt he paused to snatch a length of wood left leaning against a wall – he had no positive use for it but a wise man collects his weapons as he sees them, and maybe he could use it as a form of lance or spear to unseat the driver in case he did not get above the coach in time. Anyway, it was better than nothing; he would figure out a use for it when the opportunity arrived. Holding the wood under his arm in the manner of an old fashioned knight tilting at the lists, he could see the narrow archway, and already he could hear the sound of a coach travelling at speed. It had to be his coach. He had just made it in time. Now he was near enough to see its outline silhouetted against the street light. There was no time to think or plan, he had to get on to that raised walkway. There was no other option; using the thin wood as a pole he vaulted, forcing himself up with all the strength in his arms. His knees scraped the top of the low stone rampart and he felt a searing pain as the rough stone blocks grazed the skin of his leg. He landed heavily on the hard unyielding cobbles, but he was there, on top and above the coach. Time was running out on him already as the horses were passing through the archway below. Leaping to his feet, ignoring his damaged leg, he threw himself to the edge and dropped the piece of wood across the opening to the arch seconds before the driver passed below him – the timing was perfect. The fortuitously gathered prop dropped across the driver's knees and wedged itself across the uprights of the bridge. The driver had not slowed down for the narrow opening and paid the price for his actions: the speed of the impact snapped the thin wood like a carrot, but not before the man, totally unprepared for such an attack, was swept helplessly off the back, landing with a sickening thud on the roadway as the coach continued on its way.

Napier did not waste time observing the results of his handiwork, he rushed to the other parapet and flung himself over the top – a reckless and dangerous act without doubt, but it paid off. He landed on top of the vehicle just as it cleared the archway, managing to grasp the luggage rack to prevent himself being bounced on to the roadway and suffering the same fate as the driver. Pausing for mere seconds to catch his breath, he scrambled into the driver's seat, put his foot on the brake lever and hauled on the reins, bringing the team to a halt with hooves striking sparks off the cobbles, as the frightened animals, sweating and snorting through distended nostrils, fought for grip on the uneven roadway.

Napier leapt down off the box, drawing his sword as he did so. A very fortunate action, as it turned out. He had wrenched open the door expecting to see a tangle of bodies thrown forward by the sudden halt, but his opponents were made of sterner stuff; trained at the academy, they were used to taking instant action. As Napier flung open the door the first one was upon him, followed swiftly by his companion, both wielding their heavy cavalry sabres in a way that said they were used to using them. Suddenly confronted by blow after blow with the heavy blades Napier was forced to use all his skill to parry the attacks, glancing the strikes aside, unable to use equivalent force to oppose them for fear the strong solid weapons would break the fine slender blade of his tiny court sword. It was a weapon barely adequate for such a brutal conflict, and he was painfully aware that a broken blade in this battle would be fatal.

Napier, however, had not spent a lifetime as a pupil of the sword for nothing. He retreated slowly, allowing the men to force him back while he concentrated on defending and reviewing his battle plan. At that moment, his chances of riposting were nil; his fighting instinct told him he could parry the one and riposte with an almost certain kill, but the blows were coming so thick and fast, so there could be no question of parrying the second before he was cut in two. The vital seconds taken to withdraw his blade from the pierced body would be his undoing, it was all he could do to protect himself from the flurry of blows aimed at him, all without question intended to kill. Jacques had always taught him to regard fencing as a battle of minds as much as physical activity, and Napier was a thinking fencer; his mind was reviewing every aspect of the battle. These two were able swordsmen, well trained and battle-hardened, but they were soldiers, cavalrymen trained to fight on horseback and to military discipline. There was an almost parade ground rhythm to their actions and you could almost visualise the barked orders: *one two, one two, one two.* If he could rearrange the cadence of the fight he might stand a chance. Already they were beginning to tire. Now was the time to put his plan into action. Slowly he began to hold his parry just that split second longer on the one side and gradually they began to fall into the trap. The parade ground rhythm began to change until, without realising it, they began to strike separately at their target. Now was Napier's chance, before they became aware of what was happening; he parried the one but deliberately missed the second, swinging his body to one side to avoid the strike. He got away with it, but it was very close, too close for comfort, in fact – the razor-sharp sabre slashed down the side of his sleeve, cutting off a piece of his turned back cuff. The man, taken by surprise that he had not been parried, hesitated for a split second and thereby tolled his own death knell. Napier without pausing saw his opportunity and flicked his blade across the undefended throat. The needle-sharp point opened up a gash from ear to ear and the defeated swordsman dropped his weapon; clasping his hand to his throat, he fell forward, gasping for breath, as his lifeblood spurted through his fingers.

One down, one to go; Napier knew the battle was his. He could dispose of the other man as he wished, but he claimed victory too soon. The soldier, seeing his companion disposed of and lying in his own blood, had the fire of battle rekindled in his veins, with a wild fearsome cry he hurled himself at his opponent slashing away like a demented demon. Napier was forced back knocked off his feet by the impetuous attack, but as he fell he had the presence of mind to place his point in line, and the man impaled himself on the blade. Napier, laying on his back with the heavy body on top of him, still held on to his sword beneath the weight, he could clearly see the blade sticking out of the man's back, having passed clean through the body.

Suddenly a dark shadow loomed over him, there to his horror stood the soldier he had swept off the coach, now recovered from the stunning impact of his fall, despite the blood oozing from a cut on his temple. On his face was a demonic expression of hatred and above his head a glittering cavalry sabre was poised to strike a fatal blow. Napier was hopelessly trapped, pinned down by his opponent's body, his sword arm grasping a weapon he could not withdraw. There was little he could do but to make the futile gesture of shielding his head with his free hand, a pointless gesture against such a blade: it would take off his arm and split his skull down to his teeth with a single blow. This was it; he was totally helpless. He could do little but wait for the end, which would swiftly come.

Strangely, the end did not come. The blade remained poised,

the expression of hatred softened and faded, the eyes seemed to glaze and look upward showing the whites. The glittering blade, about to arc downwards and snuff out Napier's life like an extinguished candle, fell from lifeless fingers and tumbled to the ground with a metallic clatter on the hard cobbles. With a twitch of the mouth that looked suspiciously like a smile the soldier's knees gave way and he crumbled to a heap on the ground, lying motionless alongside Napier who only seconds before he had intended to dispatch without a moment's hesitation.

Napier was dumbfounded. Miraculously he had escaped certain death, but how? He had heard no shot or flash of a blade; the man had collapsed for no apparent reason. He was not a church-going man, but certainly divine intervention did flash across his confused mind. Then, as he gathered his scattered senses, he saw a figure standing just behind the spot where the man had stood. It was Victoire, looking slightly dishevelled. Her elegant hat normally precisely tilted at a fashionable angle now hung on crazily to the back of her head; her mouth set in a determined expression, hands on her hips, she stood there surveying the pile of bodies like a hunter standing triumphant over her prey. When she spoke it was with a mocking reprimand: "Shame on you, Napier," she said. "Where are your manners? Don't you normally stand in the presence of a Lady?"

Napier, once again in control of his senses, pushed the limp body to one side, jumped to his feet, put his foot against the man and with a mighty heave extracted his sword to stand instantly in the *on-guard* position, looking for further assaults.

Victoire laughed and said, "It's over, Napier. Sheath your sword, between the two of us we have accounted for all three of them."

Napier did as he was bid, and with a questioning expression on his face put into the words the confusion still buzzing through his mind.

"But how did you do it? Without a weapon, how were you

able to drop him so quickly and so efficiently? He was about to strike the killer blow, even if you had shot him he would still have had the time to get in the final strike."

Victoire made a face and in her deceptive little girl voice declared, "You men, with your talk of battle, your swords and flintlocks, think there is no other way to fight but hacking away with a blade or blasting with powder and shot, but we women have subtle but just as effective methods."

So saying she bent forward and pulled something out of the man's side, it was a hat pin with a mother of pearl and silver head – the same pin that she always wore regardless of which of her many hats she favoured on the day, the one consistency was always that pin to hold it onto her head. At that moment Napier realised that this trait something that in the past he had always considered an eccentricity was far more than just a fad on the part of this very remarkable woman: it was a very effective defensive weapon! She had thrust the long needle below the ribs and upwards into the heart, killing the swordsman instantly before he was able to despatch the helpless Napier with his sabre. The man was dead before he hit the ground.

"Come, Napier," she said, showing a flash of the steely efficient Victoire beneath the veneer, "let us find my coachman and go home, I am sure a cup of hot chocolate and a glass of brandy will not go amiss."

Leaving the bodies as they lay for the night watch to find, Napier drove the coach retracing its route at a more sedate pace until they found the coachman sitting on the side of the road holding his head. They helped him into the coach still dazed and protesting doggedly that it was his place to do the driving and he should be allowed to do his job, but Victoire would have none of it. She kept him in the coach and tended his wounds as best she could. Napier for his part sat on top of the coach, took the reins and headed the horses at a slow trot back to the Faubert house.

Alone on the box in the night air Napier was able to marshal his thoughts and come to some sensible conclusions. Looking down on the sleek backs of the horses pulling easy and strong on the traces, he reflected that he was not much of a driver, having never driven a coach before, but the horses seemed to know what they were doing and were heading in the right direction. With what little light there was gleaming on the polished brass of their harness they seemed so confident of finding their way home along an often travelled route so familiar to them that he gave them their head and let them get on with it, with just the occasional flick of the reins to encourage them. Now that he had gained confidence in his unfamiliar task his thoughts turned back to the events of the night. He knew the watch would not ask too many questions regarding the bodies. It was not uncommon for groups of soldiers to quarrel drunkenly of an evening, particularly if they were foreign soldiers training at the academy where nationality disputes could lead to trouble. Maybe it was the night air, or maybe it was the steady rhythmic clopping of the horses hooves coupled with the rumble of the wheels and the quiet steady creak of wooden coach work and leather harness, but Napier began to get things into perspective. He had been unfair to the Fauberts. His friendship with Alexandrine had not been of their choosing; in fact, they had actively discouraged it. Victoire in fact had been completely blameless and now he owed his life to her impromptu action with improvised weaponry. Now he felt he was going home and looking forward to renewing his friendship with Victoire. As for Françoise, he was still wary of him, but slowly trust was developing and maybe he was on the way to understanding the complex character of the man. Whatever, he was now ready to let bygones be bygones, forget the past and get on with his new life, whatever the future might bring.

12

The Return of a Legacy

Time, they say, heals all wounds, but it also has a way of changing people and Napier was no exception. He was unrecognisable as the ragged urchin of his birth and a world away from the youth who had fled the tragedy of Mulgrove Manor. In appearance he was the typical wealthy Parisian: suave in manner and slightly haughty. His clothes, chosen with infinite care – although not quite so flamboyant as his peers – were always at the forefront of fashion, and his association with Victoire Faubert had refined his manners to a point where he could fit into any company, comfortably conversing over a range of subjects, moving easily through the spectrum of talk, from the pointless chit chat of the affluent, uneducated to the intellectual and serious discussions of the leading political and scientific minds of the day.

He moved with consummate ease through all the levels of society, a familiar figure who inspired both respect and fear. A man pointed out with awed whispers as a dangerous and deadly duellist, though none suspected he was paid to be so by Françoise Faubert and even they who suspected it might be so were wise not to voice to their suspicions. Even his facial appearance had changed; gone were the boyish good looks, the honest open expression to be replaced by the hardness and lines etched there by experiences gained on the harsh traumatic fields of the duel.

Nowhere does a man undergo the heady mixture of excitement, fear, exultation and sadness than during the intense atmosphere of a single conflict, and Napier had endured it more than most men. Not that it worried him much, after the collapse of his relationship with Alexandrine and the mental anguish involved, he had adopted a 'what will be will be' attitude to life. Even death itself he approached with this cavalier attitude, his conclusion being that Fate will guide your steps rigidly regardless of how hard you fight to oppose her will. For him it had always been so. It seemed her guiding hand had pushed him on from the stinking mud of the Thames where he was born, then his stumbling steps to the countryside and Mulgrove Manor and his first fateful meeting with Jacques Gerard, right through the events leading to his flight to Paris and on to what he had become today. He saw the hand of Fate every step of the way. Small wonder then that he saw his future rigidly mapped out in front of him, totally inescapable and set waiting for him regardless of how hard he might try to escape it.

The accumulation of wealth was not an issue with Napier. Apart from his allowance from Françoise Faubert and the secret cash payments for services rendered in the dawn light of the duelling field, he had the same attitude as his mentor Victoire. If he needed money he would win it a little at a time on the gaming tables and, though he would readily admit he could never hope to attain the level of expertise she possessed, he was still a match for most of them he met across the green baize.

Thus his life rolled on aimless but exciting, happy in a way and sometimes exhilarating, but most of the time rather pointless. Much of his time was spent where he felt at home and comfortable: at the fencing school, passing on his skills to the pupils. In a strange way he felt that this was what Jacques would want him to do and the old man was there in spirit, approving of the fact he was giving his time and expertise, passing on the knowledge the old fencing master had worked so hard to instil in him. In this way if Jacques' knowledge was passed on then the memory of Jacques would continue to live, and that was what Napier wanted more than anything.

Thus it was as his alter ego, Napier Feray, nephew of Victoire Faubert, fencing master, duellist and gambler, that he entered a gambling house one fateful evening – not necessarily for recreational purposes but more with the intention of supplementing his income to pay off some household bills. As was his custom, he adhered faithfully to Victoire's doctrine of *'win a little then move on'* thus avoiding the possibility of his opponents realising his winnings were gained by skill and knowledge and not luck, and thereby ensuring a ready supply of willing victims. Everything as usual went according to plan. Sensing the time had come to move on, he collected his winnings, made a polite excuse and with profound apologies prepared to move to another venue. Rising to his feet he was about to leave when he glanced up and saw a scene at the far end of the room which made his muscles tighten, and a feeling of hatred and anger rise within him.

The image he saw across the room cancelled out everything around him, almost like looking down a corridor with all the surrounding activity blurring into the sidelines with the scene at the end standing out with stark clarity, almost like a charade played out for him alone. There, across the room, ignoring the colourful bustle of the crowded tables, his gaze focussed on the entrance door where a man had appeared, surrounded by his fawning entourage. The man was the Fifth Duke of Mulgrove, Napier's sworn and hated enemy, the man who had hounded him across two countries and whose father had been the direct cause of the death of Jacques Gerard. He was older and thicker about the body than Napier recalled, but it was he without question. He looked more like his father now, with the long thin nose giving him the cruel hawk-like appearance Napier remembered so well. There were other distinguishing features he had not seen before, although he was well aware of their origins, for example, the disfiguring scar down the side of his face. Obviously he had not been rescued quickly enough to prevent the fire from having a lick at him and the sleeve of his elegant jacket ended in a left hand encased in a black velvet glove, which could not disguise the fact it was little more than a rigid, useless claw. Napier reflected grimly that a blow with a morning star does not do much for the flexibility of the fingers.

He moved across to the far corner of the room in order to consider the situation. Here he could wait his chance and slip out quietly when they moved away from the door. He did not think the duke's presence had anything to do with the hunt for him. Surely by now they would have considered him to be well gone to some foreign clime.

Suddenly he saw something that made him go hot and cold all over, something that made a cold grim sense of fatality come over him and gripped his very soul. There, hanging on the duke's hip, was a sword. Nothing unusual there – most of the men in the room carried a sword of some sort. However this was no ordinary sword; Napier would have recognised it anywhere and at any distance. It was Jacques' sword! The one he had sacrificed when he had so reluctantly placed it in the cart as a decoy to delay the hunt. So, it had not been lost, and here was this man with the audacity to wear it and claim it as his own! Now all the past events of his youth come flooding back surging into his memory, bringing a searing anger, and he knew with absolute certainty that from this day he would stop running and hiding; he would cease to be Napier Feray and face the world as he really was – Napier Gerard, regardless of the consequences.

Now that he had made his fateful decision he squared his shoulders and began to mingle with the crowd. Gradually he moved closer to the duke's table and finally stood watching the play directly facing his quarry. The duke neither looked nor noticed another face in the crowd. When a chair became vacant

Napier enquired if he might join the game, with an affirmative answer he sat down fatalistically expecting to be denounced the moment he did so. The duke barely glanced at him. As an aristocrat he rarely noticed people and never looked at servants. All the years they had spent together in the Salle he had never looked at the lad he had considered as nothing more than a piece of equipment to be used and disposed of at will. Therefore it was not surprising that looking at Napier so vastly changed in appearance and persona he did not recognise the man whom he had ordered his minions to catch and chase so persistently and with such vicious intent, the man he hated so intensely for inflicting on him the crippling disfigurement he now displayed, and now they were face to face.

Ironically he did not recognise him. All he saw before him was a man who he perceived as not of his social standing. Normally he would not have given him the time of day; however, he was bored with the company of his entourage and was only too aware they always let him win, therefore he welcomed the possibility of a challenge which this stranger presented. Thus he was prepared to stretch a point, and just this once play with a man who was not his social equal.

Napier for his part quickly realised his disguise had not been penetrated and decided to play out life's game to a finish and cope with whatever the fates decreed was to be his future, for better or for worse. As the game progressed the other gamblers dropped out one by one leaving the two old adversaries as the only players, the duke still blissfully unaware that the man quietly relieving him of his money was the quarry he had hunted so relentlessly since the days of their youth. Napier had realised as soon as they began to play that the duke, although a powerful aristocrat and a fine swordsman, was a very average card player, one he could beat whenever he chose to do so. It would give him the greatest pleasure to strip him of every Louie he had on his person. This he proceeded to do with a single-minded determination.

As card followed card the duke's money began to transfer to Napier's side of the table. Although he had initially welcomed a challenge as a relief from boredom he had not expected to be so comprehensively beaten; as a man always surrounded by toadies the duke was a man who always expected to win, therefore it was not surprising that he began to get more and more angry and frustrated.

Now at last he began to look directly at his opponent who he now found to be perplexingly familiar. However his attention was brought swiftly back to the game as with a triumphant flourish Napier turned the final card and deprived him of his last coin. Immediately the duke called for a marker, insisting with a promissory note he be given the chance to win his money back. Like all gamblers he believed he had been beaten by bad luck and, given the chance, his luck would change. He had failed to recognise, as most people who play the tables fail to recognise, the skill and expertise ranged against him to bring about his downfall.

Looking back Napier could never say, or understand why he did what he did, why he did not take the note and deprive his enemy of a fortune and still preserve his anonymity. Obviously his disguise was perfect and had not been penetrated; to stay as he was, represented freedom from pursuit for the rest of his life. The icing on the cake was the chance to strike a financial blow at his enemy without his enemy knowing whom it was who had struck it.

But the sword was there across the table, Jacques' sword, his sword, his legacy, the only link he had to his father apart from his memories. He could not allow it to remain in the hands of such a man. The sword spoke to him and demanded he threw all caution to the winds, his honour was at stake – Jacques' honour was at stake – his father would not have been proud of him skulking behind the charade of a strutting popinjay in order to preserve his anonymity.

Napier had made up his mind, he could not and would not continue this deception, he was Napier Gerard and no one else, his father had given the name to him and he had been extremely proud when he had received it, whatever the consequences he would carry it proudly to the jaws of death itself if needs be.

Looking fearlessly into the eyes of the duke he pronounced the words that would commit him to the wiles of fate regardless of the consequences.

"No, your promissory note is not good enough for me, but I will stake all of my winnings against my father's sword, a weapon you have neither the integrity or the right to wear!"

The duke looked startled at first. He could not believe the audacity of this upstart to refuse his marker. Was he not one of the richest and most powerful men in England? No one had ever dared to oppose him in this way before. Then, slowly, the truth began to sink in. At first he had not fully comprehended the full meaning of his opponent's statement, *'my father's sword!'* The duke as much as any man knew the recent history of the weapon he wore, he had taken it as the spoils of war, a small compensation for what he had suffered. He was also aware that the sword was unique. Even he with all his wealth would not have been able to buy such a weapon. His own father had tried many times to buy it from Jacques but to no avail. He had even attempted to have it reproduced by the very best sword makers but none could quite match the materials and workmanship. When it came into his hands he had paid the reward without quibble and claimed it as his own, a practical work of art, he knew no one would ever be able to match. Now, those words echoed through his brain, *'my father's sword!'* No – it could not be and yet it must be. For the first time he really looked at the man facing him, when recognition dawned he stood up knocking over his chair as he did so.

"Well, well, well," he repeated the words savouring the feelings of triumph and satisfaction that surged up inside him,

"Napier Gerard in the flesh. I have found you at last. I must admit you are to be congratulated; I would not have recognised you. It would appear you have achieved a miracle by turning a sow's ear into a silk purse. Such deception will not save you, however, the gallows awaits for all murdering scum such as yourself."

Turning to his entourage he shouted, "Seize him, he is a wanted murderer! He killed not only my father but his own father as well."

Napier had anticipated this. "Wait!" he said, holding up his hand palm forwards towards the advancing toadies. "I have broken no law in France. You have no authority here. Do you think an English aristocrat, not the most popular personage as far as the French are concerned, would be able to drag me in chains across half of France. I think not and I would guarantee to give you a considerable amount of trouble. I have a much simpler solution."

So saying he rose to his feet, smoothly slipping a pair of leather gloves from his waistband as he did so, before anyone could move he delivered a stinging blow across the duke's face, the time-honoured ultimate insult and a direct challenge to a duel.

"You and I," he said quietly and without emotion, "will fight a duel to the death."

The duke's face went red with anger and took on a demonic expression. It was not so much the stinging pain of the blow that upset him but more the insolent audacity of this man, once a servant who dared to strike him who had once been his master. His face contorted into a mask of fury and Napier could see the clear resemblance to the Fourth Duke of Mulgrove, his father, from whom he had inherited this maniacal rage. The sight transported him back in memory to the manor where he had witnessed the same uncontrollable emotion so many times during his life under the duke's rule.

Speaking through clenched teeth, the anger still welling within him, the duke made a great effort to control himself.

"Much as it pains me to say it, you are right," he said. "You would give trouble and the French can be so uncooperative sometimes. Even if I were to get you to England they would not allow me the pleasure of hanging you myself, I would have to stand and watch someone else having the enjoyment of placing the noose around your neck. You are lowborn and I am an aristocrat; by all the rules of propriety, I should not soil my hands on you, but for you I will make an exception. It will give me the greatest pleasure to cut you into little pieces before I finally run you through, and I will do it with this sword, the one you seem to have so much affection for."

Now it was Napier's turn to feel anger, the string of insults from this man, his sworn enemy, creating a rage within him, he spat out his response;

"That is fine by me," he snapped. "My seconds will attend yours to finalise the arrangements."

"To hell with the conventions" said the duke "Do you think I would be stupid enough to allow you the time to disappear again? We will fight now! And don't expect any of the proprieties – there will be no rules. We will fight until only one of us remains standing using whatever means we have available."

By now some of Napier's friends had gathered to give support, one of them volunteered an inn he knew of with a large walled courtyard and gates that could be shut to ensure privacy. Apparently the landlord was infamous for his willingness to hire his establishment for any purpose and turn a blind eye, providing the price was right.

The courtyard proved to be more than adequate for purpose. It was spacious enough for both antagonists plus the small crowd of spectators who had followed from the gaming house, eager not to miss the spectacle they were about to witness. Napier perused the yard with a fencer's eye; the rough cobbles were wet and here and there the evidence of the presence of horses had not been cleaned up, the chances of a trip or slip were obvious –

he would have to be constantly aware of that fact – otherwise the place was perfect. The high walls gave shade all round so there would be no possibility of being manoeuvred into a position where he was facing into a dazzling sun. He was aware the duke would be prepared to use every trick in the book in order to achieve victory, he knew that in this conflict there would be no quarter asked and none given.

Acting instinctively according to the rules the seconds set out immediately pacing out the area and preparing to bring the combatants together for the conventional start. The duke would have none of it. He had already discarded his jacket and drawn his sworn and was advancing on Napier with murderous intent in his eyes, slashing at the air with his glittering blade. He obviously had no intention of wasting time with the proprieties of the duelling code.

"Come on, upstart," he screamed, "you do not have the right to fight like a gentleman. We agreed no rules so what are you waiting for?"

Napier struggled out of his coat but the duke was upon him before he could draw his sword. He had every intention of finishing it quickly, totally unconcerned about it being a honourable fight. Taken by surprise but nevertheless acting swiftly his opponent threw his jacket into the face of the lunging fencer at the same time twisting sideways just in time to avoid the vicious thrust. As he twisted he brought his bunched fist sideways and managed to inflict a blow to the side of the ear which sent his opponent sprawling onto the cobbles. This action gave him breathing space to draw his own sword. He moved towards the man on the ground, his instincts telling him to run him through there and then but his sense of fair play and ethics were too strong, plus his own experience told him to beware: a man on the ground could still be a dangerous adversary. This hesitation over the delivery of the final thrust gave his foe the chance to scramble backwards like a crab and regain his feet. The assembled spectators had cried shame on the duke for his actions. Many of them placed their hands on the hilts of their own swords expecting to join in a general melee, an event not unknown in the history of duelling when spectators or seconds found cause to disagree. Now they saw the wrong righted, they applauded Napier for his chivalry. Napier quietly cursed himself for not taking his chance while he could, after all, the duke had been the one to cast aside the rules and set the theme for the fight. He knew the duke would not afford him the same courtesy if the roles had been reversed. This one moment of gentlemanly weakness might very well have signed his death warrant.

Only now did the full realisation of his position hit him. He was fighting for his very life in a duel where dirty tricks were totally acceptable. Rules and conventions meant nothing whatsoever. Within the first few exchanges it became clear the crippling of his sword hand (he had always been a natural left hander) had no way affected the duke's prowess as a fencer. He had merely changed over to his right hand and trained himself accordingly. Napier felt a grudging admiration for the tenacity of the man. As a master he was well aware of the difficulties he would have had to overcome. Now he was as good as ever; without question the finest and most dangerous opponent he had the misfortune to face and in his heart of hearts he was not sure he had the ability to beat him. But that was defeatism and Napier was not the man to be overawed by any opponent regardless of reputation or how skilful he may appear to be. Jacques had always taught him to believe there is no such thing as an opponent who cannot be beaten. All you have to do is find his weakness and you can prevail. Unfortunately Jacques had also taught the duke and passed on the same wisdom. However there is some comfort to be derived from such knowledge if you are wise enough: knowing the way he had been taught gave him an insight into his opponent's thinking and, to a certain degree, he would be able to predict his actions.

All these thoughts and more flashed through Napier's mind as he fought to control the bewildering series of attacks by a swordsman whom he was forced to admit, was very good indeed, in fact far better than he had thought possible. The handful of spectators privileged to watch had never seen and probably would never again see swordplay such as this in their lifetime. Lunges, incredibly fast ripostes, attacks and counter attacks passed between the two combatants with unbelievable speed, almost too fast for the spectators to count or contemplate. Not one of those present would have cared to put a bet on the outcome, as neither duellist appeared to have the upper hand. As the fight continued, the flashing swords darted in and out with such speed and ferocity sparks flew from the metal when the blades made contact.

Eventually the tempo began to slow. The two swordsmen began to circle one another warily; both knew they had to find an opening, a weakness in the other's defence if they nurtured any hope of walking away from this duel alive. Napier held his sword in front of him, keeping the point in line. He looked down the length of his blade at his opponent, considering his next move. He had tried every trick in the book. Each time it had been countered. His only consolation being he knew his opponent had done the same and faced the same impasse. He must be thinking the same thoughts: *'How do I break this stalemate? How do I penetrate a defence that appears to be impassable?'* There were some tiny signs of fatigue he could read in the menacing figure slowly circling him. The duke looked like a prowling tiger about to leap; almost too late Napier understood the body language and realised that was precisely what he intended to do. With a ferocious attack the duke hurled himself forwards. Obviously he had decided he was getting nowhere with finesse, therefore brute force could be the answer to his problem. Napier parried the attack but was unable to prevent the heavy body from crashing into him, taking advantage of the *corps a corps*, his opponent attempted to slice the cutting edge of the sword down the side of his head hoping to draw the first blood and gain a psychological advantage, but he was held off, blade to blade. Without warning the claw-like left hand came up, the stiff fingers hooked, preparing to gouge into his eyes, but Napier was too quick; he grabbed the hand and forced it away. The two men wrestled hand-to-hand, neither daring to break away in case the other had the advantage as they parted. They strained and struggled until the inevitable happened – one of them lost his footing on the manure- strewn cobbles. Both of them went crashing to the ground, their swords dashed from their hands by the impact.

Napier obeyed his instincts and rolled away from his opponent as he fell. Shaken but not hurt he scrambled to his feet; as he did so his hands felt the hilt of a sword which he grabbed gratefully. To face such an opponent in this conflict without a weapon would mean instant death. This was a fight in which he could expect no mercy. Dropping instantly into the *on-guard*, position a swift look around told him his opponent had found his sword and done the same. Only then did he realise the sword he held felt different, it seemed to mould itself into his hand and became a part of his arm, it's lightness and perfect balance had to be experienced to be believed. Looking down at the weapon in his hand he felt a thrill of joy go through him. Without knowing it and by pure accident he had picked up his father's sword, his legacy. Now he knew he could win! The psychological boost was amazing; he felt a surge of energy flooding through him, almost as though the weapon had magic powers. It occurred to Napier that King Arthur must have felt the same feeling of invincibility when he wielded Excalibur!

The duke who must also have realised the exchange of weapons had given his fellow duellist an advantage, did not continue his attack, but stood waiting for his opponent to come to him. He was more careful now, relying on the skill and finesse his years of training had given him the ability to master. Napier was a different fencer now: his tiredness had gone, his movements were quick and sharp. Now at last he was beginning to dominate the fight, and for the first time his opponents confidence began to wane and a nagging fear for his own safety began to develop.

Holding the sword brought back memories and Napier began to hear his father's voice whispering in his ear, '*Look for his faults. Remember the many patient hours I spent trying to eradicate them. Does he still have them? Does he still lift his elbow when forming a low line parry?*' Napier saw it clearly now – *Yes, of course that had been one of his main faults. Jacques had managed to get rid of it but maybe when tired and under stress he still does it. Worth a try.* A couple of low line attacks were met with perfect low line parries, the third produced dividends: a low line parry with a clear lifting of the elbow. *Yes he was tiring and the fault was still there.* A definite weakness – he could use that! His antagonist was a highly skilled fencer and not likely to fall for a simple trick. He would have to allow him to tire a little more before he tried his ploy, then a low line attack and there it was, a lifting of the elbow. It meant he was not holding the attack properly on he parry, giving his opponent the chance to slide over the top of his guard and thrust at the upper body. Realising the danger, the duke ducked out of the way but not far or quickly enough. The razor-sharp blade missed his head by a hair's breath and sliced into his left ear. He put his hand to the side of his head to find the ear hanging by a shred of flesh. Blinded by the blood pouring from his wound and, enraged by the agonising pain, he could not subdue the temper that had blighted and controlled his life. With a scream of anger, one ear hanging by a shred, the crimson blood streaked across the burn-marked face, the hooked nose and the demonic eyes, he looked like a fiend rising from the fires of hell as he flung himself, his blade slashing wildly in one last desperate effort to eradicate the foe he hated so venomously. Napier remained calm in the face of such ferocity. He knew that terrifying as this gruesome figure hurling itself at him appeared, it was basically a man out of control and could be easily dealt with.

Taking a step backwards to give himself space, he executed a perfect lunge so low that his leg and body appeared parallel to the ground and the duke impaled himself on the needle-sharp point, the tempered steel cutting deep into the body. The Fifth Duke of Mulgrove fell to the ground, his heart pierced by the very weapon he had threatened to use on Napier to wipe him from the face of the earth.

Napier looked down on the gory mess that was once a duke, his foe. The hunted years were over. He could discard the name Feray and proudly become Gerard once more; no one would be chasing him now. He pulled the sword from the duke's chest. It had saved his life. Without the psychological boost it had given him the outcome might have been very different. Wiping the blood off the steel on the duke's shirt he found the scabbard his foe had discarded and slipped the blade into it's accustomed position. When he got home he would clean and polish it properly.

The small crowd who had been stunned into silence by the dramatic events began to gather round. The duke's men began to stare in disbelief at the figure on the ground. They had held him in awe, considering him to be virtually immortal and certainly unbeatable as a swordsman. Even now they found it hard to believe he had been defeated. Who now would they fawn over and flatter now that their master had gone? Their toadying had no meaning now. There was no one to accept their praise or soak up their adoration. Their idol had crumbled and their protector gone – they had no choice now but to go home and seek out other masters.

The hangers-on from the gaming house, who had just come

to see the fun, felt humbled and privileged to have witnessed a duel that would go down in he annals as one of the greatest ever fought in Paris. Now they crowded round to see the body. Eager to remember the smallest detail, events to be recalled and relived, over the dinner tables for years to come. Only Napier appeared to have seen enough. He pushed his way through the jostling crowd and walked quietly away. He carried the sword in both hands, the hilt cradled in the crook of his arm almost as though he were carrying a baby. He looked down at the weapon and took in all its detail. The faultless craftsmanship, the simple yet exquisite design, the perfect balance and the unique materials of which it was made caused him to think of Jacques: his humour, his wisdom, his patience. *Would he be proud of me now?* he thought, *I have done nothing but what has been forced upon me. Fate has made me what I am and I have coped with it in the best way I know how, yes I am sure he would understand and be proud. After all he was a duellist himself.*

The old fencing master had often speculated which of his protégés would be victories if ever they duelled. He had come to the conclusion that the duke with his pronounced killer instinct would have the edge. However he had failed to recognise that time and fate would harden Napier and the duke's temper would let him down at the final hurdle. If he had been alive to see it he would have been delighted to be proved wrong in this instance. He would have smiled in his good humoured way and said, 'Well done, my boy!"

As Napier walked back to his house alone with his memories, he took no pride in his victory. He knew that he would become a hero but alone in his triumph, as men would fear him even more now. In the future, he would be surrounded by acquaintances masquerading as friends just as the duke was. The Fauberts would be the only friends he could rely on and they would be the instruments trapping him in his despised lifestyle. He had no option but to make the best of it, as he had no other life on offer.

He looked down at the sword, it had come back to him and he had felt its power. He was a duellist, son of a duellist and was now its owner as Fate had intended. It was indeed the legacy of a duellist.